Range

Of

Darkness

Range Of

Darkness

Adele Hewett Veal

www.adelehewett.com

Range Of Darkness

Copyright ©2021 Adele Hewett Veal

ISBN-978-0-578-90826-7

Other books by Adele Hewett Veal

Shadow in the Mirror

Reflections From Within

For Taylor and Moriah

Know the importance of having

your footprint imbedded in the sand of life. Continue

to make a difference.

1

SURVEILLANCE WAS NEVER Gee's favorite part of the job, especially when she had to go it alone. It was nights like this, slow and unproductive, that dredged up thoughts of the future—thoughts that were uncomfortable and frightening. She found herself dwelling on the unfamiliar shape her life was going to take once she hung up her badge and became the wife of Keith Jenison. These thoughts usually made her stomach do flip-flops, and tonight was no different. 'Fear of the unknown' was what she called it. However, others, including her best friend, Reese, called it 'cold feet'. It was fear of not being in control, fear of depending on someone else, and fear of what's on the other side of *I do* . . . pure, unadulterated 'cold feet.' There was no question that she loved Keith, she did. But would Keith consider her worth the wait after giving up everything to be with him? She looked at the engagement ring on her finger, remembering the last time they were together. A faint smile pulled at the corners of her mouth. She closed her eyes, imagining Keith's arms about her, and she stretched her neck at the thought of his warm breath dusting the side of it. The feeling was so real, she had to shake her head to pull herself out of it. "Concentrate, Gee. Concentrate."

She wiped the fog from the car window and peered out. Nothing much had changed since the last time she'd looked. A few drops of rain fell, enough to annoy the average Californian, but not the die-hard jogger, who paused beside the car to catch her breath and stretch before continuing her run. Gee sighed as the jogger disappeared down the road. It was the most exciting thing she'd seen all night.

She rested her elbow on the armrest and palmed her chin, then spied the pizza box lying partially open on the passenger seat. She reached over and lifted the lid. *One piece left.* The cold cheese stuck to the bottom of the box as she pried the piece loose and lifted it to take a better look. The slice took on a translucent sheen that covered the crust. It was stiff and uninviting, and a stale odor filled the air.

"Yuck," she shuddered, and dropped it back into the box, then powered down the window for a breath of fresh air. Movement caught her eye, and she focused to follow it. Her eyes narrowed as she scanned the area. *Had it been her imagination? No. She was sure she'd seen movement.*

She squinted through the eerie darkness, sure that whatever or whoever it was would move again, and they did. A figure sidled the apartment wall to the stairs. Gee's eyes followed it, while feeling clumsily behind the passenger seat for the binoculars she'd tossed in the car the night before. When she touched the cold steel and the rough leather, she grasped them, careful not to lose sight of the figure, while she pulled the binoculars up and fumbled to turn them right side up. She lifted the binoculars to her eyes and zoomed in. It was just as she thought-the same person she'd seen the other night—a woman. Gee watched as she tiptoed up the stairs and stopped to listen at the door. She reached into her pocket, pulled out a white envelope and placed it into one of the mailboxes that flanked the door, then slipped down the stairs and left as quietly as she had come. Gee slid a pen from behind her ear, picked up her notepad and wrote, *Thursday, 11:00 p.m. suspicious woman. Could be African American. Second time this week. Left note again. No verbal or physical contact.* She put an asterisk at the beginning and end of the next question. *Note?*

The suspense got the best of her. She glanced around the area, then carefully opened the car door and slid out from behind the wheel. A cool breeze swept over her as she paused, studied the area again, then darted across the street and up the stairs to the mailboxes. Adrenalin had every nerve in her body, standing at attention. Breathing rapidly, she reached into the pocket of her oversized sweater, removed a small flashlight, and moved closer to the mailboxes. There were four of them. She flipped on the flashlight to read the names. When she got to the fourth one, she spied the edge of the white envelope protruding from it. Sliding the flashlight between her teeth, Gee pulled out her pen and wrote on the palm of her hand, 'Deke Henderson, apartment 4B'.

She removed the flashlight, her gaze crushing on the note as she toyed with the thought of taking it to the car – just to read it—that's all. Of course, she'd return it. She glanced behind her, then back at the note, and convinced herself, there and then, that it was the right thing to do. *Necessary for the investigation.* Gingerly, she pulled the envelope out of the mailbox, folded it in half and slipped it into her pocket, then rushed back to the car. Her boss's words rang in her ears with every step: "Don't be a hero, Gee. Just sit there and observe. Don't approach anyone, don't ask questions. Hell, don't even get out of the car. Do you understand?"

Gee gave a satisfying smile, wondering what he would say when she told him what she'd found. Excitement, coupled with curiosity built inside her.

She laid her hand on the door latch and gave it a quick lift, but a loud thud and flash of pain cracked against her skull. Her curiosity overcome by rapidly, ensuing darkness took over as her body fell forward and hit the ground.

***

Muffled voices met her at the edge of a dense fog of nothingness, and someone lifted her body from the cold ground into a sitting position. She tried opening her eyes, but blaring flashes of light stabbed at them and forced them closed again. At first, the voices reminded her of the Charlie Brown cartoons she watched as a child, "Wah, wah, wah, wah, wah, wah, wah, wah," slow, unclear, but audible. She was comforted against the warm chest of the person holding her and talking to her. Gee turned in the direction of the voice and blinked her eyes to focus. It didn't work. She opened them wider then blinked again. *What was he saying?* The inside of her head was on fire, and the flames had no specific direction. She lurched forward and vomited.

"It's okay. I gotcha. I gotcha."

Gee held her head and turned toward the voice again. "Wh-who are you? What happened?"

"Someone walloped you a good one, young lady. Have any idea who would've done that?"

"What do you mean? Done what? Why's my head hurting?"

He yelled over his shoulder. "Sam, call an ambulance, will ya?"

Gee put up her hand. "No. Wait a minute. Just give me one min— Wh—Who are you?"

"Name's Ellis, ma'am. Officer Wayne Ellis."

"Officer?"

"That's right, and over there's my partner, Samuel Richards."

"Listen, officer. If you can just help me to my car?"

"That's a negative, ma'am. The only thing I'm willing ta help you do is raise up off this cold ground into an ambulance and to the closest emergency room we can find." He turned to his partner again. "Sam."

"No—wait—. Please, not an ambulance. Scripps Mercy isn't far. Can you just take me there? Here—" Gee moved slowly with the help of the officer and opened her car door. She leaned in and slid her bag toward her. "My name's Georgie Haynes. I'm a private investigator." She handed him her ID, and then lifted her hand to her temple.

He reached up and pushed the button for dispatch. "Uh, dispatch, I got a 10-15 here. Going to Scripps Mercy. Her name's Georgie Haynes. I repeat, I got a 10-15, and I'm takin' her up over ta Scripps Mercy."

"Copy that," the dispatcher answered.

He helped Gee to his cruiser and slid her carefully into the back seat.

"Sam can follow us in your car?"

"Th-Thank you, officer. I-I think my keys are still—"

Before she could finish, Ellis whipped around to his partner. "Sam, look in the car there and see if Ms. Haynes' keys are still in it?" He waited for an answer.

"Yeah. They're here," Sam yelled back.

"Great. Follow me ta Scripps Mercy. It's just up around the corner." He slid behind the wheel of his cruiser and sped off with Sam following close behind.

The movement of the car caused a queasiness that lurched in her stomach again, and she leaned forward, surprised that such a small change in position could ease it. "How'd you find me?" she asked.

"Someone called in a 10-53. I believe it was another officer. He said there was a person down, and we needed ta get to 'em ASAP."

"What's a 10-53?"

"That's the code for 'person down.'"

"Who called it in?"

Gee sat back, laying her head on the soft leather of the back of the seat. She swallowed the bile threatening to come up, and she leaned forward again. "What do you think they hit me with? A two-by-four?"

"By the look of the bump, it just might've been."

"H-how can I get the name of the officer who called it in?"

"Dispatch might know. Hold on." He picked up the microphone. "Dispatch, do you have a 4-1-1 on the person who called in the 10-53?"

A woman's voice came on the radio. "Yes, it was an officer out of Arizona, Keith Jenison. He called and reported it."

"Arizona? Okay, thanks."

"I should've known," Gee whispered.

The officer turned sideways and glanced back at her. "You know him?"

8

"He's my fiancé."

"Dispatch says he's in Arizona. How'd he know where you were?"

"It's an app," she said, rubbing her temples.

"An app? You mean like on your cellular phone?"

"Uh-huh. When I'm on a stake-out alone, I turn it on. He can track where I am."

"That's technology for you. Something's new every day."

"I thought it was silly when he first suggested it, but now I—" She didn't finish the sentence, just sat back and stayed as still as possible for the duration of the ride.

Officer Ellis pulled into the parking lot of Scripps Mercy and drove around to the Emergency entrance. He put the car in park, slid out and rushed around to the passenger side to help Gee. Cupping her elbow with his hand, he eased her out of the car.

"Now, you just take your time. Don't try ta rush it."

The emergency doors whooshed open. Rushed footsteps could be heard on the pavement as two men dressed in scrubs approached the car with a wheelchair.

"Looks like you can use some help."

"Yeah, thanks. We found her lying in the street. Out cold. Somebody hit her in the head and took off. She's complaining 'bout a headache. Concussion, I'll bet."

They eased Gee into the wheelchair.

"Ma'am?" said a voice behind Officer Ellis.

Gee's reply was strained and hoarse. She lifted her head slowly, "Yes?"

Sam stepped around Ellis and placed Gee's cell phone and purse on her lap.

"You might want this. It's been going off like crazy. I dropped your keys inside your purse."

"Thank you," she said.

The interns wheeled her through the doors to triage.

"Can you tell me your name, ma'am?" one intern asked.

"Georgie Haynes," she whispered. Her head stayed buried deep inside her hands while flashes of light that felt like burning embers singed against her skull.

"Do you remember what happened to you?"

"Yeah. Somebody hit me."

"What did they hit you with?"

"I'm not sure. I didn't see it coming, but the way my head feels, it could have been a bat."

"If you can stand up for me—"

"Why? Can't I just sit here? I don't want to move, if I don't have to." The thought of it made her stomach toss.

"I can help you, but I think you'd be more comfortable on the cot. We'll dim the lights for you, and someone will be right in to get your information. Are you allergic to any medication?"

"No," she said, lifting her head slowly to look around. "Where's Officer Ellis?"

"Gone, ma'am."

"Gone? I wanted to thank him."

"Knowing him, he'll be back after his shift to ask about you. He's off in a couple of hours."

"How do you know that?"

"He's my dad."

"Your dad?" She rubbed the side of her temples. "I think he's my hero."

He smiled. "Yeah, mine too."

He pulled a clean hospital gown from the cabinet and turned to her. "I'll have the nurse help you with this. It'll make it easier for them to run an IV if you need one. We can put your clothes in the closet over there."

Gee nodded slowly then stood to remove her sweater, but her knees wobbled fiercely and buckled underneath her.

The intern rushed to her side before she tumbled to the floor. "Whoa," he said, catching her and easing her back into the chair. "I'll get someone to come help you."

"I just want to take off my sweater."

He helped her slide her arms out of the sweater, and she folded it over her lap.

Gee thought of her boss, Regis, and how angry he was going to be when he got wind of what she'd done. Then a sudden surge of accomplishment washed over her, when she remembered the envelope. She slid her hand down the side of the sweater and deep into the pocket. It was empty.

"No," she whispered.

A familiar voice filled the corridor. Gee groaned. It was Regis.

"Miss, are you all right?" the intern asked.

She yanked her sweater around and slid her hand into the other pocket. Nothing.

The voices got louder as they approached the door. Someone tapped, and Gee turned to the door as it opened.

"This gentleman says he knows you?" the nurse inquired.

A sting of embarrassment crept up the back of her neck and across her face.

"Yes," she admitted, "He's my boss."

The door opened wider, and Regis's large frame filled the portal. He froze, riotously, his gaze fierce, but observant. The muscles in his jaw clenched, making the crease in his forehead more pronounced. Gee watched his expression change from fright to anger, and then to relief, in one fell swoop. When he finally moved, it was only to shake his head and give a thankful nod. His eyes never left hers, and when he spoke, his words were slow and deliberate.

"Helen and I have been beside ourselves. I have been on the phone with Keith all night. We called every hospital and every police station in the area. When Keith called to let us know he had dialed 9-1-1 and they'd found you, you have no idea the relief that gave us. " He shifted his weight, and wiped a hand across his face.

12

"I haven't had the chance to call anyone. I-I just got my phone back. The officer—"

Regis held up his hand. "Gee, you need to call Keith."

Gee's eyes widened and brimmed with tears, feeling like a scolded child.

"Yes, I will—"

"You need to call him now. He's been a nervous wreck."

"I was going to call as soo—"

"Call him. Now."

She tensed at his sharp tone. Then she fumbled with the phone, to put it in the right position, and punched in Keith's number.

He answered on the first ring.

"Gee?"

"Yes, it's me, babe. I'm okay. I'm so sorry."

Tears spilled over and streamed down her face. "I didn't mean to worry anyone. I'm sorry." She touched the side of her head. The throbbing was intense. "I haven't seen the doctor yet, but I'm sure I have a concussion."

"Don't cry, Gee. It's okay—you're okay."

"I know, but I should've— "

"Don't do that. I'm just relieved that you're safe. After you didn't answer my calls, I checked the app. It showed your phone was still in the car, but you weren't answering my calls. I knew something had to be wrong, so I called 911. Have you talked to Regis or Helen?"

"Regis is here."

Keith chuckled. "That doesn't surprise me. He was so worried. Everybody was. So, what happened?""

"Someone hit me from behind. I didn't see it coming, but they got me good. I'm sure I have a concussion."

"God, Gee. You have no idea how good it is to hear your voice. I've been going crazy over here."

She nestled the phone closer to her ear and closed her eyes, wishing she could erase the distance between them, touch him, feel his arms around her.

"Call me as soon as the doctor sees you, okay, babe? I want to know what he says."

"I will."

"Let me talk to Regis."

Gee held out the phone. "He wants to talk to you, Reg."

Regis took the phone and stepped into the corridor, closing the door behind him.

While he was gone, Gee let the nurse help her change into the hospital gown and start an IV drip. The nurse explained that the drip would quell the nausea. She nodded, happy that she had taken the intern's advice and lay on the cot with the lights dimmed. She took another deep breath and closed her eyes, waiting for them to come take her to x-ray. Regis came back in before they got there.

"Keith said to call him as soon as you know something, and he loves you."

"Thank you, Reg."

He answered with a curt, "Uh-huh," and cleared his throat. "We're not going to talk about it right now, but I want you to be prepared, when this is over, to tell me what the hell you were thinking."

"Regis . . ."

"Not now. It can wait."

"Regis. I found something."

"Something more important than your life, Gee?"

"No, but I'm sure its important for the case."

"Does it prove that Deke Henderson is selling guns illegally?"

"I'm not sure…"

"I want to be done with this case, Gee. It's simple. Casandra McClure hired us to prove that he's selling guns illegally. If he's not, write it up, so we can be done with it. This whole business is frustrating."

"To me too, but I think I'm on to something."

Regis shrugged. "Show me."

"I can't."

"Why?"

"I put it here, in my pocket, but it's gone."

"Then, we're finished with this discussion."

A tap at the door drew their attention away from the awkward conversation. The doctor opened the door and entered the room. He nodded at Regis and walked toward Gee.

"Hi, Georgie?" he said, checking her wristband. "I'm Doctor Miller. You mind if I take a look at that bump?"

Gee sat up and leaned forward. She winced when he touched around it.

"Uh-huh," he said, then took an ophthalmoscope from the wall. He flashed the light quickly in one eye and then the other. When he finished examining her, he stepped back and gave a slight nod.

"Okay, here's what we're looking at. You definitely have a concussion, but I want to run more tests and get a CT scan to make sure that's all we're dealing with, so I want to keep you overnight—"

Gee lifted her hand in protest, but the doctor rushed on.

"Just to watch you. You can probably go home tomorrow if all goes well."

"But, Doc –"

"She's happy to comply." Regis's gaze bore into hers.

Gee closed her eyes and sighed, then nodded in silent surrender.

"Good. Let's get the tests started." He left the room.

Within minutes, a nurse came in and took Gee's blood pressure, which was a bit elevated, but not unusual, given the circumstances. After getting all the vitals, the nurse recorded the information in the hospital computer beside Gee's bed.

Regis monitored the rest in silence and every so often, Gee glanced in his direction. She had only seen him like

16

this a few times since they began working together, and each of those times she knew it was best not to say anything.

Finally, the technicians came in. "Ms. Georgie Haynes? Time to go take pictures."

His attempt at humor was futile as he pulled up the brakes on her cot and wheeled her out of the room.

She heard the faint ring of Regis's phone.

He answered.

"Helen? Yes, I'm with her now. She's on her way to Cat scan, but she's going to be fine. They're keeping her overnight."

Gee felt a warm tug in her heart.

***

After the ordeal in the emergency room, they found a bed for her on the second floor. The intern teased her on the way up- telling her the room was one of their most requested, because 80 percent of the people who stayed in it recovered quicker than others. She didn't feel much like laughing, but hoped the detached smile would reflect appreciation for his attempt at levity. When Regis left, Gee spoke one last time to Keith. Then settled back on to her pillow and stared out the window.

The moon resembled a huge pearl illuminating against the backdrop of a starless, black sky, as if God had composed it especially for her, soothing her and helping her regain some semblance of wellbeing. Still, as she slipped off to sleep, she grappled with one burning question:

Why didn't I just stay in the car?

2

IT SEEMED AS if Gee had just closed her eyes, when shards of sunrise streamed through her hospital window. She smiled and turned toward it, but as soon as she opened her eyes, a sudden bolt of fiery pain shot through them and burned into the back of her skull. Suddenly, she recalled where she was, and why. Her lids snapped shut and she cradled her head, desperate to stop the pounding. She felt around the bed for the call button and pushed it several times.

"Please, someone —anyone . . ." she whispered. Soon, a nurse entered her room, pushing a machine ahead of her. "Good morning," she smiled.

Gee couldn't smile back. She shielded her eyes, and the only word she could utter came out in a whisper, "Please."

The nurse checked Gee's wristband, and quickly took her vitals. "On a scale of one to ten, how severe is your pain?"

Gee groaned, "Twelve."

"Well, you're in luck. Your doctor left an order for pain meds as needed. And, this bright light can't be helping." She swiveled around, snapped the blinds shut, then left the room. "I'll be right back," she called over her shoulder.

Gee slowly lowered her hand, but kept her eyes closed as she relished the absence of that abominable light.

The nurse returned with a syringe and jabbed a needle into Gee's IV line. Almost immediately, Gee felt the medication's welcomed effects. She sighed and rested her head back against a cool pillow. As the medicine worked its magic, she glanced over at her IV, then made a pinched face, and muttered, "I really blew it last night." After a low groan, she succumbed, and slipped into the drug's cozy, painless corridor.

***

"The doctor wants to see if you can handle a little food. It's a soft diet. You want to try?"

Gee opened her eyes. Thankfully, the room was still dark, and Gee managed to focus on the nurse's movement as she placed a tray on Gee's table and rolled it toward her.

She yawned. "How long have I been sleeping? Was it you I saw earlier?"

"That was about three hours ago. It's 9:00 now, and yep, that was me. I'm Kate. Do you think you can eat a little something?"

Kate helped her sit up. Despite the renewed pounding and the room spinning, she replied, "Okay, I'll try. But . . . no promises."

"Just eat what you can. I'll be back."

Gee looked over the tray. Dry toast, warm coffee … and something resembling jello. She wasn't sure, so she left it untouched. After a few minutes, she gave up and pushed the tray to the side. She'd have to give eating a little more time. She lay back on her pillow and closed her eyes again. As she did, thoughts of yesterday reemerged, and with it came a heavy dose of self-castigation. She'd been foolish, and she felt every bit of it. She disobeyed orders, and was paying for that, too.

Okay, so much for that. I can't undo anything about it now, so it's time to move forward.

"It is what it is," she murmured, stubbornly. "I'll dish out some serious apologies and promise that this will never happen again… and this time, I mean it."

Someone knocked.

"Who's there?"

"It's me, Regis."

Gee sat up. "Come in, Reg."

The door opened and she stifled a laugh at the sight of Regis's hulking 6 foot 4 inch frame, as he stepped through the door with six get-well-soon balloons in tow. He saw her mirth, and his eyes narrowed. "Don't," he warned.

That did it. Gee covered her mouth and her body shook with the riotous laughter she had tried so hard to conceal. Something about her big, gruff, no-nonsense boss, standing in the middle of her room, with balloons bobbing about his head defied restraint.

"Are you quite finished?" His own mirth belied his composure, and his shoulders trembled with laughter. He thrust the balloons toward her. "Here. Helen told me to pick these up for you."

Gee took the balloons, still chuckling. "Sorry, Reg, I couldn't help it. I really needed the distraction." She lowered her voice in false secrecy. "You see, I just happen to know the heart beneath all that muscle and masculinity."

"It was Helen's . . ."

"Yeah, yeah, yeah." Gee chuckled and gave him a knowing look. "Well, thank her for me," she said. Helen might have made the suggestion, but Regis Ovalton never did anything he didn't want to do.

"How are you feeling?"

"I had a rough morning, but you made my day. It's amazing what a little levity will do. I'm listening to the doctor."

"I'll bet."

"I'm glad you're here, Regis. I've had plenty of time to think about the incident yesterday and— I should never have— I feel like I need to apolo . . ."

22

He put his hand up. "I know what you're going to say—"

"Then, let me say it and get it over with."

"You don't have to do this, Gee. Don't, please." He walked over, took the balloons from her and tied them to the bed frame.

"But, I do . . ."

"Leave it alone."

"Oh, for crying out loud! I'm trying to apologize,"

"For what?"

"*Yesterday*."

"Don't want to hear it."

Her mouth fell open in disbelief. "Why?"

"Because you always apologize."

"I can't believe you're saying that to me. I do not."

"Every time your ass ends up in the hospital, you apologize."

"Stop it." She folded her arms and looked away.

"What? You think I'm exaggerating?"

"You know you are."

"Was I exaggerating when you went to Arizona, on vacation, by the way, and ended up with a bullet in your chest? If I'm not mistaken, you apologized for being careless and for worrying everyone then, too. Exactly the way you're doing now. You almost died, Gee."

She rolled her eyes toward the ceiling.

"And how about the time you almost got your ass fried in a fire?" His brows shot up. "Huh?"

"That was five years ago."

"But, you apologized. Right?"

"There was a little kid trapped in the building."

"Yeah. The firemen got her out, then they had to go back in for you. You put people's lives in danger."

"Okay, so that wasn't my finest hour . . ."

"No, it wasn't! What about when you confronted the gang leader?

"You can't use that one. That was different."

"How so?"

"He was in my personal space."

"Y-Your personal what?"

"Come on, Regis. I couldn't let him get away with that. What about my street cred . . ."

"Well, let's not have the big gang leader with a gun damage Gee's street cred, shall we? Are you listening to yourself? Thank God we were able to find you after he dumped your ass in the desert. No shade. No water! Do I exaggerate, Gee? Because I remember an apology then too." He laughed and lifted his hand to his head. "I don't think old age has anything to do with these gray hairs on my head."

She groaned, putting a hand to her aching forehead.

"That's a bit extreme. I just wanted to say I was sorry."

"Keep your *sorries..* I'm sure you'll need them for the time you decide to unmask your next villain or save the world from the next foe that dares to come up against the invincible Gee Haynes."

"Has it been that bad?"

Regis sighed deeply. "Not bad. Frustrating. Gee, you gotta stop taking chances. You're like a daughter to me and Helen, and you're going to have a husband soon. You have people who love you, who worry about you. We want to keep you around."

A moment stretched between them.

Gee lowered her gaze. When she looked back up, she gave a nod.

Her brow furrowed. "Not to change the subject, but do you have any idea who my replacement is going to be? The wedding's only a couple of months away, you know."

"Yeah, I know. I've got a few prospects."

"Not as good as me, though."

"Let's hope not." Regis laughed. "Are they sending you home today?"

"They're supposed to let me know any minute. I've been waiting for someone to get back with me. I can't imagine what's taking them so long."

"How's the head?"

"It still hurts like hell. They said it would if I don't stay ahead of it with the pain meds. So far, a shot goes a long way, but I'm concerned about how well I'll do when I get home."

Another knock at the door had Gee hoping it was a nurse with her discharge papers, but when the door opened, Keith popped his head in.

"Can I come in?" he smiled.

"Keith?" Gee shrieked, and held out her arms to him. "What are you doing here?"

In a few quick steps he was at her bedside. He carefully gathered her in his arms and planted a warm kiss on her lips. "Did you really think you could be in a hospital, and I wouldn't come to see about you?"

He pulled back, and his palms gently flanked her cheeks. "Let me look at you!"

His gaze roved every inch of her face. He lifted a finger and touched the bandage over her head wound. She winced, and he pulled her close again. She clung to him, breathing in the heady mixture of masculine fragrance and his leather jacket. She wanted his scent to linger forever. Keith had come for her.

"God, it's good to see you," she whispered.

He caressed her cheek, and nodded, then looked at Regis.

"How you doing, Regis?" He straightened and offered a hand.

Regis shook it. "Great, now that you're here. Maybe you can make this woman behave."

26

Keith chuckled. "We *are* talking about Gee, right?"

They laughed.

Gee grimaced.

"And Helen? How's Helen?" Keith asked.

"She's good. She asks about you all the time. Hope you're going to be here long enough to keep Gee out of trouble."

Keith glanced over his shoulder at her. "Is that even possible?"

"No," Regis laughed.

Gee intervened. "Hello, I'm still here, you two. I can hear you." She swept her bangs to the side, and tucked them behind her ear, then gently rubbed the side of her head.

The door opened again.

"Well, look here. Let me guess," the nurse smiled, "dad and husband. Right?"

"Almost." Gee answered. "Finance' and boss."

"Oh, I see," she said, moving to Gee's bed. She placed the discharge papers on her lap and read through the discharge instructions while Keith and Regis listened in.

"What about follow-up appointments?" Gee asked.

"You can follow up with your family doctor if you need to. Dr. Miller spoke to him last night. He's the one who ordered the neurological examination and CT scan. But everything looks good. If it was left up to Dr. Miller, he would've kept you another day. So, make sure you go home and rest. I wouldn't try to watch television or read today. Looks like you'll be well taken care of." She glanced up at the two men. "Also, your doctor called in your prescriptions, so they should be ready to pick up at your pharmacy. I suggest that you take them as prescribed and stay on top of the pain. Someone's going to be home with you, right?"

"Yes, I'll be there." Keith said, giving Gee's shoulder a gentle squeeze.

She reached up and covered his hand with hers. "But, what am I going to wear out? My clothes were ruined."

"Oh, I forgot to tell you." Regis straightened and opened a small closet. "Helen sent these, along with some house shoes. She brought them up when you were getting the CT scan. They'll get you home."

Gee fingered the pink jogging suit, and mused, "These are brand new."

"Yeah, she went out and got them yesterday. I told her that yours were soaked and muddy."

"Please tell her I said thank you. I'll pay her back." Regis waved her away, and left the room so she could get dressed.

When the door opened again, it was an attendant with a wheelchair. "Ready to go?"

Gee chuckled. She stood, slowly. "Yes, but I don't think I need that thing."

"Oh, yes you do," Keith said. He grabbed the chair and wheeled it closer to Gee's bedside. "Not today. Your chariot awaits, madam."

Gee protested. "Keith…."

He held up his hand. "I'm in charge for the next couple of days, Georgie Haynes." He nodded toward the wheelchair. "Your chariot."

She took in a breath and stood from the bed, allowing him to help her into the chair. The attendant untied the balloons and wrapped the strings around her wrist.

Keith opened the door wide, and the attendant navigated toward the elevator.

Once outside, Gee's eyes scanned the parking lot. "Where's your car, Keith? How did you get here?"

"I flew in and Uber'd from the airport to the hospital."

"Looks like you thought of everything."

Keith winked at her and carefully helped her from the wheelchair into her car, then he fought with the balloons until they were secure in the back seat.

Regis pulled his car up beside them, and rolled down his window. "I'm gonna give you two lovebirds time to get situated. Helen's making soup for Gee, so we'll bring it by later."

"Sounds like a plan," Keith said, waving his hand out the window. "I'll see you then. Thanks for being there for me, man."

"No problem at all, Keith. She's like a daughter to us. You know that."

Keith nodded. "Yeah, I know. We'll see you later."

"Yep, we'll call when we're on our way," Regis said with a nod and drove off.

Relief washed over him as he steered his car through traffic and instructed his Bluetooth to call his wife and bring her up to speed.

"Helen? Okay, Gee's going home. Yes, I gave her the balloons. Six of them just like you asked. You're not going to believe who came in after I got there."

"Yeah, how'd you guess?" He listened to Helen's reason and smiled. "You're right. He loves her. I told them you were making the soup, and we'd be over later. I'm on my way to the office, then I'll come pick you up.

I love you too, Helen." He hung up.

3

THE DAYS THAT followed Gee's return home from the hospital sped by, and before she knew it, it was time for Keith to leave. But during his stay, he helped her through the pain and suffering by applying ice packs, and making sure she rested and stayed medicated, until the last of the prescription was gone. He even cooked for her, and today, she lay in bed, watching him roll his freshly washed clothes and arrange them in his carry-on bag.

"I don't want you to go," she sulked. "I've gotten use to you being here."

He moved the bag out of the way and eased down beside her, gently pulling her close to him. "Soon, you're not going to have to worry about that. We'll be together every day as husband and wife. We're never going to be apart again." He gently stroked her hair.

Gee loved that. Her body arched. "Is that right?"

"Right as rain," he whispered against her forehead.

She wrapped her arms around him and nestled closer. "You're so warm," she purred.

"Yep." His eyes were moist with desire.

"What's that look?"

"What look?"

"The one that's telling me I might get lucky."

"I don't think luck has anything to do with it."

"Hmm, you may have a point there," she said, lifting her lips against his.

Keith's need for her rose as their kiss deepened. He paused, and leaned back, drinking in her unique essence, and willing her to open her eyes. When her lids fluttered and lifted, her eyes were brimmed with hunger for him too.

"You're so beautiful," he whispered, and pulled her closer.

She leaned up and kissed him again. His arms tightened about her as the couple gave themselves over to the throes of passion and then to the depths of despair when Gee's phone rang.

Keith let out a low growl. "Don't answer it," he whispered against her hair.

"Okay," she whispered back.

It continued its relentless chime.

"Don't even look at it."

"I won't," she laughed.

"They'll leave a message."

"I know."

They released sighs of relief when the ringing stopped.

"Now, where were we?"

"I believe we were—here." Gee lifted her lips to his.

Her phone rang again. They tried to ignore it, but on the third chime, Gee scowled and reached for it.

"I just want to see who it is."

"No, you're gonna answer it."

"No, I'm not. I just want to see who's calling."

"Gee. . ."

She turned the phone around to look at the caller ID.

"It's Reese. I'll tell her I'll call her back. If I don't answer it, she'll think something's wrong and come over."

Keith heaved a sigh, and relented. "Well, answer it. We don't want that," he chuckled, rolled out of bed, and headed for the bathroom.

Gee hit the button. "Hey, Reese."

"Hi, Reese!" Keith yelled from the bathroom door.

Forty-five minutes later, Gee was saying goodbye for the third time.

"I mean it, Reese. Keep it short and sweet. That man's a bully. I don't like him. Why do you feel like you have to have dinner with him, anyway? Tell him you have other plans. Say, you're coming to see me."

She paused.

"Okay then, have dinner and go home. Don't let him talk you into anything else. We'll talk later." She said, walking into the kitchen. She sat at the table across from Keith. "Keith's waiting for me to have breakfast. I've got to go."

Keith looked up from the newspaper and smiled. The breakfast they'd ordered earlier had come thirty minutes ago, and Gee's was untouched. His plate left only crumbs of a breakfast long gone.

Gee hung up and looked guiltily across the table to Keith.

"Sorry, Keith. She really needed to talk."

"Of course she did."

"Breakfast looks delicious."

He gestured toward his empty plate. "It was. So, what's going on with Reese?"

"She's going out with this guy. His name is Daxden."

"Good for her."

Gee shook her head. "No, not so good. I have a bad feeling about him."

"Why? Has he done something you don't like?" Keith sat forward with interest and laid the paper aside.

"I don't know. I can't put my finger on it. I just don't trust him."

"You know him well enough to say that?"

"I've met him a couple of times, and each of those times, I've walked away … concerned."

"You don't think Reese is smart enough to see him for who he is?"

"Sure I do, and she's tried to break it off, but Daxden's clever."

"How so?"

"He makes her doubt herself, and I've never known Reese to allow someone to do that. And he arranges situations that make it difficult for her to say no. Like tonight. She thought about it and decided to call him and break a date. Like a hundred times before, what does he do? Before she can even get the words out of her mouth, he starts guilt-tripping her. He tells her that he has reservations for them at this new waterfront restaurant she's been dying to go to, after, of course, railing about the hell and high water he had to go through to secure them,"

"So, she's going?"

Gee nodded. "Yep."

"Maybe not." He held up the newspaper. "Stormy forecast for tonight. Supposed to be pretty bad. She might be able to get out of it."

"Hope so."

"Be careful, Gee."

"Oh, I'm very careful." She reached up and rubbed her head. "I think I've learned my lesson." She picked up a slice of cold bacon and took a bite. "He's calling it, 'their special dinner.' Wonder why?"

"What do you mean?"

"That's a pretty fancy restaurant. He's up to something?"

Keith shrugged, "You said she's been dying to go there. . ."

"It's manipulation." She picked up her last piece of bacon and pointed it in Keith's direction. "This guy is so controlling. He's up to no good. I can feel it."

Keith gave her a long look. "Gee, you've got to relax. Give yourself time to recover."

"I'm trying to. I am worried about Reese, though."

"Listen, you know I'm here for you, but you've got to let this go until you're better. I'm leaving tomorrow, and I don't want to be in Arizona worried about what's going on here."

She considered him. "You're right, Keith. I'm letting it go." She waved her hand in the air.

"Good. How's your head?"

"Better. I've been thinking about going back to work on Thursday. I was going to call Regis later, and get his thoughts on it."

"Actually, they want us to come over for dinner tonight. I told them I'd check with you and see if you felt up to it. What do you think?"

"Yeah, I'd love to go. When did they call?"

"Yesterday, while you were napping."

"Did they want us to bring anything?"

"I'll call and ask, but first—" Keith stood and walked around to her side of the table. "I believe you owe me a minute of your time." He held his hand out.

Gee smiled, wiped her hands with her napkin then placed them in his. When she stood, she moved closer to him and whispered against his chest, "I think I can rally up more than a minute."

"I'd like that."

They walked, hand in hand to the bedroom.

4

REESE DISCONNECTED FROM her call with Gee and sat back on the sofa. She lifted her cup and took a long sip of coffee, then turned toward the window. The wind had picked up, blowing harder than usual. The forecast warned there would be thundershowers toward the afternoon and into the night, but they hadn't said the storms would start this early. She watched the dark clouds in their relentless approach, promising a changing backdrop to enhance the serenity she enjoyed whenever she gazed out at the vast, California sky. Whether it hosted the clearest blue of blues, or a breathtaking sunset, or even if the tempest of angry thunderheads ripped asunder by fiery bolts of God's pure power, Reese considered it a canvas for a poet's pen and reflected a poet's heaven.

She stood, then walked to the patio doors and swept them open. She breathed in the scent of fresh rain looming her way.

Dining at the new Ocean Bay Restaurant had been a desire of hers since it opened, but she wondered if it would be safe tonight. Really, the waterfront couldn't be the best place to go with the winds they were predicting for tonight. Maybe she'd call Daxden and try to cancel again, or at least postpone for a later date … which, would give her time to think of other ways to discourage him. She liked that idea. Actually, she could get together with Gee when Keith leaves, and the two of them could go to the restaurant one night, a night with no storms and Daxden, just a bad memory. Hell, Gee's company would be a lot better. Tonight, she could just as easily stay home and curl up in her favorite spot, snuggled under a warm blanket with a good book. Especially after the way Gee had just reamed her a good one for even considering tonight with Daxden.

Reese hated the influence Daxden held over her. She didn't feel powerless, but his suggestions were strong, compelling and difficult to refuse, and she didn't know why. She'd never been timid.

Mulling that around in her head, she came to the conclusion that tonight might be just the thing . . . just intimate enough to break it off completely with him. *'Daxden, we're better friends than anything, and I think . . .*

No . . . maybe I should say, Daxden, it's not you, it's . . . me. I think we should explore other options because this dating –thing isn't working for us.'

She clutched her hands behind her back and watched as big raindrops began to dot the patio floor. It quickly turned into a deluge that sprayed against the screen door, forcing her to step back and close it. *'Oh, make up your mind, Reese!'*

She went back to her place on the sofa and picked up her cell phone, then punched in Daxden's number. She had no idea what she was going to say, but she needed to prove a point.

"Morning, Reese," he said.

"Hi, Dax. Do you see how hard it's raining?"

"Yeah. Not like we didn't need it, right?"

"I know, but I'm thinking about tonight."

"What about it?"

"You know. We're supposed to go to that restaurant?"

"Oh, hon, the rain will be over long before then. I wouldn't let anything ruin the surprise I have planned for you tonight. Especially a few raindrops."

She cringed at the title of endearment. *'Hon'*—. She could see there was no changing his mind. *'Plan B.'*

"I guess we should leave around 6:30?" Daxden suggested.

Reese was quiet.

"Reese?"

40

"Yes?"

"What time do you think I should pick you up? I made reservations for 7:00. I think we should leave around 6:30, That way, we'll get there a little early."

"No, I was thinking I'd meet you there."

"Meet me?"

"Yeah. I want to run by and check on Gee first."

The silence on the other end of the phone was packed with disapproval.

Finally, he said, "I can't believe you're letting Gee interrupt the special evening I planned for us. I mean, I was looking f-forward to picking you up. You don't know, I-I could have had flowers for you or something special like that. I-I had the whole evening planned out. It's-It's a special one. A-And you gonna let Gee and a-a little bump on the head interfere with our plans?"

Reese took in a breath, not surprised at how quickly his mood changed. When they first met, his mood swings frightened her, now they just left her exasperated, knowing the conversation would suddenly become one-sided. His. Nothing ever got accomplished with Daxden stuttering and talking over her. It was like trying to reason with a child. And just like most frustrated mothers, she'd give in and let him have his way, but not today. She waited for an opening.

"Dax?"

"...And all you can talk about is going to check on Gee? W-What? I-Is Gee your lover now or somethin'? W-Why, you gotta be the one to check on her? I-I thought –"

"Dax"—

"W-What's Gee d-doing for you? Uh-Uh, every time I turn around, I hear Gee needs this, or Gee needs that. Wh-What about wh-what I need? Do you ever th-think about that? You-you are ma-making m-me d-d-disdain th-th-that girl! W-w-what about *me*!"

"Are you finished?" she yelled.

"Wh-What?"

"Are you finished?"

"Wh-What do you mean, am I f-finished?"

"Are you finished, Daxden? With your tantrum."

"N-no tantrum! I'm just saying!"

"Then this is what I'm going to do!" This was her firmest voice. "I will be at the restaurant tonight, but I'm driving myself because I'm going by to check on Gee!"

Daxden was furious. He bristled under her tone. He thought, '*she's talking to me like I'm stupid, like I'm a child!* But he bit back his explosive reply and decided to let it go. The night would take care of itself. Put everything in its perspective.

Still, there was a certain edge to his tone when he said, "Fine."

She hung up and took in a breath, embracing this temporary victory. As small as it was, it made her feel confident and in control, and even less willing to share his company tonight. She had silenced Daxden Green and he wouldn't take that lying down. In some passive aggressive way, he would exact payback. Woe-is-her. Or better yet, as Gee would say, *"Why the hell are you putting yourself out there like that?"* What bothered Reese most was, she didn't understand why she kept doing it.

She didn't like the way she felt around Daxden. She didn't trust him, and she despised his unpredictable mood swings. He had been handsome when she first met him, but as she got to know him, his physical attraction faded along with a rapidly diminishing set of social skills. All because of a personality that literally sucked.

Gee was convinced he could be dangerous and was afraid for Reese. Nevertheless, Reese swallowed her own misgivings, and murmured, "Well, at least we'll be in a public place."

She walked to the door again to watch the rain.

5

DAXDEN WAS OBLIVIOUS to how long he held the phone after Reese hung up. Women were not supposed to talk to men the way she just spoke to him, and he was having a hard time holding his composure. This was another thing he was going to have to teach her. And, it would have to be taught in a profound and lasting way. She simply could not continue like this. Suddenly, his composure slipped, and he slammed the phone down. He couldn't move. He just stood there allowing his anger to wrestle self-control, then he took a couple of deep breaths and walked to the window.

Daxden Green's house sat in the center of a cul-de-sac. He was surrounded by rows of single level and two-story homes that, for the most part, looked alike. Daxden lived in one of the two stories, and he prided himself as having the only house with an immaculately manicured lawn that stayed green, even during the winter months.

He didn't know his neighbors and didn't want to know them. Every now and then, he'd see someone walking a dog or strolling a baby, and that was enough for him. He didn't speak to them, and he exuded discouragement that they speak to him. The last thing he needed was nosey people snooping around his house. They should be able to tell from his antiseptic surroundings that he was a notch above them and had no desire to descend to their level. Or anyone's, for that matter. That is, until he met Reese.

The first time he saw her was at the grocery store in the produce section. He watched her pick around the oranges until she found the perfect ones and dropped them into a bag, then into her cart. He followed her to the deli counter, where she requested a pound of freshly cut turkey slices, and laughed excessively with the young man behind the counter. Daxden didn't like that.

He frowned. *'She's flirting.'*

He watched her sway up one aisle and down another. He liked watching her. She was beautiful, and her fair-skin was not only flawless, it also had a bronze glow to it, as if she'd spent the sunny part of the day lying by the pool. Her high cheekbones complimented the structure of her face, and he imagined her auburn hair matched her eyes, or maybe they were a fawn brown. He'd have to get a closer look to know for sure.

He rushed in front of her and waited for her to push off with her cart and, when she did, he purposely struck hers with his, then feigned shock and embarrassment.

"I am so sorry."

"No. Really. It was my fault." Reese insisted.

"It's unusually crowded here today. Isn't it?

Reese laughed. "I've seen it worse."

"You shop here often?"

"I feel like I live here sometimes."

"Me too," he laughed. "It's my neighborhood store."

"Oh," was all she said.

He waited, hoping she'd say it was hers too, to confirm she lived in the neighborhood as well. She didn't.

"Well, it was nice—uh—bumping into you." Reese laughed, extending her hand. "It was nice meeting you."

Daxden took her hand and covered it with his other one. He especially liked the way the corners of her eyes crinkled when she smiled.

"But we really haven't met, though. Have we? My name's Daxden Green, and I hope you won't think me out of line if I say you're the most beautiful woman I've seen in a long time."

Reese didn't know what to say; a bloom of color swept her cheeks, and she whispered, "Thank you."

"Will you tell me your name?"

"Reese. Reese Cunningham." She felt the heat of her blush move up her neck and around to her cheeks again.

46

"Reese? I like that." Daxden stepped closer and made a mental note – her eyes were hazel. "Reese, do you think it would be possible for us to meet for coffee one morning?"

"Coffee? Sure. I'll have coffee with you."

"How about later today?"

"No, can't today. I'm meeting friends. Maybe tomorrow." She reached into her purse for a small tablet and pen then jotted down her number. She ripped off the page and placed it into Daxden's hand. "Give me a call. I'll try to work something out this week."

He was satisfied. *Mission accomplished,* he thought with a smile, then he nodded, and the two went their separate ways.

Daxden didn't let any time pass. That night he called her number. She didn't answer.

That was six months ago. Since then, Daxden felt like he and Reese had grown closer, but now it was time to take their relationship to another level.

6

AT 5:30 THAT evening Gee and Keith were ringing the Ovalton's doorbell. Regis answered it. He greeted Keith with a stern handshake and Gee gave him a quick hug and rushed past them to the kitchen where she was sure she'd find Helen.

Helen Ovalton was an older woman in her early 60s, she had one grey streak that started on the side front of her hairline and traveled to the back, giving her a stunning, but unique appearance. She stood no more than 5 feet tall, and her thin frame gave her a chic look that could place her on the cover of a fashion magazine even at her age.

Gee watched her take a pot out of the oven and place it on the stove. She removed the oven mitts and wiped her hands on the apron, covering her teal blue pants suit.

"Helen, you look fabulous, as usual."

She turned to see Gee standing in the doorway and smiled. "Hello, dear. Dinner is just about ready. Where's Keith?"

"He's in the other room with your husband."

"Well, come on over here and talk to me while I finish up."

"What do you need me to do?"

"Sit," she said firmly.

Gee sat at the kitchen island and the two women fell into friendly chatter. Their conversation was only interrupted twice. Once when Keith came in to say a quick hello and give Helen a hug and again, when Helen handed Gee a stack of plates. "Now you can do something," She said.

Gee smiled. "Gladly! But first, I'd like to ask you something." She set the plates down and pulled Helen to the seat next to her.

"What is it, dear?"

"Helen, my wedding is just a couple of months away. I don't know what I would've done without you. You and Reese have been there every step of the way. I mean—the way you took it upon yourself to go to the bridal shops, looking for the perfect dress for me, when I had just about given up, was monumental. Not only did you find the dress, you also went with me to every fitting. It's no secret how I feel about you and Regis, and you did say you'd help out wherever I needed you."

"Of course, what do you need me to do?"

Gee's mood changed, and Helen reached over and laid a hand on top of hers. "What is it, dear? What do you need?"

"You can say no if you want to. I'd completely understand, but you're the closest I have to a mother, and I was wondering if—you'd sit in for her."

Helen's speechless stare was unwavering. She took in a breath and slowly lifted a hand and pressed it against her trembling lips. Her eyes filled with tears and a slow smile spread across her face. "I would be honored," she whispered.

"Thank you." Gee smiled. She leaned over, and drew Helen into a loving embrace. "That means so much to me."

"Of course, dear." Helen removed her apron, dabbed the tears away from her eyes, and then discarded it onto the back of a chair. She picked up the plates and handed them to Gee, then followed her into the dining room to set the table.

Dinner consisted of roasted pork tenderloin with rosemary and garlic, mashed potatoes, and sautéed asparagus.

"Everything looks so good, Helen," Gee said.

"Well, I hope it's as good as it looks," she laughed fondly.

Gee put a forkful of the tenderloin into her mouth. She closed her eyes to enjoy the way the flavors blended on her palate.

"This is delicious. How do you make it so tender?"

"I believe it has something to do with the white wine I add. I'll send you home with the recipe. It's foolproof."

"It's delicious," she said, shoveling another forkful into her mouth.

Regis glanced over at Gee. "I know you don't want to talk about this now, but I got another call from Cassandra McClure."

Gee rolled her eyes toward the ceiling, "And? What does she want now?"

"She wants to be done with the case. We know that this Deke character is involved, so we need to write up the report and give it to her."

"Why is she in such a hurry? She needs to get off my back and let me do my job."

"Well now, Gee. If this Deke is selling guns illegally--"

"We know he is, Regis, but I don't think she cares about that. He's just the go-between. I'm sorry. Deke doesn't have enough sense to be in this alone. I may be wrong, but I really believe she's trying to implicate him for some other reason or to cover up for someone else."

"Who? And if that's the case, why are we following him?"

Gee shrugged. "Because I think he's going to help us. We're closer than we think, and that's why she's going nuts about it. My gut tells me, she's expecting us to stop now, write the report and put all the blame on Deke, but I believe he's going to lead us to bigger fish."

"Really?"

"Really. You know me, Regis. I'm not one to give in so easily."

Regis lifted his fork to his mouth and paused, "We don't have a choice. She's the one signing the check, and she wants the report now."

"Well, I'm not ready to give it to her."

He laid his fork down, sat back in his chair, and studied her.

"What, Regis? Come on, I think I've earned the right to follow this through. I'm the one who ended up in the hospital while working on it, and I believe I had it right in the palm of my hand."

"You're talking about the note?"

"Yes."

"Hey, you two. We're having dinner here," Keith warned.

Helen chimed in. "No more talk about work, Regis."

Gee held up her hands. "This is the last thing I'm going to say, and then I'm done. Cassandra McClure is a bitch, and I can't wait to be done with her, but I'm not going to let her ruin my reputation by turning in some half-assed report. You taught me better than that."

"Then stop digging. Just turn over what you have. McClure wants the proof that Deke's involved, and we have that."

"Why?"

"Why, what?"

"Why does she want a report that only proves Deke's involvement, when we can give her so much more? If I turn in what I have, I'm just scraping the surface. It goes deeper than Deke, and she knows it. I don't know who she's protecting, but, before I'm finished, she's going to wish she had hired a different firm. We don't work like that, Regis. Don't expect me to stop before my job is done. My reputation is at stake here. I can't do that."

"What do you mean, you can't? If I tell you to—"

"Don't pull rank on me, Regis. Let me do my job, or I'll quit."

"You'll what?" Regis shouted.

Helen's hand came down hard on the table, and the loud thud brought everyone's attention to her.

"Enough!" she said, never taking her eyes off Regis.

Regis cleared his throat, picked up his fork, and lifted a forkful of tenderloin to his mouth. To say another word, after Helen's reprimand, would be foolish, and he knew it.

"No more, Gee—It's over," Keith said. "We're here to enjoy dinner, damn it."

"Okay. I'm done."

"Me too." Regis said, holding his hands up in an 'I surrender' type motion, to reassure his wife he was true to his word.

"I'd just like to know which of 'em hit me." Gee said quickly, looking around the table, then lifting her shoulders in a half shrug, "I'm just sayin'."

By 6:30, they'd finished dinner, and Gee helped Helen clear the dishes, glancing down periodically to look at her watch. At 6:45, she glanced at her watch again, then searched the room for Keith.

He was still talking to Regis, but instinct had him look up and around until he met Gee's eyes. He knew that look. As soon as he could, he excused himself and quickly closed the distance between them.

"What's wrong?" he asked.

"I just happened to look at my watch. It's almost time for Reese to meet Daxden for dinner."

"Okay? And?"

"Keith, I'm worried about her. I don't know why. I just am."

"So, what do you want to do?"

"I want to make sure she's okay."

"You gonna call her?"

"If she's with Daxden, she's not going to answer her phone. He doesn't like it."

Keith grimaced. "What do you mean, he doesn't like it?"

"He asked her not to take calls or make calls when they're having their quality time."

"That's bullshit, Gee. Where's your phone?"

Gee reached into her purse and pulled out her phone. She found Reese's number and hit the button, then she handed it to him.

Keith held the phone to his ear while it rang and went to voicemail.

She gave him an 'I told you so' look.

"I want to go, make sure she's okay. Can we?"

"You want to go to the restaurant?"

"Yeah."

"No, Gee."

"Keith, she's my best friend."

"I understand that, but—"

"Please."

"Woman, you are relentless. You can't just barge in on Reese like that. What if she doesn't want you there, or what if your being there makes matters worse?"

"Then you go. Daxden doesn't know you."

"What? Me?"

"Yes. You. I'll wait here for you, or I can go and stay in the car."

He tilted his head back and pinched the bridge of his nose. "Woman," he said, shaking his head in disbelief while fighting to control the tone in his voice. "I can't believe I'm agreeing to this, but you're not going with me. I'm taking your ass home. We all know what happens when you're told to stay in the car."

7

DAXDEN LOOKED AROUND the restaurant, pleased with himself. The ambiance was exactly what he needed. The warm, inviting glow in the room boasted of an expert designer and a proprietor's talent to know what draws the best clientele and keeps them coming back. Every detail addressed, from the most attentive waiters, to the soft mood lighting that washed over each table. A huge window wrapped from one end of the room to the other, and beyond it was a breathtaking view of the magnificent bay front that reached to the end of the horizon, until it met the sky. As the sun lowered, it rested on the far edge of the water, promising a fitting sunset for what Daxden had planned tonight. He couldn't wait to see Reese's face when she walked through the doors. She was late. And just as the thought formed, he caught sight of her, making her way to the hostess desk, and craning her head to locate him.

It's about damn time, he thought, but feigned a smile, and stood to greet her. "Well, look who finally got here." He took her hand and guided her to their table.

Reese barely looked at him, her attention captured by the splendor around her. "It's as beautiful as I imagined," she said, and he adjusted the chair for her.

"I'm glad you like it. We have the best seats in the house. I insisted upon it," he smiled.

"Thank you, Daxden. It's beautiful."

"I've already ordered drinks for us. What took you so long?"

"I told you I was going by to check on Gee," she lied.

Daxden shifted, malevolence sparked. "It's always about Gee, isn't it?"

Reese raised a brow. "Meaning?"

Daxden considered her. He swallowed the angry words that rose much too quickly, and said, instead, "We'll talk about it later."

No. I want to know what you meant by that?"

He lowered his gaze and said a low-voiced. "I said, we'll talk about it later."

When he looked back up, Reese chilled at the menace she saw in his eyes.

Things with Daxden hadn't started out this way. He was very different from the man she'd met in the beginning. But, it hadn't taken long for her to see a break in what she now knew was a façade. The change had been gradual, but consistent, and lately it had gotten even worse. He held a fury inside of him, which seemed even more pronounced tonight. It was deeper and unyielding, especially when it came to Gee. In fact, it had become scary, which bolstered Reese's resolve even more to stay on task.

He leaned forward. "Listen, Reese. I don't want to fight. Not tonight. I have special plans for us. Can we just put our differences aside and have a good time?"

"I'd like that, Dax." *What did he mean, special?*

The evening had not started well. Their conversation had suffered. They barely spoke. Then, when the waiter arrived to take their order for appetizers, Daxden's mood suddenly lightened. "I'll have an order of potato skins with sour cream, and the lady will have a shrimp cocktail."

The waiter scratched the order onto his pad and turned from the table.

Reese frowned at Daxden. "Wait. I don't want shrimp cocktail?"

Daxden's brows furrowed.

Reese straightened in her chair. "You didn't even ask me, Daxden."

She was fed up. And, he was so utterly self-absorbed he couldn't see it.

His eyes flashed as she summoned the waiter back to the table.

Daxden straightened and leaned forward. "I've already ordered for both of us. Don't make a scene."

"She turned to the waiter. "Can you please bring me an order of your stuffed mushrooms? I hear they're amazing," she smiled.

The waiter scratched it on his pad. "Sure."

Daxden laughed. "Stuffed mushrooms? They're hideous. I hate stuffed mushrooms."

"They're not for you," she said.

The waiter glanced between the two. "Do you still want the shrimp cocktail?"

"You can bring it for the gentleman."

"Yes, ma'am." The waiter smiled and left the table.

Daxden stared at her. "Why couldn't you have just left it alone?"

"Because that's not how this is going to work tonight, Daxden. You ordered my wine *and* my appetizer. What next? My entrée?"

Anger colored his cheeks "It's the gentlemanly thing to do."

She sighed, "No, it isn't. It's the controlling thing to do, and Daxden, that's not happening anymore."

"You should be thankful that I even brought you here in the first place."

"You brought me here? Daxden, that's my car outside in the parking lot. You may have invited me, but I brought myself. Don't get it twisted."

His eyes darkened. Hardly able to conceal his irritation, he heaved a sigh and leaned back. Even though his mouth smiled, his eyes continued to glare.

"F-Fine." He said.

The single-word answer made her wonder what thoughts might be going through his mind, which placed an additional strain on the rest of the evening. Reese took in a breath and dropped her shoulders, wishing she had said no to his invitation. Gee would have been much better company. Hell, a baboon would have been better company. But, here she was. She shifted in her chair and studied him across the table. Tonight she would break it off with Daxden Green for good. No ifs, ands, or buts. She was breaking this off tonight.

"Dax, let's put our differences aside and enjoy the rest of the evening."

"Fine," he snapped again.

She rolled her eyes, knowing that the sharpness in his tone was intended to rip her suggestion to shreds and smear it right in her face, but she refused to play his game. She picked up the menu and read every entrée available, determined to ignore his tantrum.

With so many delicious entrées listed, it was difficult to decide, so she summoned their waiter to the table again. She had chosen two entrees she thought she'd like to try, but couldn't decide between them. The waiter took his time, describing both entrées in question –explaining how it was prepared and stating whether it was marinated, or if it contained a special sauce. He even suggested the manager's prime choices for the evening. Reese listened intently, allowing his descriptions to paint mental pictures of the mouth-watering cuisine.

Daxden watched, his blood boiling. He was furious. *She's flirting right in front of my face.*

8

KEITH THREADED HIS way through the throng of prospective diners waiting to be seated. As he stepped into the main area of the restaurant, he paused to marvel at the splendor surrounding him, then he whistled softly through his teeth. It was everything the advertising and word of mouth claimed it would be. Definitely a place he'd like to bring Gee one night.

He dragged his attention back to the task at hand and scanned the dining room. It didn't take long before he spotted Reese, and across from her had to be the infamous Daxden Green.

What kind of name is Daxden anyway? He thought. He sampled the name, rolling it off his tongue with various pronunciations. He kept coming up with Dagwood, which put him in mind of two things. Endora's hilarious mispronunciations of Darren on Bewitched, or Blondie's bumbling husband, in the comic strip. He chuckled softly to himself.

Keith looked around at absolute sophistication: the art on the walls, the exquisite seating . . . the view. His gaze shifted back to Daxden, remembering Gee's warning about this Daxden not playing with a full deck and could blow up if provoked. *Really?* He thought. *Here? Could he really be that foolish?* On the other hand, he and Gee had both agreed that the entire dinner could turn out to be just that, a very nice dinner. If that's the case, there would be no reason for Reese to know he had been there at all.

He found an inconspicuous seat at the fully stocked bar, in the far corner of the room. He sat and ordered a beer.

He could see that Reese was captivated by her surroundings by the way she kept looking up from the menu to glance around, absorbed by the beauty of the restaurant and fascinated by the presentation of each dish that passed by their table. After a while, she motioned to a waiter, who quickly came to the table. Reese appeared to be asking questions about the list of entrees.

Keith thought about ordering an appetizer for himself, but the dinner at the Ovalton's had been so filling, he decided against it. Also, he and Gee had been sent home with enough leftovers to feed them for a week. He picked up his cell phone to call Gee.

"Hey, babe."

"What's going on?" Gee asked.

"Looks like Reese is enjoying herself. The restaurant is gorgeous. Somebody sank a lot of money into this place."

"So, Reese looks happy?"

"No, she looks—fascinated."

"By Daxden or the restaurant?"

"I'm not sure."

"Take pictures and send them to me."

"I can't do that."

"Yes, you can, Keith. I need to see her face."

Keith rolled his eyes toward the ceiling. "Okay, I'll call you back after I send them." He moved to an area where he could get a full shot with his camera, took several pictures and sent them to Gee. He waited a few minutes and called her back. "So, what do you think?" He asked when she answered the phone.

"Keith, look at the second picture. Do you see how Reese is looking at Daxden? The first picture is when she's looking around the restaurant; she likes it, but there's tension in the second picture. She's angry and saying something to Daxden. Something's wrong. I don't like it."

"Okay, what do you want me to do?"

"Nothing yet."

Keith went back to the bar to continue watching the table, with the phone to his ear. He trusted Gee's instincts. If she said something was wrong, it was. After the waiter left the table, Daxden reached across and grabbed Reese's arm, yanking her toward him, and spat words in her face. Reese snatched her arm free and gestured a sharp warning back in his direction.

"Uh-oh."

"What is it?"

"Daxden grabbed Reese's arm."

"He did what?"

"Uh-huh. But she snatched it back. Whatever happened over there, she's not backing down."

"What do you mean? What did she do?"

"She folded her arms on the table, and she's leaning in on him. Like she's telling him off. Gee, has she ever said anything about this guy grabbing her?"

"No. What do you think she's saying to him?"

"I'm too far away. I can't make it out. It's not exactly cozy over there, I'll tell you that."

"Get closer."

"If I do, I'll blow it."

"At this point, so what?"

"I'll try to get as close as I can, but if he's as unpredictable as you say, I don't want to set him off." He stood slowly.

"Be careful."

"Hold on, Babe. Reese just got up. She's moving toward the restrooms. They're arguing, there's no mistake about that. Daxden looks like he's about to explode. It's obvious he's struggling to control himself. Listen, I'm

66

going to go stand by the restroom door. I think it's time that Reese knows she's not alone."

As Keith passed their table, he saw Daxden take a deep breath and relax with it, then he reached into his pocket, pulled out a ring box, and set it on the table in front of him.

Keith whispered into the phone. "Gee, Daxden just pulled a ring box out of his pocket."

"A what?"

"You heard me. You don't think he's stupid enough to propose to her. Do you?"

"I *wondered* why he kept calling this their special dinner. Keith, this won't end well."

"Okay, I'm standing outside the restroom alcove waiting for Reese."

Just then, Reese emerged and almost ran into him. She was surprised at first, but then she relaxed.

"What are you doing here?" she whispered.

"Seriously? Your friend's name is Gee Haynes, and you're wondering what I'm doing here?"

"Gee sent you?"

Keith slid the phone into her hand. "She wants to talk to you."

Reese took it and ducked back into the bathroom.

"Gee?"

"Yeah, it's me, Reese. You okay?"

"You were right, this was a terrible idea."

"I kind of figured it would be. No worries, though, Keith is there. He's won't leave you."

"That makes me feel better. Thanks."

"Reese, Keith said Daxden grabbed you. When did that shit start?"

Reese sighed. "I'll talk to you about it."

"This isn't the first time?"

Reese was now holding back tears.

"Reese, do you have some kind of psycho love for this goon that you're not telling me about?

"Noooo. I loathe the man. And, I did tell you things have been escalating,"

"Keith saw how he grabbed you, Reese. That's not escalating, that's full-fledged abuse."

"I know. And, I know it can only get worse. That's another reason I came tonight. I came to end it, thinking I'd be safer in a public place."

"Ok, then there's a bigger problem. Keith saw Daxden put a ring box on the table. If he's already putting his hands on you, your refusal tonight is going to really set him off."

Reese sighed, closed her eyes and rested her head against the wall. That was the last thing she wanted to hear. "Okay. I'll handle it."

She left the bathroom and handed Keith his phone.

He put the phone to his ear and said, "I'll call you back, Gee," then he hung up and slid the phone in the case on his belt.

68

"Gee told you about the ring?"

Reese pulled in a breath. "I don't know what he could be thinking. We've hardly made it to that level. This is so weird."

"No, it's not. You know the scale of escalation in these matters."

She gave Keith a miserable nod. "That's why he kept calling this our 'special dinner.' I thought it was because of the restaurant. I never thought it was to ask me to marry him! You saw the way he grabbed me."

"Oh, yeah. I saw it."

"Why would I say yes to a marriage proposal after that?

She shifted nervously and lowered her gaze. "Daxden's looking at us. He sees us talking."

"He doesn't know me."

"That doesn't matter." She glanced up. "Oh, God. He's coming this way. And, I can tell, he's flipped out."

Keith turned toward him, but Daxden whisked past him to Reese. "Get back to the table," he ordered.

Reese turned her head. "You don't tell me what—"

Daxden cut her off. "You heard me!" He glanced furiously up at Keith. "Are you trying to push up on my woman?"

"No, man. Not at all. I thought she was somebody I knew." Keith put his hands up. "I didn't mean to offend, sorry."

Daxden turned to Reese, "Get your ass back to the table."

Keith dropped his head. His voice low, "Is it necessary to talk to her like that?"

"W-who the hell are you to t-tell me how to talk to my woman?"

Reese moved in between the two men. She tried to control her voice. "This is not going to happen here, Daxden. I won't be treated this way."

Daxden grabbed her arm and shoved her in the direction of their table. "D-Didn't I t-tell you to get back to the t-table?"

Keith stepped forward and wrenched Reese's arm free. He looked at Daxden. "You're making a scene, man."

Daxden was a shadow of Keith's tall, lithe frame and his face streaked red. He summoned his most ferocious regard, and sputtered, "What the- what the- what the f—? You're trying to t-tell me w-what to do with my woman?"

At Daxden's back, Reese whirled around to Keith. He looked subtly at her table, then the exit, with his message clear. *Get the hell out of here.*

Keith bore Daxden's furious regard and let him rant on . . . and on, while he quietly watched Reese gather her things and exit the restaurant. He folded his arms as Daxden

70

railed about his rights with *his woman* and all other kinds of medieval nonsense. When he was sure enough time had passed for Reese to locate her car and get well on the way home, Keith allowed his gaze to grow steely and forceful. He dwarfed Daxden as he leaned close to the smaller man. "Are you done?"

Affected, Daxden struggled to hold onto his swagger, but took an involuntary step back. "Y-Yeah, I'm done. W-Why? You got something else to say?"

Keith gave Daxden a withered look. "No."

He unfolded his arms and walked back to the bar, leaving Daxden to figure it all out.

Daxden whipped around to throw a glaring look at Reese, but she was nowhere in sight. He barreled across the room to their table and, after noticing that her purse was gone, he rushed to the front of the restaurant to look outside. Still nothing. A sneer creased deep grooves into his face. He'd been duped. Completely outwitted. By a woman! He stormed back to the table and sat alone for a while, then asked for the bill and a take home box.

Keith watched Daxden, breathless with anger, pay his bill and stand to leave.

As Daxden walked across the room, he noticed Keith sitting at the bar and walked over to him.

Keith turned and looked Daxden full in the face. His eyes slid over to the empty table and retraced the path

Daxden had to have taken to approach him, and then he met Daxden's glare again, "Lose something?" he asked with a smile.

"M-Man, y-you better be glad you're ass is in *here* because, if I see y-you outside—"

Keith reached inside his breast pocket, pulled out his badge, and laid it carefully on the top of the bar in full view. He gave a methodical chuckle and returned Daxden's icy glare. "I honestly don't think you want any of this," he said coolly, nodding toward the badge. "Seriously—just walk away."

Daxden's glare turned into thin slits, and the tiny twitch of his lips let Keith know he had hit his mark. He watched Daxden's hands drop to his side and form clenched fists, but there were no more words spoken between them –just one last tilt of Keith's head, as though he was daring Daxden to throw his best punch. Instead, Daxden let out a long, angry breath, then turned and stormed out of the restaurant.

9

KEITH PULLED INTO Gee's driveway and reached up to push the button that opened the garage door. He watched it slide up and as usual, when Gee heard the garage, she made her way to the door to wait for him.

He looks tired. she thought

He made a mock face as he kissed her. "The things I do for you, woman."

She smiled back. "Reese is here."

"I figured that."

He walked through the kitchen into the dining room and greeted her with a hug.

"Reese told me what happened," Gee said. "I should've gone with you."

A deliberate look washed over Keith's face, and his words sifted through his lips like sand. "No. You shouldn't have."

"What would you have done, Gee?" Reese asked.

"I don't know, but I felt helpless, just sitting here."

Keith did a half turn and looked at her. If Daxden had seen you, no telling what he would've done. He's out of control."

"I told you." Gee said.

Keith opened the refrigerator and pulled out a beer. "No, it's worse than we thought. You want a beer, Reese?"

"No, thanks. I'll take a soda, though." She sat down at the dining room table.

Keith turned to Gee. "Babe?"

"Nothing for me, thanks."

Reese groaned, "I'm afraid I've gotten myself into a real mess."

"It's nothing you can't get out of," Gee said, sitting next to her.

"I know, and it's not like it's going to break my heart to see it end, either."

Keith joined them and took a swig of his beer, then handed Reese her soda. "You just watch your back, Reese. I wouldn't put anything past this guy."

"I'll be fine. Daxden's no fool. I'm sure he knows it's over."

Gee rubbed Reese's shoulder, "Guys like that don't take hints, Reese. You're going to have to come right out and tell him it's over."

Reese opened her soda and took a sip. "I had planned to do that tonight."

Keith shifted, uncomfortably. "Don't be cavalier about this, Reese. When you say things like that, it lets me know you've seriously underestimated this guy. He's possessive, physically and mentally abusive, and has already decided you'll marry him despite all the red flags. That's an over-the-phone break up if I ever heard one ... and then a restraining order, because he's not just going to leave it at that."

Gee looked at Reese, whose face bore the truth of what Keith had just said. "You've had these same thoughts. Haven't you?"

Reese looked away as she studied the moment. She looked up at Keith first and said, softly, "I'd so hoped I could just . . . end it. Hoping he'd understand and we could go our separate ways."

"And after tonight?" Gee asked.

Reese lowered her gaze again and slowly shook her head. "I'm afraid that . . . Keith is right."

Gee felt a shiver deep inside. She looked at Keith, then Reese. "Reese, this behavior didn't occur in a vacuum. You told me about the verbal abuse. But, when did the physical stuff start?"

"Not too long ago. I never let him get away with it, though. He'd snatch my arm, I'd snatch it back and stand up to him. But once he was on a rant, there was no stopping him, and he could say some terrible things."

Gee studied the deep hurt in her friend's eyes. "God, Reese. I mean, look at you. No one should treat you that way."

Reese gave her a long look. She slapped her hand against her lap and brandished a wide grin. "You know, you're right." She shook away the encroaching heaviness. "I don't have to take this. I'm worth better than this. As of tonight, I'm finished with him."

"And you can just turn off your feelings?"

"What feelings, Gee? Feelings didn't even have a chance to develop."

Gee grinned, relieved. "There's my girl."

Keith took another swig of his beer and shook his head. "I still have my concerns, but I'll hold them at bay."

Reese chuckled and finished the last of her soda. "And on that note, I think it's time for me to get going." She said, picking up her purse, she moved toward the door.

Keith gave her a guarded look, "Reese, I'm leaving tomorrow, and I'd love to know that there's someone here with Gee, after what happened the other night. You might want to consider staying here until things blow over."

Gee's eyes brightened. "That's a great idea."

"As much as I appreciate it, I think I'm gonna just go home. I can't let Daxden scare me like that, but thanks."

They said their good-byes. Gee and Keith stood in the doorway, until Reese was safely in the car and pulling out of the driveway.

76

10

SO, WHAT DO you really think?" Gee asked.

"I think Reese bit off a little more than she can chew."

"Me too, but what can we do?"

"Just be there for her. Daxden's not playing with a full deck, and Reese is giving him too much credit. I mean, he actually wanted to fight me when he thought I was trying to—" he lifted his hands and made air quotation marks with his fingers, —'push up on his woman.'"

And, after everything that happened tonight, he was still going to ask her to marry him. What fantasy world does that man live in? What could be going on in his head? It's obvious Reese isn't into him. Why can't he see it? He thinks that a shiny ring is going to make Reese love him? He's crazy"

"Don't underestimate him, Gee. Be careful."

"You don't have to worry about me."

"I don't?" Keith said, clearing his throat sarcastically.

Gee looked up at him. "What? You don't believe me?"

He took in a heavy breath. "Just be careful."

Gee studied him. "You think Dr. Alex can help?"

"With what?"

"He might be able to answer some questions for us. Can you do me a favor?"

"Uh-oh,"

"What?"

"Your favors have grave consequences," he chuckled. "What is it this time?"

She gave him a snide look. "Just contact Dr. Alex for me. See if he'll give me a call."

Keith studied her and nodded. "Okay. I don't think he'll mind. Sure, I'll do that for you."

"He might be able to help us understand what Reese is dealing with and give us some kind of an idea on how to proceed if we need to."

"He's definitely the best person to talk to."

"I know."

"I'll call him in the morning. So—what reason are you going to give Regis for pursuing *this*?"

"Curiosity."

"And you think he's going to go for it?"

"Of course not," Gee laughed.

Keith laughed too and shook his head. "Did you talk to him about going back to work?"

"Yes, I meant to tell you. We agreed I'd return on Thursday. He thinks it's still too early, but it's been a full week and there's work I need to get back to."

He nodded. "I agree with Regis. It might be too soon, but I know you're about to go stir crazy."

"And you would be right," she laughed. "What time does your plane leave tomorrow?"

"Two. Why?" He raised a curious brow and smiled.

"Just making sure we don't have to get up early."

"I can Uber to the airport."

"You certainly will not Uber, Keith Jenison. I'm taking you."

"You don't have to."

"I want to. What's the matter with you?"

Keith closed the distance between them and pulled her close. "I'm gonna miss you, woman."

She snuggled close to him. "I'm only an hour away by plane."

"I know." He leaned in and kissed her gently, and when he tried to pull away, Gee moved her hand to the back of his head so he couldn't. The kiss deepened, and Keith moved his hands slowly, down her back and over the small mound of her butt. He felt her arch upward with desire, and every cell in his body tingled with pleasure. He opened his eyes and studied her. "You're so beautiful," he whispered.

Gee's eyes fluttered open and she felt a slow burn of desire in the pit of her stomach. "So are you," she breathed, unable to peel her eyes from his.

"I'm so turned on right now." The last part of his words came out husky and on a heavy sigh.

Gee bit down on her bottom lip. "Me too."

"What do you say, we take this conversation to the other room?"

"Which one?"

"Pick one."

He found her lips again, and this time he slid his tongue across them, urging them to open and welcome his inside. When they did, their tongues met, and she gave his a teasing lick. She felt around for his hand then led him to the bedroom, where he sat impatiently waiting for her to join him. Her body, warm and sensuous, sank onto his, and she kissed him softly, reaching up to unbutton the first button of his shirt. The small act created goose bumps across his skin. Then she moved to the second button.

Keith's whole body shook with desire, and he pulled her closer, skimming his lips along the line of her cheek and down her neck, laying pools of wet kisses at her collarbone. He needed to look at her— absorb every bit of her intimacy; he needed to see the way her eyes glossed over and danced with mischief and sweet surrender. As though she read his mind, her eyes lifted to his, and there it was—so many facets of yearning summed up in one word—love. There was no mistaking it, as though someone had taken a chisel and permanently etched the word there, and she continued to caress him.

"Gee," he breathed against her mouth.

She unbuttoned the last button on his shirt and let it slide off his back, down his arms, and onto the floor, leaning in, she placed wet kisses on his bare chest, trailing downward until he couldn't stand it. "Gee, please," he breathed.

She reached over and pressed the button on the radio, filling the room with the sound of Teddy Pendergrass' sultry voice, singing, "Close the Door." Gee stood, swaying in time with the music, her body enticing and seducing him, as she slowly and deliberately removed her clothes, never once averting her eyes from his.

"I love watching you," he said.

"I know. I can tell."

"I'll bet you can," he said, following her gaze to the undeniable erection in his pants. "I can't get enough of you."

"I'm glad."

He removed the remainder of his clothes and lay beside her, then leaned down and trailed butterfly kisses from her neck to her ear, where he whispered in a deep growl. "Do you know how sexy you are?"

"No," she whispered back. "Tell me."

He pulled her closer. "I'd rather show you."

Their lovemaking was hot and desperate that night. With the need to let the other know, their present and future were wrapped in their oneness. This was a memory that they would hold on to until the next time they were together.

***

Gee looked at the clock.

"It's 3:00 in the morning," she said through a yawn.

Keith lay with his eyes closed, and his arms crossed under his head. "I know."

"Don't you think we'd better get some sleep?"

"I really love this music."

"It's an oldies station I found.

"I'm lovin' it," he said, singing along with Ray, Goodman, and Brown.

Gee smiled. "I like hearing you sing. It lets me know you're happy."

He turned to her. "I couldn't be happier."

"Me either. What's this song?"

"Come on. You've got to remember, Ray, Goodman, and Brown's, "Special Lady."

"I do. I just couldn't think of the name."

He turned to her and sang the words, then reached up and brushed her bangs away from her eyes, tucking them behind her ear, then he pulled her down and kissed her.

"I love you, Gee."

She nodded. "I love you too."

They lay in each other's arms without speaking, enjoying the music and the realization that they belonged to each other in every way, and everything was good.

It wasn't until another familiar song came on that Keith broke the silence by chuckling softly.

Gee lifted her head to look at him. "What?" she asked.

This song has to be one of my all-time favorites."

"Why's that?"

"Remember me telling you what my family went through with my mom? Her problem with D.I.D? My dad said this was the song that was playing when she walked through the door at his party, and he knew immediately she was no longer the evil alternate personality, Lee, who put us through so much grief." He sighed and raised his hand to his mouth as he yawned.

"It's hard to imagine your mom being anyone other than the sweet woman she is."

"Oh, I've got memories."

"Yeah?"

"I remember Lee. I don't like remembering her, but I do."

"You say she was evil?"

"She was worse than evil."

"Because she abused Kelly?"

He turned toward Gee and lifted himself on his elbow. "Not only that."

"Did she abuse you too?"

"Oh yeah. When I got in the way."

"Of what?" Gee asked.

"Her beating Kelly. I tried to stop it. Sometimes, when I knew she was on the warpath, I'd take Kelly and hide her away in what I thought would be a safe place, begging her to stay quiet until things cooled down."

"You're such a good brother."

"Not nearly good enough. I couldn't stop it."

Gee turned her head and looked at him. "You were just a little boy."

He gave a quick nod. "I know."

"What more could you have done?"

"I guess I feel like things wouldn't have gotten so bad if I had told Dad sooner."

"No, Keith, you're not going to lie here and tell me that after all these years, you still blame yourself for what happened. Kelly's an accomplished woman, a great wife, and a wonderful mother, *despite* what Lee did. All because of you. It wasn't your fault."

He nodded. "She has Pen now. He'll take care of her."

"You and Pen. You two have been friends for a long time. Haven't you?"

"Oh, yeah. Since our police academy days." Keith chuckled. "Jeffery Pennington. He was my brother long

84

before he became my brother-in-law. It's good to know you've got someone to depend on. Our motto has always been, 'You jump. I jump.'"

Gee laughed. "I know. I like the dynamics between the two of you. What did your parents say when Kelly and Pen fell in love?"

"They were all for it. I was the one who had the problem. Pen was my friend. No man wants his best friend dating his sister."

"Why not?"

"Guys have –you know—guy talks. Pen had never had a serious relationship. He couldn't settle down. A different girl every weekend and I knew about it. I didn't want my sister to be his next conquest."

"But that's not how it turned out."

"No. It's not. He loves her."

"Yes, he does," Gee said, cuddling closer. She lifted her eyes and studied him. "You're lucky to have such a wonderful family."

Keith sat up on his elbow again and looked down at her, "What do you mean? They're your family too, now."

"I know, and I love all of you. It's hard to explain. I'm crazy about your mom, but I get envious sometimes, wishing mine was still here. Your dad is an amazing father, but I have a hard time dealing with the fact that mine walked out on me before I was even born. I miss having that biological connection. You know what I mean?"

"Aw, come here, woman," he said, wrapping her in his arms. "I'm the next best thing to biological."

Gee chuckled, "Yes, you are," she whispered against his neck. "You know, I still can't imagine your mom being evil."

He lifted his head and smiled at her. "She's not. We had to get to the place where we could separate the two. Mom is not Lee, nor the other way around. They're two different people. A lot of therapy went into making sure we understood that. Dr. Alex was amazing."

"I know. That's why I'm looking forward to talking to him. I look at your mom and dad. They are so in love."

"Yeah, they are," Keith said fondly. "Dad said, when he saw her walk through those doors, he swore his feet wouldn't work, but his heart seemed to sprout ten thousand wings that glided him to her. He said he knew instantly that she was Les, and hoped Lee was gone forever. I always said that I wanted a love like that one day, and now I have it."

"We both do," Gee whispered, kissing him softly on the cheek and nestling her body closer to his. "This is the kind of love my mother used to tell me to hold out for. She always said, 'don't settle,' and I'm so glad I didn't."

Keith held her close and hummed the tune of, "If You Don't Know Me By Now," by Harold Melvin and the Blue Notes.

It didn't take long before they were sleeping soundly.

11

REESE BACKED INTO the garage and sat, watching the garage door close before getting out of the car. She let herself into the house and turned on every light she passed, on her way to the living room, then she stopped abruptly, irritated with herself.

"This is silly. I'm not going to be afraid in my own home."

Her house was located in a new community near the freeway, one of the many perks that helped her make the decision to move there. The exquisite open floor plan offered three bedrooms and two and a half baths; the half bath was considered a powder room, but the other two were full baths. One was located in one of the guest bedrooms, and the other in the master suite. The house came equipped with a tandem garage that she thought would make a perfect office one day, but, for right now, her office was in the third bedroom. Warm beige colored the walls inside Reese's house contrasting with the Natural Brazilian Cherry wood floors. This was *home*. She loved it, and she was not going to let the likes of Daxden Green make her afraid to live in it.

She made her way to her bedroom to get comfortable. When she returned to the living room, she was dressed in a gold and black caftan that wrapped around her thin frame and flowed to the floor. She sat on the sofa and turned on the television. A little TV before bed would help her relax enough to fall asleep. It wasn't long before she realized she was just staring at the screen. The late news had been playing. She fumbled for the remote to change the channel.

"Something funny," she mused as she flipped through the channels. "I need to laugh."

Her phone chimed, and she glanced over at the coffee table where it lay face up, with Daxden's name emblazoned across the screen. She shifted back to the TV and let it ring. She couldn't take any more of him, not tonight. She knew what she had to do, but right now, all she needed was the time to recharge.

Daxden hung up and called again.

"Get a hint, Daxden. I'm not answering."

This time, when it stopped ringing, the voicemail notification sounded.

Five minutes later, he started calling again, several times, back to back. Each time he left a message. Reese ignored the calls. Then they finally stopped completely.

It was after midnight when Reese decided to turn off the television and the lights and go to bed. The darkness highlighted the usual hums and vibrations she called her 'white sounds,' a symphony of house sounds that comforted her. However, her comfort was suddenly marred by the unexpected slam of a car door that clipped the silence and sent an avalanche of uncontrollable shivers up her spine. She tensed and took an involuntary step toward the door.

"He wouldn't dare," she whispered.

Distant footsteps echoed on the pavement outside and leading to her front door. Panic mingled fear and the unknown with her blood, as she scrambled to the door and pressed her back firmly against it.

"Reese!" Daxden yelled.

His fists banged on the door so hard she felt it jolt and vibrate through her back. "Reese! Are you in there?"

Reese held her breath and remained pressed against the door.

"Reese, I didn't mean what I said on those messages. I just need to talk to you. That's all."

She could see the flashing blue light of her cell phone on the coffee table. In her haste to get out of sight, she'd left it there. *What kind of messages could he have left that made him think he needed to come over, at this time of night, to apologize for them?* She asked herself, cursing under her breath; *I can't even call the police if I need to.*

"R-Reese, please o-open th-the door?" he stuttered.

She stayed put, barely breathing. Fear trickled like ice water through her veins.

"D-Damn it, R-Reese." He hit the door one last time, then he walked away.

Reese heard his quick footsteps leaving the door and she took a quick peek through a long side window. She could see him walking toward his car and hoped he was leaving, but, she couldn't be sure, so she scurried across the floor to the coffee table, snatched up her phone, and dashed back to the door just as she heard his footsteps coming back.

A bright beam of light flashed through the window and, like a bullet, hit the opposite wall, then it bounced from corner to corner in an attempt to find her. The light danced its way from the base of the floor to the ceiling and then it crawled back down again. Reese kept her back pressed firmly against the door, watching the stream of light wash over the fireplace and bounce again from corner to corner. The room went dark, just to brighten again, when Daxden shined the flashlight through the window on the other side.

Reese's whole body shook with fear so violently she found it difficult to hold the phone and press 9-1-1.

"9-1-1. What is your emergency?"

She gave her name and address. "There's a man outside my door with a flashlight," Reese whispered. "He's shining it into my house. Please, send someone quickly. I'm afraid."

"Are you somewhere safe, ma'am?"

"I'm inside my house, but I have no idea what his intentions are."

"Do you know this man?"

"Yes."

"Okay, I'm sending a cruiser your way. Stay where you are and stay on the phone with me until you hear them."

"Please hurry," she whispered.

Daxden moved to the windows on the side of the house and shined the flashlight through them, then she heard him rattle the gate leading to the backyard, but a padlock kept him from going through.

He made his way back to the front door and pounded on it again, yelling her name, "R-Reese! Reese! Damn it, R-Reese, open t-the fuckin' door!"

Reese threw her hands over her mouth and pressed tightly stifling a scream that threatened to escape, when Daxden hit the door hard one last time.

She was relieved when she heard voices outside. Pressing her ear against the door, she to listen.

"Good evening, officers," Daxden said.

"Is this your house, sir?"

Daxden tried to laugh, "No, sir. My girlfriend lives here. I was trying to make sure she was –safe."

The other officer looked over at Daxden's car. "That your car?"

"Why, yes . . ." his voice trailed off when the officer walked to it and shined a flashlight through the window.

"Is there a reason your girlfriend wouldn't be safe?"

"What?" Daxden asked, shifting his weight. He turned his attention from the officer looking in his car and met the gaze of the one standing in front of him. "Oh, we had a little tiff at a restaurant tonight, and I was trying to make sure she was okay."

"Doesn't look like anyone's home. What is your name, sir?" The officer took out a pad and a pen.

"Name's Daxden. Daxden Green. I tried to call her, b-but she's not answering her phone."

"Well, you're scaring the neighbors. We got calls about you yelling and pounding on the door. They're not happy. If she's in there, I'd say there's a pretty good chance she doesn't want to talk to you. What's your date of birth, Mr. Green?"

"Is th-this necessary?"

"You can give it to me now, or I can take you down to the station and . . ."

Daxden rattled off his date of birth. "N-Now, what?"

He fell instantly silent, trying to calm his temper. The last thing he needed were cops snooping around in his business. He watched the officer snatch a paper free from his pad. He walked over and handed it to him.

"What's th-this?"

"Disturbing the peace. It's a warning. Go home, Mr. Green. It's on record now, so don't come back here tonight. Go home, sleep on it, and maybe she'll talk to you tomorrow."

Shaking with fury, Daxden snatched the warning from the officer's hand and stormed to his car. He ripped the car door open and slid behind the wheel, tossing the flashlight and the warning into the back seat, then he slammed the door shut and waited.

The officers went to their car and waited too. When Daxden didn't leave right away, they hit their blue lights, with a *woop-woop* of the siren.

Daxden started his car, threw the gearshift into drive, and sped away.

Reese watched through the window as he disappeared down the road. After a few moments, the officers got out of their car and came to the door. Reese opened it.

"Thank you, officers. Can you just stay around the neighborhood to make sure he doesn't come back?"

"Sure, we'll cruise back around from time to time."

"He was pounding and yelling through the door like a crazy man." She held her hand over her heart. "I've never been so frightened in my life."

"What was he yelling?"

"For me to open the door. He said he wanted to apologize for some messages he'd left on my phone." She

94

opened her voice mail and hit the speaker, so the officers could hear the messages.

"You c-can't answer my c-call, Reese?" He screamed through the phone.

She pushed the button to go to the next message. "I-I'm gonna c-call back in one m-minute, bitch. Y-You'd better answer the phone."

The next message was, "Y-You know, it wouldn't be difficult, Reese, for me t-to put my hands around y-your scrawny little neck and sq-sq-squeeze the life r-right out of you. I-I'm so ready t-to do that. Y-You have no idea what you r-r-ruined tonight. E-every th-th- thing was p-p -p . . . everything was p-p-per f-f-fect. And you r-r-ruined it, you whore!" The stuttering got worse with each message.

The next message said, "I'm gonna make you w-wish you were d-dead, bitch."

She pushed the button again, and Daxden's voice changed to a deep unfamiliar bellow that thundered through the phone and frightened her so badly that she almost dropped it, "Answer the fuckin' phone, bitch!"

The officers glanced at each other and then back to Reese. "Ma'am, we're going to finish writing this report, and in the morning, if I were you, I'd get over to the station and get a restraining order. Don't take these threats lightly."

"I won't, officer."

"When you go to the station tomorrow, they'll be able to pull up our report. Attached will be a copy of the warning he was issued as well."

"Sounds good," Reese said, still shaken.

"And whatever you do, don't erase those messages."

"You're still going to stay in the neighborhood. Right?"

"Yes, ma'am. Especially after listening to that."

"Thank you. I feel better knowing that."

That night Reese had a fitful sleep. Even though she knew the police would be monitoring the area, she jerked herself awake several times at the slightest noise. What she didn't know was, Daxden had circled back and parked in front of her house more than once and each time the cruiser pulled quietly behind him and flashed their lights. He cursed the last time, when they pulled beside him and powered down their window, Daxden did the same.

He chuckled, nervously. "I-I just n-need to make sure she's alright, officers. I-I-I'm so w-w-worried." He shook his head. "I won't b-b-be able t-t-to s-s-sleep tonight. I'll j-j-just be p-pacing the f-floor all n-n-night. . ."

"Then the only other thing we can offer is a cool night in the county jail on a stalking charge, because that sure is what it looks like to us."

Daxden's eyes widened. The reply had caught him up short. His fingers gripped the steering wheel, his notion to schmooze the officers crushed.

The officer went on. "Sir, the whole precinct knows what's going on here and what you've been told. Another incident and you're in lock-up for the night. You'll have a huge tow bill, fines to pay, not to mention court costs . . . All kinds of problems, Mr. Green, when all you have to do is leave the area and stay away. And, just so you know, our cars are marked . . . and unmarked." The officer looked at Reese's' house and nodded. "Any car that drives up to that house tonight is going to be checked out. Go home."

Daxden clenched his teeth. It took everything within him to keep from screaming at them to leave him the hell alone. Instead, he forced a smile and a nod and closed his window. He didn't need trouble with the law, not now. He drove away and didn't come back that night.

12

IN THE MORNING, Reese got dressed and rushed to the courthouse to get the order of protection. She had to wait her turn. In front of her was a woman holding a small child. Her eye blackened and almost completely swollen shut. Her bottom lip split with dry blood caked around it. She consoled her little one by cuddling her gently to her chest and hissing a rhythmic, "sh-sh-sh-sh," in the toddler's ear until she was fast asleep. Reese could only imagine the night of horror, she had endured, and by the looks of it, she figured the young girl's problems were much worse than hers.

When she left the courthouse, she had an official restraining order filed, with a copy of it in her hand. She hurried back to her car and headed home. Somehow, having the paper in her hands and knowing he'd be served sometime today, made her feel safer, until she glanced into the rearview mirror at Daxden's car, trailing behind her. Icy terror ran through her body as she rechecked the mirror. It was definitely him, following as closely behind her as he could. He was glaring at her. *How long had he been there? Had he seen her go into the courthouse?*

Her hands shook as she pressed the Bluetooth on her steering wheel and asked to be connected to 9-1-1.

The dispatcher answered. "9-1-1, what's your emergency?"

"Yes, I just left the police station. I got an order of protection against someone."

"Yes?"

"Well, I'm on my way home, I look in my rearview mirror, and he's right behind me. What am I supposed to do, hang it out the window and show it to him?"

"Ma'am, do not approach the perpetrator. What do you mean, he's behind you?"

"His car is behind mine. I'm at a traffic light. I look in my rear view mirror, and he's right behind me. He's following me. What – should – I - do?"

"He'll be served with the order today."

"But what am I supposed to do right now?"

"Where are you?"

Reese told her.

"Pull into a public parking lot that has an attendant. Do you see one?

"Yes. I'm pulling into it now."

"Wave at the attendant. Have him come to your car."

She did as she was told and watched Daxden speed off in a different direction. "He just took off. He's gone."

Reese was shaking.

"Now, before you leave the lot, look around and make sure he's gone. Give me your address and I'll have a cruiser meet you at your house. Be careful going home." The dispatcher said.

"I will. Thank you," She gave her the address and hung up. She explained to the attendant what had happened, and he let her pull over to the side to make another phone call.

***

Gee answered. "Hi, Reese,"

"I need your help."

She sat up and motioned to Keith.

"What's wrong?"

"I had to call the police last night."

"What? Why?"

"Daxden kept calling, and he showed up at my house. The police came, and they made out a report. I can tell you the rest later, but I think I'd better take you up on your offer. Can I come stay with you for a couple of days?"

"Of course. Come on. I'm taking Keith to the airport at 12:30. Do you want me to pick you up on my way back?"

"Can you?"

"Sure. I'll call you when I'm on my way."

"Hurry, Gee. I'm scared."

A chill chased up Gee's back. She had never heard Reese admit to being afraid of anything. She hung up and turned to Keith.

"She said she's scared. Nothing scares Reese. I need to go get her now."

"Then let's go."

Gee called her back. "We're on our way, Reese. Get some clothes together and be ready when we get there. It sounds like you're in the car. Are you?"

"Yes, I am. I'm on my way home from the courthouse. I'll be there and ready by the time you get there."

"The courthouse?"

"Please, just come. I'll tell you everything when you get there."

At 9:00, Reese watched Gee's car pull into her driveway, she opened the garage door for her to back in. And she waved to the officers in the cruiser to let them know it was okay. They waved back, but stayed put.

Inside, Reese had two suitcases, a carry on and her purse ready to go.

Keith eyed the luggage. "Looks like you're staying longer than a couple of days." He laughed.

Gee smiled, remembering the trip to lodge the night she'd met Keith. Reese's luggage is what made everyone late and she chuckled at the memory.

Reese rolled her eyes, teasingly, "So funny, Keith."

101

She helped put the luggage in the trunk and then hopped into the back seat. They drove out of the garage and slowed down long enough for Reese to let the officers know what she was doing.

"Good move," they said and they left the scene.

Reese relentlessly scanned the area to make sure Daxden was nowhere in sight. He wasn't.

Gee turned sideways and asked, "So, what happened?"

Reese sat forward. "You're not going to believe this. He started calling after I got home from your place, and I wouldn't answer his calls. So, he came to the house. He's pounding at the door and yelling for me open the door.

Reese told them the details of her horrifying night and about the police coming. She told them of their suggestion to go the courthouse for the order of protection.

When I was leaving the courthouse, I noticed his car behind me and pulled into a public parking lot. As soon as I motioned for the attendant, he took off, like a bat out of hell. That's when I called you."

Both Gee and Keith exchanged glances, then slowly checked their side mirrors to make sure the coast was clear."

Just as they pulled into Gee's garage, Keith's cell phone buzzed. The caller I.D showed it was Dr. Alex. He answered it.

"Hey Doc, thanks for returning my call. Doing just fine. They're doing great too. Well, we've got a weird situation we'd like to run by you and get your opinion about. No, me and Gee. I'm at Gee's, in California—. You're kidding? For how long? Can we meet up? Great. I'll text you the address and look forward to seeing you."

He hung up and typed in Gee's address and hit send, then turned to her.

"Doctor Alex is here for a speaking engagement. He's coming by."

"Fantastic."

"Who's Doctor Alex?" Reese asked.

"A psychiatrist from Arizona who specializes in mental disorders."

"And you know him; why?"

Keith glanced at Reese, "he's a friend. He kinda helped our family through a serious crisis more than one time, and we'll always be grateful to him."

Reese shrugged nervously, realizing the subject was an uncomfortable one for him. "Sorry, I didn't mean to pry."

"No problem, Reese. You're family. I'm sure Gee will fill you in on everything." He smiled with a nod.

***

Gee prepared a light lunch for everyone but before Alex got there, Reese took a sandwich and soda and excused herself.

"Where are you going?" Gee asked

"I'm just going to rest a little and give you and Keith some time with Dr. Alex."

103

Keith stepped forward, "You don't have to leave."

"I know, but I want to. I'm tired. I hardly got any sleep last night. I'm going to lie down and take a little nap."

Gee understood, and nodded.

"But don't hesitate to join us if you want to. I'd really love for you to meet Dr. Alex."

"Maybe next time. I'm really tired," Reese said.

She entered the guest room, closed the door and glanced around. Reese was envious of the way Gee could take an empty room, add color and the perfect furniture, and make guests feel she designed it especially for them. The queen size bed invited her with its elaborate mahogany headboard and a plush Champaign and gold comforter. An excessive amount of pillows in various gold patterns and shapes adorned the head of it. Two high backed chairs sat in front of a bay window with a small table between them, giving Reese the enjoyment of viewing a beautiful sunset at night or an exquisite sunrise of dawn. The room also contained a matching mahogany dresser with mirror, an armoire, and a small vanity that sat beside the entrance of the door. Gee even designed the guest bedroom with a full bath for the comfort and privacy of her guests. Reese stood in the middle of the floor. She glanced around the room again, allowing it to do precisely what Gee intended it to; welcome her with a hug. She laid across the bed and closed her eyes just for a second. She thought.

A strange voice coming from the other room stirred her and she wondered how long she'd been asleep. She checked the small clock on the nightstand. It was noon, so the strange voice must belong to Dr. Alex. She sat up on the side of the bed and listened.

"Hey, young man." Keith teased.

Dr. Alex greeted him. "What's this? Food? Uh-oh, you might not get rid of me now." He laughed.

"It's just a few appetizers. I figured you might be a little hungry."

"You figured right." Alex laughed again.

Reese eased herself off the bed and tiptoed to the small vanity by the door. She pulled out the seat and sat down, then leaned her ear toward the door.

Dr. Alex's voice was pleasant enough, she thought, hoping he would understand the situation without thinking her a silly woman, easily deceived by someone with apparent problems. Especially when the red flags were so blatant and in her face.

She sat listening to the exchange of small talk, and then Alex said.

"Okay, what's up? What's this about a weird situation? Are you two working on a case together?"

"Not exactly. It's more of a personal situation involving a friend, but it could very well turn into a case. We thought you'd be the best person to talk to about it."

"Why so?"

Keith explained about the night at the restaurant. Describing what he witnessed. "I don't know, Doc, this guy seems unhinged. Like he lives in his own world. I mean he really believes this friend of ours is in love with him and if anyone tries to come between them, look out. She actually had to leave her home because he showed up there, insisting she let him in. It got so out of hand that she had to call the police."

"Hmm—this friend? Is she a reliable source?"

Keith sat forward. "What do you mean?"

Doctor Alex shrugged, "I mean, maybe this friend isn't telling you everything—the whole truth. Could she be leading him on?"

"She wouldn't do that." Keith said.

"How do you know?"

Reese emerged from the bedroom. "I'm sorry I couldn't help overhearing." She turned to Dr. Alex. "No, I'm not leading him on. I admit, there were times that I questioned myself --wondering if I was standing in the way of a growing relationship, but then I realized it was him trying to manipulate me into thinking that way. When I tried to show that his controlling ways were not working on me, things got worse, and I'd find myself giving in to keep the peace. Who wants a relationship like that? I'm not sure how I even allowed it to get to that point, but suddenly there I was, trapped by his intimidating manipulation. I wanted to break free of it but then he'd do or say something to

106

override me. Like the other night. I had no idea he was planning on proposing. I never gave him any indication that I would ever consider marriage with him. I don't know what I would've done if Keith hadn't intervened."

Dr. Alex sat, caught off guard when Reese entered. Later, he would have to admit that he was so mesmerized by her beauty and engrossed in the way she moved about the room that he barely heard a word she said. He was sure that he must have looked like a damn fool, sitting there with his mouth gaped open, believing he had just walked into somebody's unexpected dream. He had to physically jerk himself out of his trance and force himself to speak.

He cleared his throat. "He –um –he proposed to you?"

"Well, he was going to. Keith saw the ring on the table, but he never got the chance because I took advantage of the first opportunity and got the hell out of there."

"Uh-huh. So, you have no feelings for this man at all?"

"At first, I thought I did. Daxden was charming, and I got swept away by all the attention and compliments. He had plans—big plans for us, but, I soon realized, it was all talk. He didn't really have any plans except to control my every move. He eventually became more and more demanding—suddenly showing up at the supermarket when I was buying groceries, or at restaurants when I was having lunch. I couldn't go anywhere without him suddenly showing up."

Gee shifted in her seat. "Like the time we were eating lunch, and he came into the restaurant."

"Right." Reese said, "Daxden called my phone, but I didn't answer. I needed a moment to myself—just me and my best friend, having lunch. Then, he walks into the restaurant and comes over to the table. He sees my phone sitting there, so he knows I saw his name on the caller ID when he called and he was livid. Suddenly, he didn't like my friends, especially Gee. He kept saying he was the only loyal friend I had."

Gee shifted in her seat. "So childish. Thank god you didn't believe him."

"Of course not. I knew it was just another one of Daxden's control tactics. You and I have been friends too long for someone like Daxden Green to come between us."

"So, you started seeing through him? How long did you say you dated?" Alex asked.

"On and off for about six months."

"And, how did you end up at the restaurant with him?"

"Well, I knew I didn't want the relationship, but I thought we could at least remain friends. My plan was two-fold, I had been wanting to dine at that restaurant anyway and, I thought it would be the perfect place to make it clear to him that it was over."

Alex sat back and thought for a minute and then took a long breath and ran his thumb lightly across his bottom lip.

"Did you ever get the chance to meet any of his family? Friends?"

"No. But, I knew he had friends. A couple of times, when we were together, he'd excuse himself to answer his cell. I could hear a woman's voice on the other end and thought maybe it might have been a relative or friend, but I never met them. At one point I thought he was seeing someone else." Reese shrugged. "No real evidence of it— just a hunch. I didn't care." She said, fanning her hand through the air.

"What made you think that?"

"You know, the woman's voice-- secret phone calls." Reese fanned her hand again. "Sometimes he'd disappear for a weekend or two and resurface and be upset that I hadn't tried to call to find out where he was or question what he was up to. He was fixated on the idea that I felt the same as he, no matter what I said."

"Reese, you never told me that," Gee said, sitting forward.

Alex sat forward too. "Did you tell him how you felt?"

Reese nodded. "Plenty of times. That's when he'd go ballistic -- yelling and stuttering—saying things that made no sense at all." She shook her head. "It became exhausting around him, so I made the decision to break it off completely. I thought, if we were in a public place, he'd watch his temper. So, I told him I was going over to check on Gee and I would drive myself to the restaurant. I used that excuse in case things got out of hand, I'd have my own car, and I'd be free to leave, if I needed to. He didn't like that at all."

Alex nodded. "Smart move." He said, allowing his gaze to drift up to meet hers. Her hazel eyes held him hostage.

"I don't know what else I could have done. It's like, now Daxden's angry and I'm the one responsible for that anger, so I have to pay the price and become a prisoner in my own home and now, I can't even be there. Who lives like this? I want my life back." She said, blinking back tears.

Alex noticed her eyes pooling, and his heart sank. He felt the urge to go to her, but his body remained glued to its spot. He was relieved when Gee rushed over and crouched down in front of her.

"It's going to be okay, Reese. It will. I promise. You know you can stay here for as long as you need to."

"Yes, I know, Gee, but that's my point, I shouldn't have to. Why can't he just go away?"

As the conversation continued, Alex became oddly aware of the animation in Reese's voice and the expressive way she described an incident. He was also attracted to the way her nose crinkled at the sides when she expressed her dislikes. It made him smile, and he gave a light chuckle.

"It sounds like your describing a clear case of narcissistic behavior. Of course, I'd have to see Daxden and talk to him to make a definite diagnosis, but that's what it sounds like to me."

"What does that mean? Narcissistic behavior?" Reese asked.

He explained. "I don't know why, but we usually find narcissistic behavior more in men than women. I'm not saying that's what he has. I'm just saying it sounds like it. Someone with a narcissistic behavior has an inflated sense of self-importance and can't tolerate rejection. These people don't care anything about your feelings. It's all about them. They have an excessive need for admiration and, for God's sake, don't dare criticize them."

Reese moved to the sofa closer to Alex. "It sounds like you're describing Daxden Green. He especially has a problem if he thinks a woman is putting him in his place."

Alex went on, "They need to feel that they're your sole provider. They want to be your one and only, and if that means they have to isolate you from everyone who cares about you, so be it."

Gee looked at Reese. "That's why he didn't like it when you'd tell him you were coming to see me. He wanted you all to himself."

Dr. Alex shifted in his chair. "There's more."

They turned back to him.

"They use words as tools to get what they want, and they can be quite manipulative. To put it differently, they are very clever con men. They lie, they exaggerate, and they see themselves as superior. That's where the danger lies. We, as psychiatrists have to be careful in our diagnosis of the narcissistic behavior because we can get caught up in the treatment of a narcissistic personality when the truth is, we've been dealing with a sociopath.

Nervous silence filled the room.

Keith took in a breath, "Doc, is it possible for a known narcissist to also be a sociopath?"

Alex nodded. "Yes."

Reese pulled her phone out of her pocket. "I need you all to hear something."

She played the messages.

Gee's hand went to her mouth, and she sat back in her chair.

Alex sat back too, examining their faces as each message led right into the other. He turned to Reese. She was frightened, and from what he heard, she had all the reasons to be.

After the messages were played, Reese slid the phone back into her pocket, then turned to Alex and described the night of horror that led to her packing clothes and coming to stay with Gee.

"I never thought anyone could run me out of my own home, but I don't trust him. I don't know what he's going to do next. I never know what's going to set him off. He – just—explodes." She made an explosion type gesture with her arms.

112

"You made the right decision, staying here. And you say you have an order of protection?"

Reese nodded. "Yes."

"Stay away from him, Reese," Alex warned. "I'll be here for a couple of days. I have a speaking engagement this evening and tomorrow, but I'm free in between those times. Let's stay in touch."

He pulled out his wallet and removed two business cards, handing one to Gee and the other to Reese, then he turned to Keith. "You already know how to contact me."

"Yeah, and I'm leaving to go home in a couple of hours anyway, but for some reason, I'm feeling relieved knowing you'll be around."

"I'll be in touch this evening after the seminar."

"That sounds wonderful," Gee said, nodding her head.

"So, in your seminars, do you talk about these disorders?" Reese asked.

Alex nodded and smiled, pleased that Reese was the least bit interested in his work.

"I do."

"Sounds interesting. Are the seminars just for doctors?"

"Usually. Anyone else would be too bored to attend."

"Not me," Reese admitted.

Alex cocked his head. "Would you—like to attend one of them?"

"Is that an invitation?"

Alex shifted his weight nervously, "I'm sure I can pull some strings and get you in."

Gee met Keith's gaze, and they both smiled.

Alex continued. "Just let me know which one you want to attend, and I'll make it happen."

"He's famous too, Reese," Gee interjected eagerly. "He's written a few books."

Keith nudged her as a warning to stop playing matchmaker, but it only provoked her more.

"You don't have anything to do tonight, Reese. Why don't you get dressed and go with him now?"

Alex's heart quickened at the thought of Reese accompanying him to the seminar. He smiled, but thought better about it and made another suggestion.

"The evening sessions run a bit long. I stick around to answer questions, take pictures, and sign books. How about tomorrow morning? The morning sessions break earlier so if you get bored, I can bring you home."

"Sounds great. Tomorrow then?" Reese agreed.

Alex nodded, his eyes never left hers, as he whispered, "Tomorrow."

He stood and moved toward the door but turned back to Reese. "Why don't you give me your number so I can call and confirm? I honestly wouldn't blame you if you change your mind."

Reese hurried to the table, scrawled her number on the back of a napkin and rushed back to hand it to him.

Adele Hewett Veal

"I won't change my mind." She said with a smile.

Her hand brushed lightly against his, and an unfamiliar warmth spread across his chest. "I hate to rush off, but—" Alex said.

"No worries," Gee interrupted, "we've got to get Keith to the airport anyway."

"But, I'll keep in touch, and you do the same. You have my card." Alex smiled. "It was a pleasure meeting you, Reese."

"No, the pleasure was all mine." Reese smiled back.

"Keep in touch." Alex nodded.

A blush stained her cheeks, and she nodded, "I will."

It was Keith clearing his throat that broke the spell between the two, reminding them that they weren't alone in the room, and they tore their eyes away from each other as Alex drifted to the door. He turned one last time and shook Keith's hand. "Safe travels this afternoon, Keith. I'll see you when I get back to Arizona. Tell the family I said hello."

"Will do," Keith said.

He gave Gee a long hug and walked out the door.

Once he was gone, they turned to Reese.

Another blush spread to her cheeks. She shrugged, "What?"

13

ON THE WAY to the airport, Keith's conversation was full of detailed instructions on what to do if anything happened. Finally, they pulled up to the curbside, and both Keith and Gee hopped out to say their goodbyes. Keith placed his hands on the sides of Gee's face.

"Be careful, Gee," he said, before he kissed her. "Are you sure he doesn't know where you live?"

"I'm sure, Keith."

"Both of you be careful," he said, crouching down to include Reese in the warning.

"We will."

"If you need me, call."

"I know," Gee nodded.

"If you can't get me, call Pen."

"I know. I know."

"Okay." He looked at her for a long time, then turned, gave a quick wave to Reese, and rushed through the doors.

Gee slid behind the steering wheel and waited for Reese to join her in the front seat. They headed back to her place.

"Okay, now tell me again what happened?"

Reese started over, telling Gee every detail of the night before and what happened this morning when she went downtown.

"You've got this, Reese. Don't worry."

"I can't wait for it to be over ...."

"I know. It will be soon."

"I hope so."

It wasn't until they entered Gee's garage that Reese was able to relax. There was so much tension built up in her that she felt her shoulders were attached to her ears.

Gee watched her. "You okay?" she asked.

Reese nodded. "I am now. I didn't realize how tense I was until we got here."

"He won't find you here, Reese."

"I know."

They got out of the car and walked into the house.

Gee let a sly smile spread across her lips

"So, you're kind of—interested in the doctor, huh?"

"What do you mean?"

"Reese, cut it out. I've known you since high school, and I know when somebody catches your fancy," she teased.

"You sound just like your mother."

Gee laughed. "I know."

"Yeah, I guess you can say he kind of caught my fancy. I'm intrigued."

Gee stepped back and studied her. She hadn't seen this side of Reese in a long time. She nodded. "He's good people. I hope it works out for you."

Reese laughed, "I just met him, Gee. After Daxden, I know to take my time and get to know the person first."

"Damn good idea." Gee laughed. "So, what do you say we make this a Margarita night?"

"I would love a Margarita."

"Then let's do it."

They popped popcorn and drank Margaritas until Keith called to let them know he'd landed in Arizona safely.

It was late in the afternoon when Gee helped Reese carry the last of her luggage from the car into the guest room.

"My God, Reese, you pack like you're moving in."

"You never know," she laughed.

"Have you given any thought to work?"

"What do you mean?"

"I'm sure Daxden knows where you work. Right?"

Reese glanced up at Gee and her smile faded. "I didn't allow myself to think that far ahead."

"You've got to, Reese. This is dangerous—he's dangerous."

"I know. Maybe I can work from home for a couple of weeks."

"Do you think your boss will let you?"

"After I tell her what's going on, I think she'll welcome it."

"You need to call her first thing in the morning. If she needs me to verify it, let me know."

"Yeah, I'll do that."

"Sorry, I didn't mean to put you in such a solemn mood."

"I know, Gee, I just can't believe I allowed myself to get in such a mess."

"Oh well, it's here, and we'll deal with it, right?" Gee moved to Reese's side and rubbed her shoulder. "Come on. One more round of Margaritas?"

They laughed and went back to the kitchen.

The two women talked well into the early evening, playing the 'oldies but goodies' station and singing along with many of the late 60s and early 70s songs.

They reminisced about school days and laughed at the dynamics that brought their friendship together.

***

They weren't friends initially. In high school, Reese was the girl everyone wanted to be; head majorette, tall, slender, and smart, not to mention her stunning looks and out-going personality. It was usually Reese who started a fashion craze, but not on purpose. She didn't have a conceited bone in her body; she was just confident and poised, and her personality reflected it. So, when she wore the latest trend of clothing, the other students usually followed suit. All, but Gee.

Gee wasn't a shopper. Unlike Reese, she was comfortable in an old t-shirt and jeans and sometimes an occasional sundress, when the weather called for it. Her hair was a dark brown shade, the same color as the huge glasses that continuously slid down her nose so much, that it became a ritual for her to push them up while reaching around to tuck her bangs behind her ear, in one swift motion. Gee struggled through school, studying hard to make good grades, and didn't care about being popular. Anyone looking for her could usually find her at lunchtime under a shade tree in the front of the school, flipping through home décor magazines or reading the latest Agatha Christie novel. And, since it was her last year, she decided to volunteer for the committee of special events.

The planning committee called all volunteers together to brainstorm for the most important dance of the year, Prom. It had to be spectacular—a memorable occasion— something they'd tell their children about. It was this day that Gee noticed Reese was among the volunteers. The students brought many ideas for a theme. They voted over and over again. Finally, they decided to go with Gee's, *The Emerald City.*

Yards of emerald green fabric in shimmery satin and tulle soon draped throughout the gymnasium with streams of golden stars hanging from the ceiling. The students decorated the big double doors leading into the room. To make the doors appear ancient, they spray painted small aluminum bowls gold. The bowls looked like studs that they hot glued around each door. Then they hung two huge letters in place so, when the doors closed the entrance became the gateway to their magical theme – OZ

The floor covering, designed to resemble the yellow brick road, would light under the student's feet as they walked into their world of fantasy. Dozens of round tables with green tablecloths trimmed in gold were scattered tastefully around the gymnasium. Each displayed three green glass centerpieces of different sizes, containing small candles to give the illusion of emerald jewels flickering throughout the room. The last thing they decided on was an air balloon, tastefully tucked off to the side, as the backdrop for Prom pictures.

Two days before the event, Gee and Reese were gluing the last of the gold studs onto the gymnasium door, when Reese turned to her and asked,

"Aren't you so excited? Did you find your dress yet?"

Gee shook her head and smiled. "No, I'm not going."

Reese whipped around. "Not going?" she shrieked. She immediately clamped her hand over her mouth and asked in a lower voice, "When did you decide not to go?"

"I never planned on it. I just wanted to help with the decorations."

Reese looked around the room.

"But you have to go. This was your idea—your creation."

"It's okay. Really."

Reese arched a questioning eyebrow. "Is it because you don't have a date? I can help with that."

"No. I don't want a date. I'm just not going to Prom. That's all."

"Gee, it's our Senior Prom –*your* Senior Prom. It's not like you'll ever get a second chance to go."

Gee took another bowl, spread the hot glue around it and pressed it in place. She heard Reese clear her throat and squirm under the awkward silence that grew between them.

"You know," Reese said, clearing her throat again, "if you don't have a gown to wear, I can loan you one."

Gee took a breath and studied her. "I didn't take the time to look for a gown, because I knew I wasn't going. I never planned on it."

"But why?" she asked again, waving her arms around the room. "Why would you be on the planning committee for something you're not going to be able to enjoy?"

Gee gave a half smile. "Knowing others are enjoying it is good enough for me."

Reese stopped working, put her tools down, and folded her arms across her chest, waiting for Gee to give a better explanation. "Nope, can't accept that one. Try something else."

Gee laughed. "Reese, please. I've just got some issues at home that make it impossible for me to attend events right now."

"What kind of issues? Parents getting a divorce? Join the club, but it's not going to keep me from enjoying my Prom."

Gee laughed again. "No, my parents aren't getting a divorce. My dad hasn't been around since I was born. Didn't want me. Walked out on my mom when she told him she was pregnant."

"Ah-ha – so, your mom's getting married to someone you don't like?"

"Nooooo," Gee laughed

"Well, if it's not one of those two things, there's no reason you can't go."

"I think I have a good enough reason."

Reese shook her head. "Nope, sorry. It has to be one of the above."

"Not necessarily."

"So, you think you have a better one?"

"Yep."

"It has to be a life-or-death situation. Let's hear it."

Gee took in a long breath. "Death."

Reese gasped. "You're dying?"

"No, my mom is."

"Your mother is dying?"

"Yes." Gee nodded.

"I'm so sorry, Gee. I didn't know."

"No one here knows. Mom was diagnosed some years ago. Pancreatic cancer. She was in remission for a while, then it came back with a vengeance, and there's nothing they can do."

"Oh my God, Gee. You must be going through hell. Where's the rest of your family?"

"It's just my mom and me. If I have relatives, I don't know them, but she pretty much prepared me for—you know. Now, we just take things a day at a time. I don't want to be away, then get home, and she's—gone. I want to be with her for as long as I can. So, I do what I can do here, then I rush home."

Reese wiped a tear from her face. "Of course, you do."

"Don't cry for me, Reese. I'm good with it."

"I just can't imagine. And here you are, working away on a project for us to enjoy."

"It keeps my mind off things. I'll enjoy knowing everyone else is enjoying it."

From then on, Reese and Gee grew closer, and the day came when Gee allowed her to meet her mother. It was Gee's mother who told Reese about her desire to see Gee go to the Prom, but she couldn't get her to change her mind.

"I'd like to see her all dressed up. Looking like a princess. But she won't budge."

124

"Leave it to me," Reese winked.

The evening of the Prom, Reese knocked on Gee's front door. She was dressed in a sleeveless, jewel-blue gown, fitted in the waist then flared into a mermaid hem that flowed to the ground. The front of the bodice was covered with tiny embellished beads, with a neckline that took on the appearance of a jeweled choker wrapping around the back of her neck. Her back was exposed to show off her smooth, tanned skin with nothing but a strap that crossed and snapped at the side. The bottom of the dress was jewel-blue satin and tulle.

Gee was taken aback, to see Reese standing on her porch with a clear plastic garment bag draped over her arm. It contained a long, ivory, satin gown trimmed in hand-beaded lace.

"Reese, what are you doing here? You're supposed to be getting ready for your date."

She held the gown out and lifted it higher in the air. "This one's for you," she said.

Gee's eyebrow arched to her hairline. "Reese."

"I had a long talk with your mom, and we agree. You have to go. She gave me the money to buy your ticket so you can't say no."

Gee's mom made her way into the corridor. Her frail body showed signs of failing health with forced breaths laboring in and out. She looked past Gee to Reese.

"Thank you." She whispered.

Gee whipped her head around. "Mom, I can't."

"Yes, you can. I need this, Gee. I need to see my daughter dressed up as a princess. This will be my only chance. You can't deny me this."

Gee rushed over to help her sit down. "But what if…"

"I'll be here when you come home…promise. I can't leave you. Especially tonight. I've got to hear about the dance. I want to know – every detail." She took another labored breath and fanned Gee away, "Now, go, get dressed!"

"I'll help you." Reese volunteered.

The two girls rushed up the stairs together.

After a couple of hours of preparation, Gee's mom watched her daughter as she descended the stairs, shaking her head slowly in disbelief. Tears brimming her eyes. "My God," she whispered. "There are no words."

Excitement funneled into Gee's heart. "Mom." She said, rushing to her and pulling her in for a gentle hug.

The moment was such a beautiful one that Reese stepped back to let them relish in it.

"Oh, I have one more thing." Reese said.

"One more thing?" Gee asked, turning to her. "Reese, you've done enough."

"Hold on." She rushed out the door to her car. When she returned, she was holding a shoebox.

"Your shoes, Gee."

When Gee opened the box, she gasped.

"Your ruby slippers!" Reese announced with a smile.

Reese removed the red sequined heels from the box, arranging them on the floor in front of her. Gee stepped into them. Then there was another knock at the door.

Reese opened it. Two male students from school stepped inside, dressed in their tuxedos. One Gee knew was Reese's date, and the other approached her with a red rose corsage and placed it on her wrist.

Gee helped her mom to the living room where she'd be more comfortable, wiped the tears from her eyes and planted a kiss on her cheek. "Mom, are you sure?"

"Yes, I'm sure. Now, go enjoy yourself, Gee. Promise me you'll have the best time ever."

"I will. I promise." She said, knowing this day would be etched in her memory for years to come.

As for Reese and Gee, they remained friends from then on.

***

They laughed, reminiscing about that night.

"What was my date's name?" Reese asked.

"You don't remember? His name was Harrison."

She laughed. "Do you remember your date's name?"

"I remember everything about that night. I still have the pictures," Gee said, rushing into the bedroom. She reached past her mom's old jewelry box to get her photo album and ran back to the kitchen.

The pictures were stained by time, yellowed around the edges, but happiness spread across each page, especially the ones of her mom.

Reese watched Gee trace her mother's face with her finger. The photo showed her mother with a group of her friends. "She was so young here—before cancer—before— me. She had friends and a normal life. I've often wondered what she was thinking here, with that far-off look and twinkle in her eyes, like she was privy to a secret no one else knew."

"Look, she's wearing the necklace." Reese gestured to the gold necklace around Gee's neck. "You still wear it."

"Yeah, I'll never take it off." she reached up and touched the wing of the gold butterfly. "It's one of the last things Mom gave me."

Reese nodded. "I know. You never found the other half, though?"

Gee shook her head. "Nope. I stopped looking a long time ago."

"If your mother could see you today, she'd be so proud of you, Gee."

"I know." She nodded with a smile. Then Gee closed the album and rushed back to her bedroom. She put the photo album back in its place, then opened her mom's jewelry box and let her fingers brush over the initials on a pocket watch. *R.G.O. Rosalyn Grace . . . what had been her married name?* They never talked about it and her mom

128

went back to her maiden name before Gee was born. She closed the box and returned, carrying a shoebox. "I kept these too."

Reese's eyes widened in disbelief. "No."

Gee nodded and opened the box. Inside were the ruby red heels Reese had given her years ago.

"I can't believe you still have them," she whispered. "Do they fit?"

"Of course they do."

"Try 'em on."

Gee sat down and removed her shoes, then slipped her feet into the ruby slippers and danced across the kitchen floor.

"They are beautiful. I can't believe you kept them after all these years."

"Did you think I'd throw them away?"

"Well, not right away, but ..."

"Reese, that was one of the most amazing nights of my life."

"You should've seen what my mother went through to find them."

Gee leaned forward, "Your mom bought these for me?"

"Yep."

"You never told me."

"She asked me not to."

"She has always been so kind to me."

"She thinks you're the bravest person she's ever met."

"Because of what I went through with my mom?"

"No. Not just because of that, but because of the way you were then, the way you are now—with everything."

Gee's eyes fell to the floor and then lifted to Reese's. "I can't say it was easy."

"I know."

"Your mom stayed with me at the hospital until after my mother took her last breath. She stayed until I was ready to go."

"I remember. She had us go to your house and get clothes for you."

"I don't know what I would have done without her. I wish she'd move here. I miss her."

Reese nodded, "Me too. She'll be here for the wedding. She loves you so much, Gee."

"I know. I love her too." Gee smiled fondly.

"Look at you now. You're a P.I., getting ready to get married to the man of your dreams, a man who adores you."

Gee thought for a moment. "I can't complain, Reese. I've had a pretty good life."

"You think you're going to like living in Arizona?"

"I'm sure I'll get used to it. I'll adjust. The same way I adjusted when I came home from Arizona and found Regis had moved our offices from L.A. to San Diego. It took some getting used to, but I did it."

"That's because I was here. Who do you know in Arizona?"

"Keith and his family."

Reese glared at her teasingly. "Seriously?"

"They're a great family, Reese. You'll like them."

"I have no doubt. I guess I'm just a little jealous." The thought of Gee moving to Arizona stung a little, but she put it aside for now. "How about another margarita before bed?"

"Coming right up," Gee said, gathering their glasses.

She was glad that Reese was there. They allowed the margaritas to drown out two completely different observations about their lives. For Reese, it was the anxiety of the past six months, but for Gee, it was the anticipation of her future.

14

KEITH DROVE TO work early the next morning and walked in before anyone got there. He made the station's first pot of coffee then sat at his desk to study a file that was lying there. Knowing Pen must've left it there for him to check out. He was still leafing through it when Pen walked in.

"Hey, you're home. I thought you would've stayed in California over the weekend. What's up? Why are you here so early on a Friday?"

Keith looked up.

"Just thought I'd come in early. That's all."

"So, how's Gee?"

"She's better. Still has a little headache, but that takes time to completely go away. She's going back to work on Thursday. You know, Gee, she's not going to let too much get in the way and keep her down."

Pen laughed. "That's for sure."

"What's going on here?" Keith asked, fumbling through the file. "Do you have any leads on this one?"

"A few. I followed up on them for you. Everything's in the notes there. Let me know what you think." He walked toward the coffee pot on the other side of the room. "You want coffee?"

"Got some. I'm good." Keith leafed through the papers until he found the notes on the bottom of the stack. "Hey, listen."

Pen stopped. The seriousness in Keith's voice made him turn around and walk back to his desk.

"If Gee or her friend Reese call and I'm not here, make sure I know about it right away. Okay?"

"Sure. What's up?"

"Maybe nothing."

Pen studied his friend. "Keith." He waited for him to look at him. "What's up?"

"I think Gee's friend is mixed up with someone who may not be playing with a full deck, if you know what I mean. I'm concerned, that's all. She's staying at Gee's for a couple of days."

"Sounds serious."

"Well, it was serious enough for her to get an order of protection against him.

"What? You're shittin' me! Why?"

Keith's shoulder flinched in a nervous shrug. "He was at her house the other night banging on her door and

133

demanding she let him in. She called the police and they made him leave. But, he still left her phone full of threatening messages, so we thought it best that she stay with Gee until this blows over."

Pen sat in the chair closest to Keith's desk. "I guess."

"That's why I'm saying, if they call, make sure I know."

Pen shook his head. "You got it, man. What do you want to do about this guy?"

"Nothing yet. Just gather some info and keep track of him."

"We can do that." Pen said with a slow nod.

"Check it out. I went to the restaurant where Reese was having dinner with this joker."

"Why?"

"Man, you know Gee. She had one of her gut feelings, and, since Daxden had never seen me, she thought I could get in there and make sure Reese was okay. So, I went."

"Daxden? That's his name?"

"Yep and he's as weird as his name too."

"Yeah? Okay, so you went to the restaurant and what happened?"

"We both know that Gee's gut feelings are usually spot-on. So, I'm sitting at the bar and right away, I notice things weren't too cool. I'm watching this guy grab her by the arm, yank her across the table, and yell in her face, and, here's Reese, trying to stand her ground. It took everything I had not to go over there and punch him in the face."

"I'm surprised you didn't."

"Gee was on the phone. She's like –stay calm, Keith. Then I see Reese get up to go to the restroom, and I follow her. And as I'm passing the table, I see this jackass take a ring box out of his pocket. He opened it, and there's an engagement ring. After everything that just happened, he was still going to ask Reese to marry him."

Pen leaned back in his chair and raked his hands through his hair, then leaned forward again. "What?" he asked in disbelief.

"Yeah, anyway, I get to the restroom door as Reese is coming out, and you should have seen her face. I don't know, it looked like shock mixed with relief. I hand her the phone and tell her it's Gee, and she ducks back into the restroom to talk to her. When she comes back out, I'm talking to her and I notice she tenses up; that lets me know that Daxden is on his way over to us. He's upset because he thinks I'm trying to 'push up on his girl.'"

"His girl?"

"My point exactly. Then he starts yelling at Reese, telling her to get her ass back to the table and shit. I told her to get out of there. While she's gathering her things to leave, he continues to call himself 'putting me in my place.' I gave her time to leave the restaurant and get to her car, and during that time, this man is yellin' and telling me off. Spittin' and stutterin', but I wanted to make sure Reese was safe before I directed his attention to the empty table. Man, you should've seen him. He looked manic."

Pen's face had gone from disbelief to anger. He lifted his hands again and rubbed his face, then dropped them back onto his knees with a slap. "So, you left the restaurant?"

"Hell no. I wanted to see what he was going to do. I watched him go back to his table, and after sitting there for a while, he asked for the check and got ready to leave. That is, until he saw me still sitting at the bar."

"Oh, shit." Pen laughed.

"Yep. This fool comes over to me and proceeds to tell me—basically—he should kick my ass. I reached in my pocket and pulled out my badge, and laid it on the bar. His eyes got as big as saucers. He wanted to hit me so bad but decided against it and finally stormed out of the restaurant."

Pen shook his head. "Man, you should've called me."

"What were you going to do? You're all the way here in Arizona."

"Doctor Alex met me at Gee's. He's in San Diego for a seminar. We talked about this guy. He agrees that he could be dangerous. He warned Reese to stay clear of him. I think he kind of likes her."

"Doctor Alex?"

"I don't want to speak too soon, but I think she likes him too."

"Really? Doctor Alex, huh? But, Reese is going to have to end it with the other guy before somebody gets hurt. What do you think?"

"I think he wants control. Reese won't give it to him, and he's mad as hell."

Pen stood up and made a second attempt to go after coffee, then stopped and walked back to Keith.

"Now that's the kind of shit I don't understand. How do these men weasel their way into women's lives? Is Reese's self-esteem so low that she'd allow a man like that to come in and control her?"

"Not at all. Reese is beautiful and strong-willed. He's—" Keith's eyes searched the air for the right words. "He's a master manipulator. And, when he realized Reese wasn't going to play his game, he reached deep into his bag of tricks and came up with another tactic that scared the living shit out of her."

Pen crossed the room and poured himself a cup of coffee then walked back to Keith.

"So, what's your game plan? I know you have one."

"Well, I told Reese and Gee, if anything happened, to call you or me. I hope you don't mind."

"Of course not." Pen sat back in the seat. He leaned forward and blew the steam away from the cup before taking a sip, then gave Keith a knowing look.

Keith lifted his shoulder in a half shrug. "What?"

"Your game plan. What is it?"

"I'm not sure yet, let me think about it. You with me?"

Pen smiled, "As always. You jump, I jump."

15

ON THURSDAY, GEE pulled into the parking lot of the Ovalton Office Building. It was a beautiful building with a quintessential floor plan. Their offices was on the second floor. Hers provided a stunning view of the Pacific Ocean. And, depending on how late she worked in the evening, she'd have the pleasure of watching the ocean view soften and transform itself into an awe-inspiring landscape of city lights.

When she reached her office, she rushed to her desk, glad to see the file she had been working was still there untouched. She snatched it open and began to read. Without taking her eyes away from the file, she made her way across the room, and, as usual, popped a pod into the coffee machine and waited for it to brew and trickle its hot liquid into her cup. She continued reading until the machine beeped, letting her know her coffee was ready. Then she picked up her cup, took a few small sips and carefully walked back to her desk and sat down.

She had turned a few pages before she spotted it. "Ah—here it is," she whispered, leaning closer to the file. She put her cup down and picked up a red felt pen, then drew a huge circle around a conglomerate of words, linked them to the previous paragraph, and drew a curved and continuous line downward to connect the words and paragraph to the name at the bottom of the page. She sat back and studied it. 'Deke Henderson'. And, she wondered how much farther she'd be in solving this puzzle, if she had been able to read the damn note.

Without thinking about it, she swirled her engagement ring around her finger, a new habit she'd developed since Keith had placed it there. Somehow, fiddling with it helped her focus—thoughts became keener and more deliberate. She swirled it around until the diamond solitaire was back in its place, then swirled it again. Suddenly, she stopped and sat forward. "Ah-ha," she said, nodding her head slowly, "Gotcha."

Her cell phone chimed. She checked the caller ID, smiled, and put the phone to her ear.

"Hey, what are you doing up so early?" She creased her brow. Her heart lurched and rapped against her ribs so hard she could hear it in her ears. "Reese, hold on. You're talking too fast. Start over—what happened?"

Gee put the call on speaker.

140

Reese's panicked voice shrieked through it. "I'm freaking out. I think I saw Daxden's car."

"He doesn't know where I live. How can that be?"

"God," she took a relieved breath, "I hate this."

"Reese, stop it. It's okay. He has no idea where I live. Plus, he can't get through the gate without the code."

"You're right. This is crazy. It couldn't have been him. It's just—I'm so jumpy after the other night, I don't put anything past him."

"You're safe at my place, though."

"I know. I get so freaked out. I'm sorry, Gee. Your first day back at work, and I call you with this craziness."

Gee relaxed. "It's okay, really."

Have you talked to Keith?"

"Yes, why?"

"I'm just wondering if he had any more words of wisdom for you.

Gee laughed. "The only words of wisdom Keith has for me is to be careful."

"That coming from a man in love." Reese laughed nervously.

"You still going with Dr. Alex this morning?"

"Yep. Already spoke to him and picked out what I'm wearing."

Gee lifted an eyebrow, "Really?" she asked.

"He's coming to pick me up, and after the seminar, we'll have a light lunch."

"Lunch, huh?"

"Stop it, Gee," Reese scolded playfully. She could hear Gee's smile through the phone.

"You like him."

"Let's just say I'm curious," Reese said.

"I've seen you curious before. I know what that means."

"What?"

"You like him," Gee tease again through a smile.

There was a knock at her office door, and she glanced up as Regis opened it and walked in.

"Reese, I've got to go. My boss just came in. I'll see you later tonight."

"Okay. Talk to you later."

She pushed the button to end the call.

"Hey, you're here early?" he said.

"Yes, and so are you."

"I'm the boss. I'm supposed to be here. What's your excuse?"

"Well, I've been out of commission for a while. This is called catch-up."

Regis gave her a suspicious look.

Gee held his gaze. "What?"

She closed the file and at a snail's pace, slid it to the far corner of her desk.

The act didn't go unnoticed.

"Gee, what are you doing?"

"What do you mean?"

"It's just a simple case. Either Deke is selling guns illegally, or he's not. Why do you have to—"

"There's more to it, Reg, and I had it right in the palm of my hand. I can't believe I don't have that damned envelope. "But, here —" She sprang from her chair, picked up the file, and rushed over to him. "Look at this."

"No."

"Come on, Reg. You can't tell me you're not the least bit interested."

"In what?"

"This." Gee opened the file and handed it to him, but Regis, giving a heavy sigh, stepped away.

"Is he selling illegal guns?"

"What the hell difference does that make? I'm trying to tell you—there's more—"

"Is – he – selling – the – guns?" Regis asked.

"Yes!"

"Then we're done here. Write it up. Call Ms. McClure and let her know we have her results."

"Regis, normally you'd be all over this. What's up?"

"Can't you just work a normal case? I mean it. Why do you have to keep digging until – we're in over our heads? We are not detectives here. We are investigators. Investigators, investigate. So, you asked questions, took pictures, blended in to follow the man. And you got all the answers Ms. McClure needs. Write it up, Gee, so we can be done with it and get paid."

Gee took in a breath. It wasn't like Regis at all to look over something as important as this. Since she'd gotten back from Arizona, he seemed guarded and entirely too careful where she was concerned. As a matter of fact, everyone at the office seemed to walk on eggshells around her. Regis wouldn't let her take chances— or go the extra mile to find the needle embedded in the haystack (so to speak). Frustrated and emotionally spent by his uncaring attitude, she took a breath. Shutting the file, she did nothing more than glare at him, then walk back behind her desk and sit down.

"You know, Regis?" she said, sweeping her bangs out of her face, "I admit I was careless in Arizona. I didn't use my better judgment. The woman took me by surprise. I was reckless and irresponsible, but it won't happen again."

"You're damned right it won't happen again! Gee, the woman shot you in the chest. You almost died. Now, here again, you're letting yourself get too close. I don't know if it's because you have other things on your mind right now, but you're taking chances you don't need to take. Look what happened the other night. My god, someone hit you and left you lying in the street."

"I've always taken chances, Regis. It never bothered you before. You know how I am. I follow my gut, and I've never been wrong. Have I?"

144

Regis broke eye contact and shoved his hands into his pockets.

Gee leaned closer, "What is it, Regis? What aren't you telling me?"

"My guess is that someone wants you out of the way. The other night was a warning. What if they come back to finish the job? Since we have the information the woman wants, let's just give it to her."

Gee's voice softened. "Regis, look at me. I'm alright. I'm okay. Let me do my job, please."

"That's all I'm asking you to do, Gee, your job. Write the report."

She breathed a heavy sigh and forced a slow smile. *It wasn't worth the fight*, she thought. A smile stretched across her face, and her eyebrow shot up teasingly. "You're gonna miss me when I'm gone."

Her words immediately suppressed his aggravated mood, and he returned the smile with a nod. "We all will."

She chuckled. "No one's going to be here to keep you on your toes."

"That, my dear, will be a welcomed relief."

"Are you trying to say you'll be glad to see me go?"

"No, not glad – relieved. I want to see you safe, Gee. Marrying Keith is going to be good for you. Go to Arizona. Start a family. Take some knitting classes and relax."

His words struck her in the gut like an unexpected bolt of lightning. "Knitting classes! Really? Listen, Regis, I love

Keith, but I don't think I'm quite ready to be put out to pasture just yet."

He took a step forward. "I didn't mean it like that."

She knew he didn't, but it still hurt like hell to have the person she trusted stir the pot that flipped her stomach every time she thought about it. She tried to put it aside with a nervous laugh. "I know you didn't mean it like that, Reg. Actually, I've been thinking about reconsidering my exit date. Maybe I need to stay on a little longer to retrain the other employees the best ways to tick you off."

"You would," he scoffed, and took in a long breath, then shook his head. "I came in early this morning to get ready for your replacement, okay? He'll be here tomorrow."

"Okay."

"I promised Keith that this last case was going to be a simple one. I don't understand why you just can't —"

"Because I can't, Reg," she interrupted. "You know I can't –and neither can you. I can't see something and not say something or do –*something*. You hired me because I'm good. You've said it a million times that we're a good team. Hell, I was one of your first employees. You trained me well. Fifteen years we've worked together. I'm not about to slack off just because it's my last case. Don't ask me to do that."

"Gee, can you–"

"What, Regis? Can I –what?"

"Can you just put yourself in my shoes? Imagine what we went through here when Keith told us you weren't responding to his calls the other night. Keith had to send out a search party. My god, Gee, we were beside ourselves. Yes, we are going to miss you around here. You're family to us, and we love you. That's not going to change. Your moving to Arizona is not going to stop us from loving and visiting you. I owe you so much."

"I love you guys too. You don't owe me a thing."

"Helen and I wouldn't be married today if you hadn't made that first phone call and shove the phone in my hand. I would never have made that call, and you knew it. We've had our share of worries where you're concerned, and I'm just asking you to let this one go. Please?"

Gee was quiet. She dropped her eyes and nodded. "Okay, Regis. Fine. I'll write the report." The room was quiet, then Gee lifted her eyes and asked, "Who's my replacement? What's his name?"

Regis released a sigh. "Ryan. Ryan Parrish. His resume shows that he's more than qualified for the job. He has the skills, knowledge, and the experience that we need. I'm impressed by him. Not to mention the fact that we can use more male testosterone in this place. I don't know how I'm going to behave. I've had nothing but women surrounding me for so long." He glanced at his watch. "He'll be here tomorrow around this time, so I need to get the paperwork in order. I'd like you to be available to show him the ropes."

"Ropes?"

"Show him around, Gee. I need you to be available to show him around. Get him use to things around here."

"I'll be available," she shrugged.

Regis studied her with a nod. "Have that report on my desk tomorrow, by the end of the day. Okay?"

"That's the plan."

He dropped his eyes and nodded again, then turned and left the office.

Gee sat with her eyes fixed on the office door expecting Regis to come back with one of his last-minute thoughts, *oh and another thing—,* but he didn't. When she was sure he was definitely gone, she eased her hand over to the corner of her desk and slid the file forward until it was directly in front of her. She lifted her eyes to the door once more, then opened the file and continued to study it.

She had the answer, she was sure of it. So she picked up the phone, punched in the number and waited for the prompt to tell her to enter an access code. When she did, someone answered, but didn't speak. She heard breathing on the other end and, after a while, Gee finally said,

"Hello?"

16

IT WAS LATE when Gee got home that evening. She left the office at six and stopped at the store to get something easy to prepare for dinner. She and Reese liked the same types of food, so it wasn't a hard decision. Rotisserie chicken, cut up in a Caesar salad, a glass of red wine, and a little conversation would go a long way before bed. She smiled and went to work preparing it.

When Reese heard Gee bustling around the kitchen, she popped her head out of the guest room. "Hey, I thought I heard you come in. How was your day?"

"Long," Gee laughed. "I just got rotisserie chicken for Caesar salad for dinner. Is that okay?"

"Perfect."

"A glass of red wine?"

"Great."

"Okay, It'll be ready in five minutes."

Reese joined her in the kitchen. "What can I do to help?"

"Cut this up and we'll be good to go," Gee said, handing her the chicken.

Reese took it, and the two went about preparing their evening's dinner.

"So," Gee said matter-of-factly, "when are you going to tell me about the seminar?"

"It was interesting. I learned a lot." She allowed a slow smile to stretch the corners of her mouth and slid her eyes toward Gee. "Is that what you really want to know?" Her eyebrow arched teasingly.

"You know it's not. Stop playing."

"I had a good time. The lunch was amazing. Alex took me to a little café around the corner from where the seminar was being held." Reese nodded. "We talked quite a bit."

"About—?"

"About—everything. He told me about his family. I told him about mine." Gee watched, a warm pink blush Reese's cheeks.

"Uh-oh." Gee chuckled.

"What?"

"I don't know. You tell me."

Reese closed her eyes and sucked in a breath then let it out slowly. "It's just that, during lunch, when I didn't think he was paying attention, I took the chance to really look at him. There's this thing he does when he's thinking. He skims his thumb across his lips, and I swear it's the sexiest thing I've ever seen in my life." A zillion butterflies took flight in her belly just thinking about it. "He must've felt me looking at him because, all of a sudden, his eyes lifted, and I couldn't pull mine away fast enough. There we were, both held captive in the moment. He was staring—no—examining me—, and I saw something there –warmth and curiosity, mixed with a little mischief and I tried to memorize every intricate detail."

"Whoa." Gee breathed.

"It was a beautiful moment. I felt like a giddy school girl."

"And what about the seminar? Were you bored?"

"Not at all. Alex isn't forceful, just sure of himself and his knowledge. The presentation was interesting to me, and I'm not even a doctor. It wasn't like he was trying to convince anyone of anything; he merely presented the facts and a standing ovation was the result. I was pleasantly surprised."

Gee stood, smiling at her. "You like him."

"Yeah. I do."

"What was it like sitting there, watching him speak to all those doctors?"

"Honestly, it was exciting. Although I knew he was there to speak to *them*, every now and then he'd turn to me. It was like he was studying every part of me. Goosebumps broke out all over my body. He is, by far, the sexiest man I know."

"So —?" She looked at Reese through curious eyes. "Where do things go from here?"

Reese turned sideways toward Gee and leaned her hip against the counter. Wrinkling her nose, she said, "I don't know. He's a great guy—but—"

"But—?"

"Things have to be completely dissolved between Daxden and me before I get involved with anyone."

"I thought they were. After receiving a copy of the order of protection, you'd think he'd get the hint."

"Like you said, people like Daxden don't get hints, Gee. We haven't been a real couple for a long time, still, no matter how many ways I say it, he only hears what he wants to hear. I thought we could just remain friends, but that thought was shot to hell the other night at the restaurant."

They sat down to eat. The salad was inviting with huge chunks of chicken.

"This looks so delicious."

"Take it from me, it is definitely my 'go-to' when I'm tired and don't feel like cooking. Tonight's one of those nights."

Reese took a bite and closed her eyes, enjoying the way the flavors blended. She swallowed. "Okay, what's the secret? You put something else in here when I wasn't watching. What was it?"

Gee leaned forward and laughed. "Just a little Poultry seasoning. That's all," she whispered.

"It's really good."

Gee took a couple bites herself then leaned forward again. "Tell me something, Reese. What was it about Daxden that caught your eye?"

"I don't know. I guess it was the fact that he was so charming at first. He always seemed to know the perfect thing to say."

"Charming? A controlling person messes with your head, just like Alex said. They are clever. They influence everything you do, and the next thing you know, they're monitoring your thoughts, and you don't even realize it. I'm glad you're finally seeing through that man. But imagine the many women out there who don't see it. I've always admired your strength, Reese. Your bright personality draws people to you. But, even with that, I noticed how you'd shrink back and get quiet whenever he was around. You noticed it too. That's why you decided to make a change. And, when he realized he was losing his grip on you, he pulled out an engagement ring. What kind of woman does he think you are?"

Reese shook her head. "What kind of woman could I have become if I didn't have friends like you and Keith encouraging me to follow my own mind?"

"Do you think you would've taken the ring?"

"Hell no, and I have no idea what made him think I would have."

Gee shook her head. "I don't like him."

"Me either," Reese said, crinkling her nose and they both laughed and finished eating in silence.

Reese studied Gee. "So, work's good, huh?"

"I'm meeting with my replacement tomorrow. Regis wants me to show him around."

Reese winced. "How do you feel about that?"

She forced a smile, "I don't know. A little bittersweet, ya know. When I think about Arizona, my stomach still flips. I'm not sure where I'm going to fit in. I have my job and my friends here. Arizona is unfamiliar territory. Some days I think about it, and I'm excited because I'll be with Keith. I love his family, but there are days, like today, when thinking about it breaks my heart."

Reese moved to Gee's side. "Breaks your heart? Why?"

"I'm going to miss everything I've worked so hard for: my job, my home, and my friends."

"I won't give you time to miss me. I'll be in Arizona every chance I get."

Gee lifted her eyes to Reese's. "I'm depending on that."

The two women hugged, then finished cleaning the kitchen and fell into comfortable chatter for another hour. Afterwards, they said their goodnights and headed off to their rooms.

Gee's house was quietly tucked away from the main road and equipped with all the amenities she loved. It was the perfect open floor plan, not too far from the new Oceanside properties. So, in the summer, on her days off, she could pack a lunch and blanket and walk to the beach to enjoy the fresh air. She was going to miss that.

In her room, she headed for her bathroom and switched on the light. She moved to the sink, turned on the faucet and went about removing her make-up, then changed into her pajamas, turned off the light, and walked to her bed. Her nightly ritual was to fold the comforter down until it neatly laid across the bottom of the bed, then she piled three pillows on her side before sliding under the top sheet. With the pillows behind her, she leaned back and allowed them to prop her up so she could read. Finally settled, she opened the file she brought home. She hadn't been reading long before the phone rang. It was Keith. She smiled and put the phone to her ear.

"Hey, you."

"Hi. You busy?"

"Just getting into bed and looking over a file, but never too busy for you." She knew her words would make him smile, and she could hear it in his voice.

"I like that. How are things with Reese?"

"Great. We had a nice, long conversation at dinner tonight. Thank God she's getting that man out of her life."

"No more Daxden sightings, then?"

"Nope. He couldn't get in here anyway. He doesn't know the code."

"Don't put anything past that guy, Gee."

"I won't."

"You sound tired. How was your day?"

Gee yawned. "Long and interesting."

"How so?"

"A couple of things happened. Maybe you can help me make sense of it?"

"I'll try. What's up?"

"Well, you know the case I'm working on?"

"Yep."

"We were hired to find out if the guy was selling guns illegally. But, I could never catch up with him to ask questions, so I didn't feel the case was completed"

"Right, I remember the conversation at Regis and Helen's."

"I think I'm onto something."

"Okay, you want to run it by me?"

"The night I got hit, I found an envelope in his mailbox. I saw a woman put it there myself. I took the envelope out of the box. The envelope has Deke's name on it. I put the envelope in my pocket and, when I get to the car—bam, someone hits me and I end up at the hospital, and the envelope is gone. What do you think?"

"Either Deke or this woman hit you and took the envelope. Simple."

"Or maybe there's a third person. Whoever they are, they didn't want me there, and they didn't want me to see what was written in the note either. I need to get some answers."

"But Regis wants you off the case?"

"Right, that's why I have to work faster. Check this out." She shifted her weight in the bed, and then flipped through the papers in the file. "Here it is. His phone records show no calls in or out, except me. Can you believe that? Who has a cell phone with nothing on it? Where are all the other calls?"

"What other calls? What's your gut telling you?"

"I'm not sure. I feel like I'm in the dark here. Regis wants me to write the report and leave it alone, but I can't."

"I know you can't." Keith smiled.

"Well, think about it, Keith. You have a cell phone. How many times a day do you make calls?"

"All day."

"To who?"

"You, Mom, Dad. Hell, everybody."

"That's right. You might even call your mechanic to ask about an oil change or a store to see what time it opens or closes—"

"What are you getting at?"

"The phone is too damned clean. Deke calls no one, and no one calls him."

Keith was quiet.

"And then today, I realize, I have an identical number in the file. I almost crossed it off because it was the same number. Except it had, what looked to be, an access code next to it. I called it, hit the number one and entered the access code. Someone answered, but didn't say anything, and when I said 'hello,' they hung up."

"Same phone with two lines."

"Bingo."

"One of the oldest games in the book."

"Right."

"Tomorrow, call the number again, but don't call too early. Whoever it is will be expecting it. Wait until after noon and call. You'll catch him off guard. This time, don't say anything. In the meantime, have someone investigate the other number. Find out who else he's been calling."

"Keith, you're a genius."

"You already had it figured out. You just needed a sounding board. Once you step back and look at it from another angle, you see things differently. I learned that from you."

She smiled. "I guess I just needed someone to validate my thoughts."

Keith laughed. "Since when?"

"Since I got back from Arizona. Regis has been handling me with kid gloves. I can't stand it."

"He's scared, Gee. We all were. And then the other night happens, My god."

"But I'm fine."

"He just wants you safe."

"Keith, don't do that."

"What?"

"You're on his side."

"There are no sides, Gee. I'm just trying to tell you, I understand what he's feeling."

"Bullshit, Keith. I'm getting ready to uproot my whole life. I'm giving up my career, my friends, and everything I'm familiar with. To do what? Sit around and do nothing? He could at least let me work this last case the best I know how."

"I don't—'

"I'm the one losing here."

Keith paused, "You're losing?"

"Yeah, my job, my independence. I'm moving to a whole different state, away from everything I know — everything. I –I built my life here in California."

"I'm sorry, Gee, it never occurred to me that you would consider marrying me—losing."

"That's not what I meant, Keith. Don't put words in my mouth."

"Those were your words, not mine."

"Well, I didn't mean it that way."

"No? Well, tell me what you meant then, because, from where I'm sitting, it sounds like you're saying, marrying me makes you a loser somehow."

She realized she had blurted out every one of the fearful thoughts she'd been carrying inside her, and her heart felt heavy.

"Oh, Keith, I'm sorry."

"Me too. I didn't know you felt this way."

"Keith—it didn't come out right."

"No. I think it did. Maybe you need time to rethink what you're about to do."

"Wait a minute."

"We're getting married in a couple of months. I'm not about to carry the burden of your insecurities into our marriage, so if you're having second thoughts, say so now."

Gee was quiet.

"Nothing to say?"

"I-I don't know what to say. I do know that I'm afraid."

"You don't think I'm afraid? I've never been married before, Gee. But, I'd never consider marrying you –losing."

"That's because you're not. Everything changes for me and I'm not sure if I want the changes."

"Wow—didn't know that either. So, what are you saying?"

"I don't know, Keith." Gee yelled.

"No? Then I guess this conversation's over."

"Keith, please don't think I don't love you."

"You love me, but you're not sure if you want to marry me. I think you'd better quit while you're ahead, Gee."

"I'm not saying I don't want to marry you, Keith."

"We need to have this conversation in person, not over the phone. You have some thinking to do, Gee. We'll talk."

"Gee took a breath and lay back on the pillows, Keith was right. She needed time to think things through. Her words were all over the place, but they were out there and there was no way to take them back. So far tonight, the only thing she was successful in doing was opening her mouth long enough to royally screw things up.

"Talk later?" Keith asked.

Gee's throat tightened. "Of course."

They hung up.

17

IN THE MORNING, Gee laid in bed longer than usual, not ready to connect the day with the awful mess she left in shambles last night. *How could she have said those things?* She tossed and turned all night with each horrific dream blending into the next, with the same outcome: she lost Keith, and she couldn't bear it. Her heart stuttered, but not only from her *own* heartache, but for Keith's too. *He has to be going through the same thing I'm going through.* She thought. "I need to talk to him," she whispered and rolled over, picked up her cell phone from the nightstand and punched in his number. It went to voicemail.

Her voice was unfamiliar, even to herself, snagging onto something deep inside her chest. "Keith, this is—me. Please call when you can. I want—no—I need to hear your voice."

She pulled herself up and sat on the edge of the bed, waiting and hoping the phone would ring. It didn't. Fifteen minutes later, she made her way to the bathroom and turned on the shower. Still, no call. After removing her pajamas, she stepped in.

She felt the tears stinging her eyes so, she lifted her head allowing the shower to wash them away, but nothing washed away the painful tightening in her throat and chest. The only relief was to surrender to it, so she braced herself against the shower walls and cried.

She had no idea how long she stood under the shower, but she did know that she wasn't willing to go through another minute feeling shattered inside. She didn't want Keith to, either. She loved him and needed him to know that. Oh, God. What if the unthinkable happened and she never got the chance to tell him? She'd never forgive herself. Stepping out of the shower, she wrapped a towel around her body and headed for her cell phone.

The blue flashing light indicated a missed call. She checked the caller ID. It was Keith. "Oh, no!" she said. Her fingers trembled, and the adrenaline pumped through her so fast that she couldn't even recall his telephone number. Suddenly, she heard a familiar voice: *just press redial, and the phone will do the rest. Whose voice was that?* She didn't care. She pressed redial and rehearsed a thousand ways to say, I'm sorry, before Keith answered the phone.

"Gee?"

"Yes, Keith. It's me. I'm so sorry about last night. I'm sorry, I'm sorry, I'm—"

"I know, babe. I know. We both said things we didn't mean. But, I can't talk right now. Pen's waiting for me, and we're rushing out. I left a message on your phone. Listen to it. I've got to go, babe, but I'll call later."

"You left a message?"

"Yes, I've gotta run."

"I love you, Keith."

"I love you too, babe."

She held the phone to her heart. All she needed to hear was that Keith still loved her. Tears of relief brimmed her eyes and spilled over, staining her cheeks. She raised the cell and hit the button for voice mail, and put the phone to her ear. The sound of Keith's voice caused a light-hearted feeling that fluttered inside her belly.

"Good morning, babe. I saw that you called, but I was in a meeting with my captain. I don't know how you slept last night, but I didn't sleep at all. I want us to talk about this. All I know is, I love you, Gee. Let's see how we can figure this thing out. I won't say I don't want you to uproot your life to be with me—that wouldn't be the truth; but I want you to want it too. We'll talk soon. Love ya, babe."

Gee listened to the message again, then got up and dressed for work. Talking to Keith and hearing his voice replaced the heavy sadness with hopeful yearning but, she still wondered where a conversation of that nature would end up. She took a deep breath and checked herself in the full-length mirror. *Black pencil skirt, white blouse, and mustard yellow, double-breasted jacket, with black stiletto shoes — perfect.* Satisfied with how she looked, she turned and left the bedroom.

"Reese," she called out, "I've got to run. I'll talk to you later."

"Okay, have a good day," Reese called back through the closed door.

Gee hopped into her car, opened the garage door, and headed to work.

As usual, she turned up her music and blasted her favorite oldies station, finding herself singing along with Aretha Franklin's, "Do Right Woman."

She chuckled to herself, thinking of the many times she watched her mother clean off the huge vinyl LP and place it gently on the turntable, then carefully lay the stylus on the track she wanted to hear. Most times, it was this song. She immediately felt a sentimental longing to go back in time, and feel the comfort of her mother's arms or hear the warmth in her voice. It was a thought she hadn't had in a long time.

***

When Gee turned seventeen, pancreatic cancer was a death sentence that her mom had beaten — twice. A month after her birthday, her mother's cancer returned for the third time—more aggressive than ever. By the time she went to the doctor, she was too weak to fight.

Her mother prepared her as best she could, making sure insurance policies were in place and her burial plot secured. Gee recalled the long bus rides to the bank, her mom teaching her to balance a checkbook and keep track of her savings. She remembered her mom's trembling hands, as she'd scratch her signature in her savings book. In a soft, raspy voice weak from exhaustion, she'd say, "Watch your finances. Always know what you're spending." Eventually, she emptied her own bank account into Gee's.

Every night before bed, her mother spoke to her about life and the ups and downs she might experience growing up: the heartaches and the joys. She removed her gold necklace from her neck and latched it around Gee's, as she instructed, "Be responsible for your own happiness. It's unfair to put that responsibility off on someone else. No one can make you happy, but someone will come along who will add to your happiness. And, for God's sake, don't chase after love. In due time, it'll find you and, when it does, hold onto it with both hands." And, the most crucial piece of advice was, "Your first instinct is usually the right one, so follow your gut. Don't second guess yourself." Then the day came when Rosalyn Grace Haynes passed away.

The funeral wasn't long, but the day seemed to drag, and pull more tears than Gee thought she had. Besides herself, only Reese's family was present to say their good-bye. No one else. Not even her mother's ex-husband showed up to say his final farewell or see if his daughter might've needed

166

a shoulder to cry on. She cried about that too. *What was it about her that made her own father walk away? She didn't understand.*

***

Gee shook herself free of the painful thoughts. It was over, and her new life was about to begin with Keith.

She wondered what advise her mother would give her about Keith, and just as she thought it, she heard a whisper in her heart. *Hold onto him with both hands.*

She smiled, "I hear you, Momma."

When she pulled into the parking lot at work, as luck would have it, the song by Harold Melvin and the Blue notes came on: Keith's all-time favorite. She remembered lying in his arms, listening to him tell the story of his mother walking through the door at a party, and his dad realizing for the first time, *it was her*. Looking at them today, you'd never guess that their relationship underwent such difficulties. They were perfect together—so in love. Their's was the same kind of love she wanted with Keith. She thought how lucky he was to have his parents with him, and a small tinge of envy surged through her; but she smiled, pulled into the parking space, and hopped out of the car.

"Good morning, Gloria," she said, greeting the receptionist as she passed.

"Good morning, Ms. Haynes."

Gee stopped and turned back to the receptionist, "Gloria? Ryan Parrish will be coming in today. Can you let me know when he arrives?"

"Sure, Ms. Haynes."

"Not, Ms. Haynes, Gloria. My name's Gee."

"Sure, Ms. – uh— Gee."

She entered her office, walked to the coffee machine and made her morning coffee. Then she moved across the room to the window, just in time to see the morning sun whisper away what was left of the dimly lit sunrise, displaying what photographers call, *the golden hour*. A glow that spread its softness against the distant mountains to reveal her very own snapshot of nature.

A tap on the door interrupted her thoughts.

"Yes?"

"Ms. Haynes?"

Gee shook her head. Gloria had worked with them for over ten years and still refused to call her by her first name.

"Yes, Gloria."

"Ryan Parrish is here."

"Oh, come in," she said, rushing to the door and opening it wide. Gee's smile fell away in confused awareness. "You're Ryan Parrish?" she asked.

Ryan stepped forward and extended her hand. "That's me," she said. Her personality light and friendly.

Gee lifted her hand, accepting her greeting. An amused expression quirked up the side of her mouth as she studied her.

"You look surprised."

"Pleasantly so. Have you—met Regis Ovalton yet?"

"Not in person. We corresponded through emails and texts."

"This day is getting better and better." Gee chuckled. "Gloria, is Regis in his office?"

"I don't think he's here yet, Ms. Haynes."

"Let me know as soon as he comes in."

"Yes, ma'am." Gloria closed the door and went back to her desk.

Gee led Ryan into her office and offered the chair in front of her desk.

"Would you like some coffee?"

"I'd love some, thanks."

Gee walked to the coffee machine and began to brew a cup. "Cream—sugar?"

"A little of both."

When the machine beeped, Gee added the cream and sugar and carried the hot brew to Ryan.

"Thanks," she said, accepting it and taking a quick sip. "It's perfect."

"Well, look around," Gee said, sweeping her hand around the room. "This office is going to be yours in a couple of months. It served me well." She walked to the window. "From here, you'll witness the most beautiful sunrises and sunsets that you've ever seen."

"Sounds wonderful."

"It is. Tell me about yourself, Ryan?"

"Well, I'm a third-generation PI. My grandfather was a PI, my dad, and now me. Their lives were always so full of adventure and suspense. I'd listen to them talk about following this lead or that one, then watch them pull pieces together, like a puzzle. Their thrill in connecting clues, solving mysteries, and finding the missing ones always intrigued me."

"I know what you mean. It's my favorite thing too."

"Well, if you love it so much, why are you leaving, if you don't mind me asking?"

"I'm getting married. Moving to Arizona."

"Can't you continue your work there?"

"I don't know anything about Arizona, except that it's hot as hell. Are you from here?" Gee asked.

"Nope. Ohio. I lived in Akron for most of my life. My parents are still there. I couldn't take the snow any longer, so I moved to Ontario about five years ago, and now I'm here. I think I'll like this much better. The bugs and I didn't get along."

They laughed.

Gee had no idea how long she and Ryan talked, but soon, it was like they were old friends, catching up after an extended absence.

"Have you ever been to Ohio?" Ryan asked.

"No, and from what I've heard, I don't want to go; hot and humid in summer and too much snow in winter."

Ryan laughed, "Don't let it scare you. It's only bad in the winter. That's my opinion. Someone else might tell you they love the snow. Definitely some parts of Ohio are beautiful. That's what keeps my mom and dad there."

"I don't think I'd mind a little snow. As a matter of fact, I was in Flagstaff at a ski resort, when I met my fiancé."

"When's the wedding?"

"August."

"Here or Arizona?"

"Arizona. He has a big family. I only have a few friends here, and they'll see it as a nice vacation."

"No family?"

Nope, my mom passed away when I was younger, and I never really knew my dad. The only family I have here is my best friend, Reese. She's a bridesmaid. And then there's Regis and Helen, of course."

Gee's desk phone buzzed, and she picked up the receiver.

"Yes, Gloria? Oh, he is? Thanks. Can you ask him to come to my office?" Gee covered her mouth to stifle a laugh.

"Why do I feel like I'm the punch line of a joke?"

Gee's face went serious for a second. "Oh, please let me enjoy this. I'll tell you all about it later."

"Okay, okay. What do you want me to do?"

"Nothing. Just stay right where you are."

Regis knocked softly at the door, then opened it and stepped in. "What's up?" His eyes darted from Gee to Ryan and back to Gee.

"I wanted you to meet someone."

"Oh," Regis said, walking over to the young woman.

Ryan stood up and extended her hand. Regis shook it.

"Regis," Gee said. "I'd like you to meet my replacement, Ryan Parrish."

Regis froze.

Gee covered her mouth, trying to hide the enormous smile that curved across her face.

"B-but your name's Ryan."

"Yes, I know." Ryan smiled.

"You never said you were a — fe —er, um —lady."

"You never asked. Is it a problem?"

"Of course not. I just thought —" Regis turned back to Gee. "I suppose this is funny to you?"

"Not funny, Regis," Gee chuckled. "Just a little humorous."

"You'll have to excuse us, Ms. Parrish. Of course, we welcome you to the firm. Your reputation precedes you. I've heard nothing but great things about your work, and I look forward to having you on our team." Then turning to

Gee, he said, "Do you think you can stop laughing long enough to show Ms. Parrish around?"

"Of course I will, Regis."

He took a breath, then turned and stormed out of the office.

When the door closed, Gee broke out in uncontrollable laughter. She laughed all the way through the explanation to Ryan as to why the whole thing was hilariously funny. By the end, they were both laughing hysterically.

Ryan sat back, taking deep breaths and wiping tears of laughter. "It looks like you two have a special bond."

"When I first came to work here, he encouraged me to go to school and get my degree in criminal justice and then he more-less coached me through my political science classes." Gee paused then cleared her throat. "He's like the father I never had. As a matter of fact, he's giving me away at the wedding."

"I love you guys already."

"Wait 'til you meet his wife, Helen. Adorable inside and out. Come on, let me give you the grand tour."

The two walked out of the office, chatting as if they had known each other for years.

18

GEE WAITED UNTIL mid-afternoon to make the call. This time she used a different phone line and punched in star-six-seven before the number. She waited for the prompt to entered the code. Someone picked up after the second ring. Gee was quiet.

"Gail?" said the voice on the other end.

"Uh-huh."

"What's wrong? Are you okay?"

"Yes, I'm okay?"

"This isn't Gail. Who is this?"

"Good afternoon, Deke. You're right, I'm not Gail. My name's Georgie Haynes. I'd like to ask you a few questions."

Deke Henderson ended the call.

"Gotcha," she whispered and leaned back in her chair.

Later, in her office, Gee skimmed down the pages of Deke's phone record to find repeated numbers. She found one that was on the sheet more than any others, and counted the times' Deke made calls to it and how many times the number called him back.

"Interesting. Let's see if this is Gail."

She picked up the phone and punched in the number. A man answered. His voice was rough and low.

"Hello, McClure residence," he said.

McClure residence? she thought. A disappointed crease gathered at her brow, but she decided it was worth a try, so, in her most upbeat voice, she asked, "Hi, is Gail there?"

"Yeah, she's here. Hold on."

He called out to her, asking her to pick up the phone, and it wasn't long before she did.

"Hello, this is Gail."

"Hi, Gail. My name's Gee Haynes. I'm a private investigator. Do you, by chance, know a Deke Henderson?"

"Private Investigator?" Gail asked, through a nervous whisper.

"Yes, can you tell me what your relationship is to Deke Henderson?"

Gail pulled the phone closer to her mouth and let out a half breath, then whispered, "P-Please—"

"Ma'am, I'm just trying to do my job. If you can tell me what your relationship is to Deke Henderson, I'll go away, and you'll never hear from me again. Otherwise, I may have to get my answers somewhere else. Was that your husband who answered the phone?"

"Please. Franklin can't know, please," she pleaded.

"Know what?"

"You don't understand. I love my husband."

"So, what's your relationship to Deke?"

"It's a personal one."

"Does it have anything to do with guns?"

"Guns?"

"Wait. What don't you want your husband to know? Are you having an affair with Deke?"

Gail was quiet.

"Are you?"

She surrendered her answers.

"Yes," she whispered. The hiss of the 's' came out long and sharp. "I'll tell you what you want to know but, please—"

"You say you love your husband? Then, why?"

"My husband is a sick man, Ms. Haynes. He's very sick."

"Was it you I saw put an envelope in Deke's mailbox?"

"Yes."

"How long have you been –?"

Gail took in a breath before answering, "Four years."

"I don't understand."

"You wouldn't. My husband has cancer—prostate cancer. I still have desires, Ms. Haynes. I never intended it to happen. Deke and my husband are best friends. It would crush him if he knew."

"Then—why?"

"It wasn't something I planned. It just happened. I was going through my ordeal with my Franklin, and Deke was upset about his illness too. Plus, he was having problems in his relationship. We decided to meet and talk—console each other. One thing led to another, and here we are, four years later."

"So, how does this work? What I see on the phone record is: Deke calls your number and the duration of the call is lengthy. Then, a couple minutes after he hangs up, he gets a call from this same number."

She took in a sharp breath. "That's our code. When Deke wants to talk to me, he calls Franklin and they talk for a while. That's my cue to call him, so when the two of them finish talking, I go into another room and call him back. The last time we talked, he told me he thought Franklin's sister, Cassandra, suspected something. She's a real bitch. She knows Deke is seeing someone, but if she finds out it's me, she'll ruin us both. My god. Please, this information can't go any farther. Please."

"So, is that why you hit me with the bat? Because I was getting too close?"

"Wait…wait—what? Hit you with a what?"

"A bat. Who hit me?"

"I have no idea what you're talking about."

"Someone hit me because I took the envelope out of Deke's mailbox, about a week ago."

"A-A week ago? So ...*you* took the note? I thought it was strange when Deke said he never got it."

Gee's cell phone rang, and she reached into her purse and lifted it out. The caller ID showed it was Reese. She texted a message that she'd call her right back and then laid the cell on the desk.

Gail continued. "I don't know anything about a bat."

"Well, let's get back to the subject at hand, Gail. I was hired to do a job, and I did it. I'm not here to destroy anyone's life. I need to write my report and get it on my boss's desk by the end of the day. My client, Cassandra McClure, wants to know if Deke's selling guns illegally. What can you tell me about that?"

"*Illegally?* Why would Cassandra say that? Deke's not that type of guy."

"What type of guy would you say he is?"

"Caring, gentle, kind... I don't understand why Cassandra would say that, when she knows what Deke does. He's been working with her and Franklin for over ten years now. He helped them build their business from the ground up."

"He... works with her? Deke works with Cassandra?"

"Yes, he makes deliveries for them."

"Can I get the name and address of the business?"

"Sure. It's called M & C Tactical.

"I think I've seen it. Is that the building near Fifth Avenue?"

"Yes, the big brown building. You can't miss it. They make most of their sales online. When my husband got sick, he stopped going into the office, and Cassandra took over the business. She and Deke used to see each other."

Gee creased her brow, "They—dated?"

"Yeah, they did. Deke broke it off with her when we started our – affair. I told him he didn't have to. After all, I was still married. Cassandra was angrier than a forest fire in a windstorm. She came over here, ranting and raving to Franklin about Deke's... infidelity. She had no idea it was me. Franklin just laughed and said, 'I can't believe you thought Deke would stay with you, you're meaner than a snake.' And he's right."

Gee nodded, and rolled her eyes toward the ceiling in silent agreement. "I'll say this, Gail. I don't know what process you're going through to deal with your husband's illness. But when my mom had cancer, I felt helpless and lost. So, I'm not passing judgment. We all try to dodge the curve balls life throws at us. But, I still have a job to do, and my boss is expecting my report. But, I'm going to follow my gut with this one. The only way your husband or Cassandra will find out about your affair is if you tell them."

"My god. Thank you, Ms. Haynes."

"I appreciate your cooperation, Gail, good luck."

She hung up and sat back, going over the facts in her head and comparing them to the notes she had taken from her conversation with Gail. She made a few more phone calls, one to her connection at the FBI and the other to the San Diego Police Department, and then she powered-up her computer to write the report.

At noon, she walked into Regis's office and laid the report on his desk.

19

THE FIRST CHANCE she got, Gee picked up her cell and called Reese.

"Reese, I'm so sorry. I was on an important call."

"No problem. Just going stir-crazy over here. I need to get out and do something. Didn't I see a market nearby? What do you want for dinner? I make a good spaghetti dish."

"The market's not a good idea. If you wait for me to get home, I'll go to the store for you."

"I was afraid you'd say that," Reese pouted.

"Come on, Reese. Don't put yourself in unnecessary danger. Call Alex. Maybe he'll come keep you company until I get there?"

"No, that's okay. He's got seminars this afternoon."

"I have some good books on my closet shelf. We like the same type of psychological thrillers. Check them out. You might find something you like."

"Okay. I'll do that. That's all I wanted, Gee. I'll talk to you later. If you think of anything you want me to cook for dinner, let me know."

Gee chuckled, "I will."

They hung up. Gee lifted her head and pinched the bridge of her nose. "Hang in there, Reese, this is only temporary," she whispered. She leaned forward to study the notes in front of her and took a deep breath, stretching her neck from side to side. *Maybe more coffee,* she thought, and then decided against it. She had already had four cups.

The office was quiet, except for the whirling of the ceiling fan overhead, offering its own rhythmic pattern of w*hoosh—hush—whoosh—hush—whoosh—hush.* She picked up another file to review but by the time she got to the third page, her thoughts were fuzzy brushes of nothing that harmonized with heavy eyelids, begging for relief. As consciousness ebbed, she surrendered to the gentle darkness of sleep.

An irritating buzz—buzz—buzz jolted her awake. *Oh, my god. Was I asleep? How long?* she asked herself, shaking the sleep away and sitting forward. *The buzzing – where's it coming from?* Her eyes darted around in a frenzy to the cell phone vibrating on her desk. 'Buzz—buzz—

buzz.' She snatched it up and checked the caller ID. It was Keith. She answered. "Keith?"

"Yeah, it's me. First time I've had a minute to call. Anything going on?"

"Going on...?" Her words were rushed, and she spoke them through a hand that covered a yawn.

"Gee, were you asleep?"

"I guess I was. How embarrassing. I'm glad no one came in."

"You didn't get much sleep last night."

"Nope. Not at all. I can't believe I said those things to you. I'm nervous about the move, but the way it came out, I—"

"I know. I know, Gee. We'll talk about it. It's fixable. So, don't lose any more sleep over it. Promise?"

"Promise. What about you, you didn't get any sleep either."

"Yeah, but there's so much going on here to keep me busy that, if I fell asleep, I'd have to do it on the run." His hearty laugh made Gee smile.

"I love you, Keith."

"I know you do. Tell me about your replacement. How's he working out?"

"She."

"She?"

"Yep."

Keith broke into hysterical laughter so contagious that Gee giggled through the nooks and crannies of her words, telling him about Regis's reaction to his new employee.

"It was a classic," she laughed.

"I know it had to have been, but I hope it didn't make Ryan feel awkward."

"It didn't. Ryan's awesome. She actually got a kick out of it too. I think she's going to fit right in here."

A knock drew her attention to the door. Regis opened it and stuck his head in. "You got a minute?"

Gee nodded and motioned for him to come in.

"Keith, Regis needs to talk to me. I'll call you back."

"Okay. Love you, babe." At the mention of Regis's name, Keith gave an audacious chuckle and Gee fought the urge to join in.

She hung up quickly. "What's up, Regis?"

He held up her report. "Can you tell me what— the-hell this is?"

"It's my report. I told you there was more to it."

"This doesn't implicate Deke at all."

"Exactly. Deke works with Cassandra McClure."

"Works with her?" Regis asked, sitting in the chair in front of Gee's desk.

"Yep. The two used to date, and when Deke broke it off, Cassandra wanted revenge. So, she tried to implicate him in her mess. Cassandra and her brother, Franklin, have a business over near Fifth Avenue, called M & C Tactical. They sell a lot of stuff online, to cover up the illegal gun operation they've got going on. They find dealers, buy guns from them, then turn around and sell those same guns for a higher price, to someone else.

"What makes that illegal?"

"They don't have a license. "M & C Tactical is one of about five million listings online, where a person can buy a gun without going through the necessary background check."

She leafed through the papers on her desk, and, when she found what she was searching for, she picked it up and handed it to him.

Regis scanned the letter. "What's this?"

"You're looking at a copy of the warning letter that was sent to M & C Tactical from the ATF, The Bureau of Alcohol, Tobacco, Firearms, and Explosives. They warned them to stop selling the guns until they got a license to do so. They've been warned twice, and they ignored the warning both times."

"The sad thing is, because they don't do background checks, these guns get into the hands of criminals and others who would never have passed one. I checked with friends of mine at the FBI and the San Diego Police Department. Apparently, we're not the only ones interested in what's going on over there. Undercover detectives set up a sting. They sold guns to M & C, and M & C turned around and sold them online. Those guns were involved in criminal cases in California, Chicago, Tennessee, and Boston. They traced the guns back to M & C. Cassandra denied knowing anything about it, of course. Then she set Deke up to take the fall. She put him in charge of local deliveries and hired us to bring him down. He was the shiny object on the hill to keep the feds from investigating their operation. That's why she was in such a hurry for us to write up the report that implicated him. Deke had no idea their setup was illegal."

Regis whistled through his teeth and nodded. "So, what happens next?"

"They're going down. It's just a matter of days. It's all there in my report."

"Damned good work, Gee," he said, lifting the report in her direction. "I'm impressed."

She sat forward. "I thought you'd be," she smiled. "And nobody even got hurt."

"Except your bump on the head."

"Oh, yeah, except that."

"I think M & C had something to do with that too," he said as he stood and walked toward the door. "I still think you came back to work too soon."

"You do? Regis, it's really not that bad," she said, rubbing the spot still tender from the ordeal.

"Yeah, but you probably need to rest more."

"Why do you say that?"

Regis opened the door and turned to her. "Because work is no place to nap." He spun back around and left her office.

Gee's whole body tensed, and her eyes widened as she watched him close her office door. She buried her face in her hands and shook her head, then she sat back in her chair and did an explosion hand gesture.

Ryan peeked her head in. "Hey, you busy?"

"Nope. Come on."

"I was here earlier, but you were napping, and I didn't want to disturb you."

Gee closed her eyes. "Are you serious? I'm so sorry. I can't believe I fell asleep."

"Hey, it happens. You want to go for lunch?"

"Sure." Gee grabbed her purse, and on the way out, she stopped at Gloria's desk.

"Gloria, if Regis asks, let him know that Ryan and I went to lunch."

"Yes, ma'am, Ms. Haynes. Oh, Ms. Haynes?"

"Yes?"

"I have some messages for you. I'll just lay them on your desk. I brought them to your office earlier, but you were napping, and I didn't want to—"

"I know...I know. You didn't want to disturb me. I'll get to them when I come back. Thanks, Gloria." She leaned toward Ryan and asked, "Does everybody in the office know I fell asleep?"

Ryan gave a nervous laugh, and a one-shouldered shrug, then nodded. "'Fraid so, and then Regis put the 'Gee's sleeping. Do not disturb,' sign on your door."

Gee stopped abruptly and shot Ryan a shame-faced look. She shook her head slowly, then the two left the building.

20

RYAN AND GEE settled on a small café near the mall. They found an empty booth and scooted in. "So, tell me, how you like your first day so far?" Gee asked.

"I'm just taking it slow. Regis gave me a few things to look over and fill out. So far, I love it," she shrugged. "I feel like I belong here. You know what I mean?"

Gee nodded. "Yes, I do. I'm glad, Ryan. I think you're going to do great things."

As time progressed, Ryan noticed an absent stare on Gee's face.

"What's up, Gee?"

"Sorry. Just a few things on my mind."

"Can I help?"

"Maybe so," Gee said, sitting forward. She told Ryan about the night she was left unconscious in the street and about the missing envelope. She shared her thoughts about the report she had written and placed on Regis's desk, and her feelings of it being half-finished.

"So, what can I do?"

"Be my sounding board?. Hear me out and tell me if this makes any sense."

Ryan leaned closer. "Okay. Shoot."

"First of all, who would've benefitted from me being out of commission?"

"Deke, Cassandra, her brother."

"Right, but Deke was in his apartment, and Franklin—" she mused, "Franklin's too sick. It had to be Cassandra. Who else would've been interested in the note I pulled out of the mailbox? If it was her, I want to nail her for it."

The server approached their table and took their order. When she left, they continued.

"How do you know Deke was in the apartment or how sick Franklin is? Maybe they're watching you."

"Because whoever hit me took the note that Gail left for Deke, letting him know that he was right. Cassandra was suspicious of their affair and they needed to cool it for a while. Deke never got the note."

"And who's Gail?"

"She's the one I got most of my information from. Franklin's wife. She's having an affair with Deke. She begged me not to say anything about their affair in my report, and I promised I wouldn't."

Ryan sat back and rubbed the back of her neck. "Whoa. So, maybe you're right, and it was Cassandra who hit you."

"That's my thought. But, here's my dilemma. If Cassandra hit me and took the envelope, she knows about the affair between Deke and her sister-in-law. Why hasn't she said anything?"

"Maybe she's waiting for the right time."

Gee considered her answer. "And when would that be?" she whispered.

Their lunches were set in front of them, and they ate in silence. Ryan glanced up every now and then to take in the folded lines of Gee's brow, knowing that she was trying to organize the container of thoughts sitting helter-skelter in her mind.

"Penny for your thoughts?"

"Regis says I get too close. He might be right, but I have to follow my gut feelings."

"And what's your gut telling you now?"

"Nothing." They laughed, and Gee glanced down at her watch. "We'd better start heading back to the office," she said, motioning for the server to bring the check. They chatted and laughed on the way to the car, then hopped in and headed back to the office, never taking notice of the silver BMW following behind them.

***

Gee peeked into Ryan's office at 5:00 p.m. "Time to go home," she smiled.

"I know. I'm just going to finish up a few things here, then I'll be on my way out too."

"You got plans for tonight?" Gee asked.

"Yep, Unpacking more boxes. You?"

"Just going home. If you didn't have such exciting plans, I was going to suggest you come for dinner."

"Sounds great, but I've got a date with the boxes in my living room. I can't stand the clutter."

Gee nodded. "I get it. If you need help, let me know."

Ryan's face lit up, "I'll buy pizzas!"

They were becoming fast friends, and Gee liked that. "Okay. It'll be fun. I'll bring my friend with me. Her name's Reese. She's staying with me for a while."

"How nice. Where's Reese from?"

"Here. Just having some problems at home, so she's staying with me until it blows over."

A knowing look washed over Ryan's face. "Got it."

"No. not those kinds of problems. She's not married. She was dating this jerk who's trying to make her life miserable, so we arranged it where he couldn't get to her for a while."

"That's even worse. How long does she have to stay hidden?"

Gee gave an exaggerated shrug. "Don't know, but she knows she can stay with me as long as she wants."

"Good friends are hard to come by. Of course, bring Reese too. We'll make a fun evening of it."

192

"Sounds good. Just say when."

"How about tomorrow? I'll get as much done as I can tonight. With all three of us working at it tomorrow, I can get finished."

"Great. I'll get your address before we leave work tomorrow."

"You're a lifesaver."

Gee winked. "Yep. That's me—sunshine on a rainy day. Don't worry about locking up. The doors are on a timer. They lock automatically at five. You'll be able to get out. You just can't get back in until 8:00 tomorrow morning. Regis will give you a key card soon. That way, you'll have free access to come and go. See ya," she said, closing Ryan's door. Gee left the building.

21

DAXDEN WATCHED GEE as she left the Ovalton Building and headed for her car. When she pulled out of the parking lot, he eased behind her and followed her through the streets at a safe distance, allowing only one car between them. He stretched his neck to look around the car, making sure he was keeping up with her. He was careful—watchful, his eyes anchored to the taillights of her automobile.

The car in front of him made a sudden stop. *Why?* He wanted to blow his horn, but that would draw too much attention. Gee's car coasted through the traffic light while it was yellow. Now, it was red. He was losing her.

"S-Stupid bastard," he said, under his breath.

By the time the light turned green, Gee was nowhere in sight. Daxden powered down his side window and passed the person ahead of him, shooting him a deadly glare, then leaned down and yelled, "Y-You idiot." After slamming his hand on the steering wheel, he turned around again and shot the driver his middle finger.

His tires screeched as he peeled away from the intersection, in search of Gee, but she was gone. He pulled over to the side of the road.

"T-That's all right, b-bitch," he said, nodding his head. "We s-still got t-tomorrow." He turned his car around and drove off in the opposite direction.

Gee drove through the gates of her community, never knowing Daxden had followed her part of the way home. She powered up the garage door and backed her car inside. Then she got out and entered the house.

"I'm home," she yelled out to Reese.

"Heyyyy," Reese said, coming around the corner of the kitchen.

"What are you doing, Reese. I hope you're not cooking."

"Yep."

"Reese, I don't want you to feel like you have to do that."

"I don't. I want to do it. Plus, I have something to tell you."

Gee met her gaze. "What's up?"

"When I got off the phone with you this afternoon, I called Alex."

"Oh, yeah?" she asked, cocking her head to the side. "You called him?"

"Yes. He was in-between seminars, so he came over."

"Shut-up. What happened?"

"The rest of the story can wait for the dinner table. Go get comfortable."

Gee kicked her shoes off and rushed into the bedroom to change. When she returned, she was dressed in a pink and white lounging outfit from Victoria's Secret. "Okay, now tell me what happened."

Reese had set the table, and the two of them went about setting the food out. When they sat down, Reese began telling Gee about her day.

"I didn't think he'd come over," she said. "I was just looking for someone to talk to."

"Start from the beginning. I want to know everything."

"That was the beginning. I called Alex, told him I was going crazy over here by myself, and he said he'd be right over. We walked around the area, just talking. I feel good when I'm with him—safe. We talked about childhood memories. I told him about my mom, and he told me about his. He has a brother and sister. Did you know that? We even talked about relationships. He's never had a serious one—too busy. And no children? How rare is that?"

Gee smiled, listening to Reese rattle on.

"So, what do you think?" she finally asked.

"The question is, what do *you* think? Gee answered.

"I like him. Granted, we've only seen each other a few times, but I can tell he likes me too. The problem is—Daxden."

"I was hoping you'd see that. You don't want to bring Alex into this situation, do you?"

"I've been thinking about that, but I don't want Alex to think I'm making excuses to not see him."

"Then tell him. He already knows most of what you've been through. Tell him that you want to know that Daxden is completely gone … is he completely gone, Reese? Have you heard from him?"

Reese picked up her phone and showed Gee the fifteen missed calls from Daxden and let her hear the messages. "I stopped answering any calls that come in 'restricted,' 'unknown,' or any call with unfamiliar numbers, in case he changes his. I don't know what else to do."

"You don't want to bring Alex into this mess. Let's clean it up first."

"You're right. I'll let him know. But, girlfriend, when this is over, I'm going to let that man court me as much as he wants."

They laughed.

"When are you supposed to see him again?"

"He's only going to be here two more days, and then he goes back to Arizona. We'll work something out."

"Tomorrow, I thought we'd go over and help Ryan unpack boxes."

Reese gave a quizzical look. "Why can't he unpack his own boxes?"

"Ryan Parrish is a girl, Reese." Gee laughed.

"Oh."

"I told her we'd come help her. You mind?" Her face lit up, and she lifted an eyebrow teasingly. "It'll give you the chance to get out of the house."

Reese's smile spread across her face. "Then count me in."

"I'll call Alex and see if we can get together the day after, before he leaves and I'll have that talk with him."

Gee nodded. "I think that's best...just until this is over." She watched a disappointing shadow wash over Reese's face, and she reached out and covered her hand. Then quietly, in her most nurturing voice, she said, "Reese, Momma used to say, 'don't chase after love. It'll find you, and when it does, hold onto it with both hands.' If Alex is that 'love,' he's not going anywhere. He'll be here when the time is right."

A tender smile touched her lips "I know," was all she said.

22

REESE LAY IN bed that night, thinking about her conversation with Gee. Of course, she was right. She couldn't begin a new relationship until the one with Daxden was completely over. It had always been over as far as she was concerened, but Daxden wasn't one to take rejection. It seemed to turn into a cat-and-mouse game for him. She didn't like it. She wanted to go home and feel safe again. How dare he run her away from what belonged to her!

She rolled over and picked up her phone, studying the missed calls Daxden had left. Fifteen today, but only three voicemails. Reese pressed the button to listen to them again. The irritated voice was laced with something unfamiliar—was it evil desperation?

"Y-Yeah Reese, y-your s-still not answering my calls. Y-You're gonna w-wish you had, because I'm gonna find

You, and w-when I do, I'm not going t-to be r-r-responsible for what has t-to happen. Th-This is y-your fault—. I-I tried to warn you. D-Didn't I? You're gonna b-be r-real s-sorry – BITCH!" The phone didn't hang up right away. There was a loud thud, a scrape, and another thud as if he'd thrown the phone and it skidded across the floor, then collided with the wall on the other side of the room. She heard him curse before he punched the button that ended the call.

The next two voicemails were just as dark and threatening. Reese sat up on the edge of the bed and bowed her head. Lifting her hand, she covered her mouth. "Why can't you just leave me alone?" she whispered into her palm. Her phone buzzed. "No, no, no," she pleaded, shaking her head. "Leave me alone." The phone lit up, and the name, 'Alex,' appeared on the caller ID. She reached for it.

Her voice cracked nervously when she answered. "Hello?"

"I hope it's not too late to call?"

She attempted to clear the tension from her tone. "No, not too late at all, Alex. As a matter of fact, your pleasant voice is one I need to hear right now."

"Something's wrong. What is it?"

She released a heavy sigh. "I just finished listening to more voicemails from Daxden. He's not giving up, and I don't know what else to do. I just want to feel safe again."

"I understand that, Reese, and I'm sure you will; but for right now, you need to stay put. Be safe."

She agreed, "I know."

"I-I want to see you, Reese."

She smiled and closed her eyes, holding the phone closer to her face. "I want to see you, too."

"So, how are we going to make this happen?"

"Alex—we need to talk."

"Uh-oh, I don't like the sound of that."

"No, I want to see you, Alex, I do; but I don't want things to become complicated. And, they will, as long as Daxden's around. It's not fair to bring you into the middle of this."

"You don't have to worry about me, Reese. I can take care of myself, and you too, if you let me. No way am I going to let this thing between us slide through my fingers because of guy named Daxden. I'm just now feeling my way around you. Finally, getting out of the stage where my words get stuck between my mind and my mouth. But, sorry to say, I'm still at the stage where, as soon as I turn from looking at you, my eyes yearn to look again. What am I supposed to do with these feelings; hold on to them until Daxden decides to back off? Don't ask me to do that." She was quiet. "Reese—don't—"

She breathed heavily into the phone. "You have no idea how hard this is for me."

"You're breaking my heart. At least say you'll see me before I go home. How about tomorrow?"

"Of course. I want to see you, Alex. Not tomorrow, though. I'm going with Gee to help a friend."

"Then, when? You tell me."

"The day after tomorrow. Before you leave for the airport. Come by then."

"Okay. I'll be there. Say, about four—or four-thirty?"

"Sure. Earlier if you want. I'll be here."

"Sounds good. Sleep well tonight, Reese. "

"You too—goodnight."

They hung up, and Reese held the phone to her chest, before laying it back on the nightstand. She laid her head back onto the pillow and lifted her eyes to the ceiling. A slight smile danced across her face, remembering the excitement that surged through her when Alex's hand accidentally brushed against hers. *When had she ever felt this way? Like a giddy schoolgirl anticipating her first real date.* She nestled under the covers and drifted off to sleep, with Alex's words echoing in her head, *I can take care of myself, and you too, if you let me.*

23

GEE WAS LEAVING for work earlier than usual the next morning. She rushed out the door and slid behind the wheel of her car when Reese came barreling out. "Gee, what time are we going to Ryan's tonight?"

"I'm not sure. I'll call you."

"Okay."

"And don't worry about dinner. Ryan's ordering pizza. We can take a bottle of wine. Choose one from the wine rack."

"Okay. It sounds like a fun time."

Gee smiled and pulled out of the garage. "See ya."

Reese waved and walked back into the house.

Gee had only been on the road for five minutes when her phone rang. She smiled and pushed the button.

"Hi, Keith."

"Hey, babe. I was thinking about coming to see you this weekend. You okay with that?"

Desire singed like hot coals in the pit of her stomach. "Of course, I am."

"I gotta come in and check on my girl." His voice was sultry and inviting.

"Uhhh, I think we're both on the same page about that. I miss you, Keith." She felt the heat of a blush on her cheeks. "What time are you coming in?"

"Not sure. I hope to get away from the office early on Friday, to get on the road. I'll let you know."

"Sounds great. I can't wait to see you."

"Same here. You got a busy day today?"

"Yep. I think the FBI is going to shut down M & C Tactical, which means Cassandra and Franklin will be getting arrested. I can't wait."

"What about Deke Henderson?"

"He actually had no part in what they were doing. He was just the delivery guy. It's the same with the rest of the employees. It's too bad they'll be out of jobs, but Cassandra and her brother, Franklin, knew what kind of position they were putting them in and they didn't care. It ticks me off to know Cassandra put the guns into Deke's hands and then hired us to bust him. Just like I told Regis, they hired the wrong firm."

"You worked hard on the case, Gee. You should be proud of yourself."

"I am— Okay, I'm pulling into the parking lot. I'll call you when I get a chance. Love you."

"Love you too, babe."

Gee hung up and walked into the building.

"You're here early, Ms. Haynes."

"Yes, Gloria. Anybody else here?"

"Nope, not a soul. Just you and me," she chimed.

Gee rushed into her office and over to the window, where she stood, taking in the breathtaking sunrise.

"My little piece of heaven," she whispered. "I'm really going to miss you." She took a breath, then moved away from the window long enough to fill her coffee cup and return.

Her desk phone rang just as she sat down. She picked it up. "Hello, this is Gee Haynes. How can I help you?"

"Ms. Haynes, this here's Officer Ellis, at the San Diego Police Department. Remember me?"

"Of course I do." Gee smiled. "How are you?"

"I'm fair, little lady. Just got a few things on my mind is all. I thought I could run 'em by you. Do you have a full day?"

"Yeah, it's pretty full, but I can make time for a hero. What do you need, Officer Ellis?"

Officer Ellis let out a hearty laugh that seemed to break from his chest. "Now, Ms. Haynes, I ain't nobody's hero. Just happened to be at the right place at the right time. The hero is that fiancé of yours. He's the one that called it in."

"Then I have two heroes," Gee said proudly.

"Okay, okay, okay, but listen here. The night we took you over to the hospital, me and Sam decided to stop back at the place we found ya. There's a coupla' things we found. Could be somethin', could be nothin'. I was wonderin' if you could swing by the station this afternoon."

She checked her calendar. "I've got appointments until 1:30. I can probably make it at two. Are you available then?"

"I can make sure I am. Just stop at the front desk, and they'll show you how ta get to me."

"Alright, I'll do that, Officer Ellis. See you at two."

"Good, good, good. See ya then." They hung up, and Gee sat looking at the phone, wondering if, what Officer Ellis had to show her, would lead to whoever it was that left her unconscious.

A knock on her door jarred her away from her thoughts. "Ryan, is that you?" she called out.

"Yeah, can I come in?"

"Sure."

"You got coffee?"

"Help yourself," Gee said, gesturing toward the machine on the counter.

Ryan rushed to it. "I was hoping you'd say that. I can't find my coffee pot amid all the boxes at home. So, I couldn't make coffee this morning."

"What a bummer. You can come in here and get coffee any time you want."

"Thanks," she said, popping in a pod and waiting for it to brew. "So, what did Reese say about this evening?"

"Oh, she's all for it, but you know, we're only coming for the pizza."

Ryan laughed. "I don't care. I'll buy two pizzas if it means I find my coffee pot." She took a long sip of the steaming brew. "Ahhhh. I needed that. So, what's happening today? What's on your agenda?"

"Very busy day and a couple of appointments. You can sit in if you like."

"I just might do that."

"Oh, and I got a call from Officer Ellis: the officer that took me to the hospital the night someone hit me. He wants me to stop by the station this afternoon. He said he went back to the place they found me, and–I guess he found something."

"What time are you going?"

"I told him I'd be there around two."

"I'm going with you."

"You can't."

"Why not?"

"Regis would kill me. What do we tell him we're doing?"

"Tell him we're going to lunch. My treat."

Gee smiled and gave a thumbs-up. "You're on."

Ryan turned to leave the office just as Gee's phone rang again. She held up the coffee cup. "I'll bring this back later," she said, her voice wrapped in a whisper.

Gee nodded and watched the door close, then she sat behind her desk. "This is Gee Haynes, how can I help you?" she asked, typing some last minute texts to Keith:

GEE: Keith, having lunch with Ryan this afternoon. I'll call you when I get back to the office.

KEITH: Okay. No problem. Love you.

GEE: Love you too.

"Ms. Haynes, It's Gail. Gail McClure."

"Yes, Gail. What can I do for you?"

"Ms. Haynes, what's going on? The police are here. They're arresting Franklin, and they even have warrants to go through our stuff. They confiscated our computers. Cassandra has been apprehended too. She's already in custody at the police station. What's happening?"

Gee raised an eyebrow. "I'm sorry, Gail. Your husband and his sister were involved in – an illegal act. They've been using M & C Tactical to sell guns illegally. They were warned several times, and they ignored the warnings."

"No, no. It wasn't illegal. It's an online store. They've been in business for years. I've made a few deliveries for them myself."

"Gail, you have to have a license to sell guns. They don't have one. Listen, is it possible for you to come to my office? I don't like talking about sensitive matters over the phone. I think we should speak face to face."

"I suppose I can. I was getting ready to leave for the police station. I need to get to my husband. He's a very sick man," she sobbed, and it tore at Gee's heart.

"Please. Come to the office, Gail." She gave her the address, and they hung up.

Regis got to the office twenty minutes later, and Gee went in search of him. She knocked, and then entered to tell him about the phone call with Gail McClure.

"How much can I tell her?" she asked.

"Well, she is his spouse. It's not like you're telling her anything she doesn't know. She just has a distorted view of it."

"Right. That's what I was thinking." She sat forward. "You know, she was so worried and protective of Franklin finding out about her affair; but he could care less about the danger he was putting her in when she was making deliveries for him. If she had been caught, she could've gone to jail." Gee stood and walked across the room, then stormed back to Regis. "The selfish bastard! I wonder how many deliveries he made in person. None. Not when he had two innocent people more than willing to do it for him. They were pawns, Reg, just pawns. He didn't care anything about them. Then Cassandra hires our firm to follow Deke and write a bogus report to make it look like he was working alone, selling guns and making deliveries without their knowledge, just because she wanted revenge. I'm glad to see the whole thing backfire in her face." Gee shook her head. "What kind of people are they?"

"Gee, calm down."

"I don't need to calm down, Regis. I get damned mad when somebody comes along and tries to use this firm for their shady exploits. I've seen how hard you worked to promote the highest standards of operation and practices in the state. This is, The Ovalton Private Investigation Firm, Don't you tell me to calm down. Why aren't you angry about it?"

"Why should I be? I think you get angry enough for both of us," he laughed.

The knock on the door pulled her attention, just as Gloria peeked in,

"Ms. Haynes. You've got an appointment waiting for you."

"Is it Gail McClure?"

"Yes, ma'am."

"That was fast. Can you take her to my office and let her know I'll be right there?"

"Yes, ma'am, Ms. Haynes." Gloria closed the door and went back down the hall.

Gee turned to Regis. "Can you please tell her to stop calling me Ms. Haynes?"

Regis laughed. "What do you want her to call you?"

"She can call me Gee, like everyone else."

"She'll call you Gee when she calls me Regis."

They laughed, and Gee stood to leave. "Regis?"

He lifted his gaze to hers.

"My time here at the firm is something that I will remember for the rest of my life. You have always been fair—brutal, but fair, and I love you and Helen so much."

"You don't think we know that?"

"I certainly hope you do—I depend on it."

"Get out of my office so I can work," Regis said in his gruff voice. Then he dropped his eyes to the mounds of paper sprawled in front of him.

Gee studied him, admiring him with a long smile, then turned and left.

When he was sure she was gone, Regis looked up at the closed door. His eyes misted over, and his heart was full. Yes, he'd miss the young girl who had come seeking a job so many years ago. The girl who would take the bull by its horns and not let him settle for second best. He was proud of the woman she'd become. Many times he almost told her the secret he'd carried in his heart, but he couldn't find the words; they just wouldn't form. Once he received the results of the DNA, his mind stayed on the edge of disbelief and wonderment. How could an unlocked secret bring such definition to otherwise questionable findings that he never knew existed? Biologically, Georgie Haynes *was* his daughter and he needed to prepare himself for the risk or the reward of telling her.

Regis opened his desk drawer and drew out a small black box. He lifted the lid and removed the other half of Gee's butterfly.

24

GEE LEFT REGIS'S office and walked down the hall to her own. When she opened the door, the sorrowful eyes of Gail McClure met her. She stood and extended her hand. "Ms. Haynes."

"Gail," she said, walking toward her. "It's good to finally meet you in person." They shook hands, and Gail sat back in her seat. "Would you like some coffee?"

"No, I'm good. Just, please tell me what's going on, Ms. Haynes." Her eyes pooled with unshed tears.

Gee sat behind her desk in full view of her. She wanted Gail to see her face when she told her the truth.

"Here it is," Gee said, "Your sister-in-law hired our firm to follow Deke, to find out if he was selling guns — illegally. She wanted us to hurry up and write a report that implicated Deke as soon as I started following him. She needed me to get pictures of him making a drop. But, to me, it couldn't be that easy… something was missing. So I kept digging—something my boss hates for me to do, but I felt compelled for some reason. Here's what I found out. Deke was only doing the same thing you did. Your husband, Franklin, had you deliver guns to local buyers. He had already been warned to stop, but he didn't. Because he knew the FBI was watching him, he couldn't take the chance on being caught making the deliveries, but you—he could use you to do it, not caring if you got caught. Cassandra, at the same time, was using Deke for the same reason. She was bitter because of the break-up, and she hired us to take him down. She wanted him to suffer."

"Wait—what?"

"Franklin and Cassandra had different reasons for using the two of you, but it would give them the same result—they thought they were covering themselves. They had no idea that the FBI was already onto them. It was just a matter of time before they would be arrested. My investigation was supposed to nail Deke but instead it exonerated him."

"But Franklin wouldn't do that to me."

"Did you make the deliveries?"

"Yes, but –"

"Then—he did it to you." She opened a folder and pulled out copies of the two warning letters, sent to Franklin from the ATF, and handed them to her. "He had been warned twice to stop selling guns until he got a license. He didn't stop. He knew what he was doing, and he knew it was wrong. He didn't care."

She waited for Gail to examine the letters and watched her face slide from heart-wrenching despair to a stunned and painful comprehension.

"Are you saying—"

"Gail, you know exactly what I'm saying. He used you, and he kept on using you because he knew you trusted him enough not to ask questions. He didn't care if you got caught. I understand he's sick –now, but he wasn't always. When did he start getting sick?"

"Early last year," she said, taking shallow breaths, hoping Gee's theory would somehow land in left field. It didn't. Everything Gee said, Gail knew was true. She put her hands over her face and sobbed. "All along? All the time I was caring for him, he was using me?"

"What about Deke?" Gee asked.

"I spoke to him this morning after the police arrested Franklin. He'd been trying to tell me something wasn't right. They considered Deke one of the top delivery people on their team but he was never allowed on the computers to check for orders. He said it was as though they were trying to hide something. I didn't believe him. I told him I was coming here to talk to you, and he said he would meet me."

Just as she said the words, they heard a commotion in the corridor.

"No, sir. You cannot go in there. Ms. Haynes has a client." Gloria's voice rang through the corridor and hit the ceiling of the Ovalton building, louder than anyone had ever heard it. Gee rushed to the door and snatched it open, then stepped quickly into the hall, closing the door behind her partway.

Deke faced her.

"Please, tell me Gail's here." He said.

Gee nodded. "She is."

"Deke?" Gail whimpered from the other side of the door.

"Gail?" he called out, rushing toward Gee's office. He pushed the door open.

"You were right," she sobbed. "You were right all along."

He rushed to her and pulled her into an embrace. His words rolled against her ear over and over again. "It doesn't matter. It just doesn't matter," he said, cradling her— shushing her. Then, he lifted her face and waited for her eyes meet his. He said, one last time with a slight shake of his head, "It doesn't matter."

Gee stood back and watched Deke gently frame Gail's face with his hands. He caressed her cheeks and wiped her tears. There was no denying it, love had found them, regardless of its forbidden circumstances. Despite the consequences, it had found them, and they surrendered to it with no more hidden guilt or shame.

"I need to go to the police station," Gail said.

He nodded. "Of course—I'll take you."

"I have to hear it from him," she said.

216

"Me too," Deke agreed. They left the Ovalton building with new direction and understanding.

Gee sat back at her desk. This is one of the many things, she loved about her job; giving people fresh or refreshed hope.

"My god, I'm really going to miss this," she whispered.

25

AT 2:00, Gee and Ryan's footsteps echoed on the travertine floors of the San Diego Police Department, and they soon found themselves standing in the center of a large room. Another room, encased behind a circular wall with windows, appeared to be the best place to get information. They approached it and asked for Officer Ellis.

"Oh, he's around here somewhere. If he's not in that crowd there, his office is around the corner. Room 105," said the woman on the other side of the glass, with a wave of her hand.

Gee turned and stretched her neck to get a quick look around, hoping to see someone familiar in the crowd of uniformed officers. Their faces resembling the ones hanging neatly on the wall, proudly boasting of the station's diverse culture.

Then she saw him.

"Officer Ellis?" she called out.

He turned in the direction of her voice, straining his neck around the people in the crowded area, until he saw her. They headed toward each other. Gee extended her hand, and Officer Ellis shook it eagerly. "I'm glad ta see ya made it."

Gee turned to Ryan. "Ryan, this is the officer I was telling you about. Officer Ellis—Ryan Parrish."

Ryan nodded and offered her hand. "Good to meet you, sir."

He shook it and turned back to Gee.

"How you doin', little lady? Looks like you're recoverin' nicely," he said.

"I am, sir. How's Sam?"

"He's good. He's right over there waitin' on me." He motioned with his hand. "Come on and follow me over ta my office. I got somethin' I wanna show ya. See if you can make some sense of it."

He had already begun to zigzag his way around the crowd and through the corridor toward his office. "I went back ta the hospital the night we took you in. Peeked in at cha'. You was sleepin' like a baby. And another time, your family was witcha, so I just got the update from the nurse, went down and talked ta my son a little, then left. Me and Sam went back ta the place we found ya, ta take another look around and see if we could find somethin'."

"Did you?"

"Picked up a few things. Like I said earlier, could be somethin', could be nothin'.

He entered his office and motioned for them to have a seat and he sat behind his huge mahogany desk and opened his top drawer. He shifted through mounds of office supplies: paper clips, pens, and rubber bands, until he came to a small plastic bag, folded neatly and hidden from sight. He drew it out and sat it on top of the desk in front of Gee and Ryan. Gee tried to make out what the items were through the bag. If she wasn't mistaken, it looked like one was a piece of wood. She sat closer to get a better look.

"Don't know if any of this makes sense to ya, but, I figured it was a long shot and picked it up anyway." He reached into another drawer and pulled out a small box of rubber gloves. After squeezing his hands into them, he used a pair of tweezers, reached into the bag, snagged the large piece of wood and pulled it out. He held it up and turned it from side to side, so Gee could view it at all angles.

"A wood fragment? Do you think –"

"Yep. That would be my guess. Could've come off of whatever it was they hitcha with. It doesn't look like it came from a bat, though. Had ta been somethin' else."

Gee studied it again and nodded. The wood fragment was jagged and could very well have splintered away from a 2x4. Her eyes slid back to the plastic bag. "What's that?" she asked, pointing to the folded paper still inside. "Looks like a receipt."

"Yep. That's what it is—a receipt." He put the wood fragment back into the bag, snagged the receipt and drew it out. He laid it on top of the plastic bag. Using his gloved hand, he unfolded it.

Gee squinted her eyes. "I can't read what it says, can you?"

"Only the name of the car wash. The rest is too smeared ta make out."

"How about you, Ryan? Can you make it out?"

"Sorry," she said, shaking her head."

"Can I take them with me?"

"I take it you don't want us ta investigate it?"

"No. I have some suspicions of my own and I'd like to follow them through. But, if I need help, can I depend on you?"

"Of course. You know where ta find me," he chuckled.

Gee and Ryan stood and extended their hands to shake Officer Ellis's, then Gee picked up the bag. "Thank you, Officer Ellis, you've been a great help. It was good to see you."

"Same here. Here, take this." He reached into his pocket and pulled out his wallet. "It's my card. If you need anything, you give me a call. Understand?"

Gee took the cards and handed one to Ryan.

"Thanks," she said again, slipping the card into her card case and pulling out one of her own. "Here's mine."

Officer Ellis took it and tucked it into his shirt pocket.

The two turned and headed for the exit.

"You young ladies be careful," he called out to them.

"Will do," Gee said with a wave. Then they hurried out of the station and back to the car.

Gee waited while Ryan buckled her seatbelt, then asked, "What do you think?"

"Not sure. There's not much to go on. Ryan reached over, picked up the bag, and lifted it to look at the contents. "Do you know the car wash?" she asked.

Gee gave a half shrug. "Yeah, but there's a chain of them. I wouldn't know where to start."

"Let's start with the nearest one and work our way through."

Gee gave Ryan a sideways glance and said, "I think I should tell you that this is the kind of stuff that gets me into trouble with Regis. He says I get too close. So, if you want me to turn around and take you back to the office, I'll understand."

"Are you kidding? This is the most excitement I've had in a long time. I'd consider this on the job training."

Gee pulled out of the parking space and started down the road. A silver BMW pulled behind them.

They had been driving for a while in silence. When she checked her rearview mirror, she noticed an erratic driver dip from behind a truck two cars back, speed up and pull behind her –directly behind her.

Gee turned at the corner then rechecked the mirror.

The car tailed right behind her.

"Don't turn around, but it looks like someone's following us." She said to Ryan.

Ryan eased over to look through the side mirror.

"Are you sure?"

"Well, let's find out."

Gee sped up and turned a sharp right at the next corner. The car behind her did the same. She eased her foot down onto the gas and made her car race forward, then turned a quick left. She checked the rearview mirror and then the side one; the BMW was catching up.

Ryan leaned over and yelled, "Get on the freeway and go back to the police station."

Gee zoomed around the block to the entrance ramp. She checked her mirrors and saw that the car was coming up the ramp too. Fast. She stepped on the gas and her car shot forward so quickly that Ryan had to clutch the assist handle above her door.

"The card, Ryan. Get the card and call Officer Ellis. Tell him what's happening and see if he'll meet us outside when we pull up."

Ryan reached into her purse and found the card. She pulled out her phone and punched in his number.

He answered. "Officer Ellis."

Ryan put the phone on speaker. "Officer Ellis, this is Ryan Parrish. I was there earlier with Gee Haynes. Looks like we've got someone on our tail and we're headed back your way."

"Wait a minute. Who's this, you say?"

"Ryan, Ryan Parrish. I was there a little while ago with Gee Haynes. You gave us your card."

"Oh, yeah—yeah. Now, what's goin' on?"

"We've got someone tailing us, sir, and we're almost at the station. We were wondering if you could meet us outside. We don't feel safe."

Gee concentrated on the road, but kept her ears glued to the conversation between Ryan and Officer Ellis. She was driving at an excessive speed, hoping to attract a police car along the way. What Gee didn't notice was her own phone lighting up and displaying Keith's name for the fifth time.

"Do you know who it is?" asked Officer Ellis.

"No, sir."

"What color's the car?"

"Silver. It's a silver BMW. Can you meet us?"

"Why, of course, little lady. I'm sure me and a few of my buddies can meet cha. You just come on in."

Gee zipped past one exit and got off at the next one. The silver car stayed close.

She felt her heart skyrocket from the surge of adrenaline. Keeping her eyes on the road and her senses keen, she continued to duck in and out of traffic. Her tires screeched as she turned the corner and skidded to a stop in front of the station.

Officer Ellis and Sam stood on the sidewalk, with what looked like every officer in the precinct. They waited for the car to come to a screeching halt.

Officer Ellis took a step toward it.

"I'm gonna need you ladies ta stay put. You alright?"

"Yes, sir."

He turned to the silver car, laid his hand on his gun, and motioned the other officers to surround it.

He yelled, "Put your hands on the wheel!"

26

ARIZONA, AT THIS time of year, is known for its high temperatures, usually hovering around the low 100s. But today, the air was stifling hot and muggy from the unexpected humidity that lingered like an uninvited friend. It caused Phoenicians to complain, crank up the air conditioners, and stay inside.

Keith sat leafing through the stack of cases on his desk. Finally, not being able to stand it any longer, he picked up a folder and fanned at the sweat that beaded around his forehead.

"God, can somebody please turn the air up? It's hot as hell in here."

Pen turned from the water cooler with a cup in his hand. He dipped his fingers into it and splashed the cold water onto his face.

"Captain said not to touch the thermostat."

"Oh, so suffering from heatstroke is better?"

Pen did an exaggerated look around the room and lifted his voice. "If somebody hadn't forgotten to turn the air conditioner back down, we wouldn't be going through this."

The officers in the precinct turned accusing eyes in Keith's direction. Keith, in turn, gave an exaggerated shrug.

"Oh so, it's my fault?"

Pen laughed. "I'm just sayin'—"

"So, I forgot. Okay?"

"And the station felt like an igloo when we came in to work the next day."

"Hey. It warmed up. I thought the thing turned off automatically."

"It didn't."

Keith fanned his hand through the air at them all and turned back to his files. Pen sat across from him.

"So, what's going on with Gee?"

"She's good, man."

Pen nodded his head, waiting for Keith to continue.

Keith looked up. "What?"

"Kelly told me about the conversation you had with Mom and Pop."

Keith stopped shuffling through his cases. "Why can't this family keep things to themselves?"

"Because we're family. You're my brother-in-law, and your sister wanted me to make sure you were okay."

"I'm fine. It was just a little argument."

"Not little, from what I heard."

Keith rubbed his hand across his face. "What did you hear?"

"Mom told Kelly that you said, Gee said, she wasn't sure she was ready to give up her life as a PI and move away from San Diego."

"That sounds pretty much how the conversation went."

"That's a major deal, don't you think?"

"Yep, but we talked again, and we both know we said things we shouldn't have –it was just a stupid argument –a difference of opinion."

Pen nodded again.

"Well, what am I supposed to do?"

"When you talked to her, how'd she sound?"

"The same as me." Keith gave a half shrug and shook his head. "I don't know."

"Gee loves you, Keith. You two just need to put your heads together and come up with a solution—some kind of compromise. I can't imagine you without her."

"I can't imagine me without her either. We'll figure it out."

"You say you spoke to her?"

"Yep, she has a lot on her plate. Dealing with her replacement, trying to finish the case she's working on, worrying about Reese . . . she's going through a lot right now."

"Does it look like her replacement is going to work out?"

"Gee seems to like her. They hit it off pretty good. They went to lunch together again today. When I spoke to her, she was busy trying to finish her report."

"So, she finished the case?"

"Not exactly."

"I'm not following you."

"You know Gee. She's got this thing that runs through her blood. If something piques her interest and there's a piece missing, she's going to follow it through until she finds it, and it drives Regis crazy." Keith laughed.

"It doesn't bother you?"

"I guess that's one of the things I love about her, her determination. She's feisty. To tell you the truth, I'm worried about her transition from San Diego to here, too. I just didn't tell her that. She's not one to sit idle."

"What are you going to do?"

"Keep her barefoot and pregnant."

They laughed. "Better not let Gee hear you say that."

"I know." Then Keith got serious.

"I'm not sure what I'm going to do, but, like you said, we'll have to come up with a solution, and quick. The wedding is just around the corner."

"Have you heard back from her today?"

"No, in fact, I— "

He pulled his cell phone out of the case and went to the tracking app –"I haven't heard any—thing." He studied his phone.

"What's up?" Pen asked.

"Whoa—"

Keith stood so fast his chair slid back and almost fell over.

"What is it?"

"Something's wrong."

"What? Keith, what is it?"

"She's driving crazy – too fast."

"Let me see." Pen rushed around to Keith's side and looked at the phone.

He watched Gee's car speed through the streets, dart around corners, and run through traffic lights.

"What is she doing?"

"You think someone's after her?"

Keith called her phone. No answer. He tapped the screen, went back to the tracking app and watched.

He called again. No answer.

"Pick – up – the phone!" he yelled.

"Maybe she can't."

Keith looked at Pen, knowing he was right. That would be the only reason she wouldn't pick up. She couldn't.

He tried calling again. No answer. He pulled his chair up and eased himself down into it, never once taking his eyes off the screen. He and Pen sat helpless at his desk and waited for the car to come to a stop.

27

OFFICER ELLIS KEPT his hand close to his gun and moved closer to the car. "I said, put your hands on the steering wheel and don't move."

The driver slammed the car into reverse and stepped hard on the gas, causing the vehicle to swerve around. When it came out of the swerve, the driver threw the car into drive and sped down the street with a dozen or more officers running after it. The car raced out of sight, leaving only long skid marks as a reminder of its existence.

Officer Ellis approached Gee's car.

"You ladies sure you're alright?"

Gee clutched the steering wheel and turned to Ryan. When Ryan nodded, Gee answered him, "Yes, we're fine. Thank you."

He turned and yelled through the crowd, "Anybody get that plate number?"

Several of the officers held up their cell phones. "Got it," they yelled back.

Ellis turned back to Gee and winked. "We're gonna find out who that was and get back wit' cha."

Gee smiled at him. "Officer Ellis, on top of being my hero, I believe you've just become my guardian angel."

"I don't know about all that, little lady, but it's always a pleasure lookin' out for ya. I don't think you'll have ta worry about him again. We're gonna get inside and run his plates ta see who we're dealin' with."

"Thank you so much," Gee said with a wave, and they rode down the street with Officer Ellis watching after them, until they were well out of sight.

Gee heard her phone ringing and looked down to see Keith's name on the caller ID. She reached out and pressed the button for the Bluetooth to answer it.

"Keith?"

"Gee? You want to tell me what that was about?"

"You were watching?"

"Damn right, I was watching."

"Keith, it was crazy. All of a sudden, he was behind me. No matter what I did, I couldn't shake him, so we called Officer Ellis and made our way to the precinct, and he met us there with other officers, but he got away."

"Who got away? Who the hell was it?"

"We don't know yet, but Officer Ellis has the plate number, and he's going to run it and get back with me."

Keith took a deep breath, "You have no idea what I've been going through over here."

"I'm sorry, Keith."

"As long as you're okay. Call me as soon as you find out who it was."

"I will."

"Is Ryan still with you?"

"Yes, she's here."

"She okay?"

Ryan spoke up. "I'm good, Keith. Thanks for asking."

Gee interjected, "We're both a little shaken, but we're okay."

"You heading back to the office?"

"Yep, we've been gone all afternoon, and Regis is going to want to know why."

"What are you gonna tell him?"

"I'm going to say, I was showing Ryan—the ropes."

"You think he'll buy it?"

"Don't know. We'll find out, though."

"Okay, I'll let you go so you can regroup. Call you later tonight."

"Sounds good. I love you, Keith."

"Love you too, babe." They hung up.

Ryan turned to Gee. "You're lucky. Sounds like true love."

Gee smiled, "It is."

"That's what I want someday."

"Then hold out for it, Ryan, and don't settle."

Ryan nodded, taking a mental note. From what she could see of Gee and Keith's relationship, if not settling meant she could have *that*, she was ready and determined to follow through on it. Each time she'd stumble into a relationship, it seemed she was always the one who ended up hurt. Now, with a new place, new job, new friends, and hopefully a new thought process where relationships were concerned, a good relationship might be right around the corner. She hoped.

They pulled into the parking lot of the Ovalton building, parked, and went inside. Gee stopped at Gloria's desk.

"Any calls?"

Gloria reached over, picked up a stack of sticky notes, and handed them to Gee.

"The phone hasn't stopped ringing, and Mr. Ovalton wants to see you in his office."

Ryan stepped forward and whispered to Gee. "Better you than me," she chuckled.

Gloria glanced up at her. "Actually, Ms. Parrish, he wants to see both of you."

Ryan's smile left her face. "Is he in a good mood?"

Gloria chuckled. "I don't think I've ever seen Mr. Ovalton in a good mood."

Gee laughed, and they walked down the hall to Regis's office.

Going to Regis's office usually turned out to be a pleasant visit. It's when he comes to her office that let's Gee know she has done something to royally piss him off. She tapped lightly at the door and waited for his gruff voice to invite them in.

"Come on."

"Regis, you wanted to see us?"

Regis smiled, "Yes, come in. Have a seat." He regarded them over his reading glasses and eventually removed them from his face altogether. "Well, Ryan, how are you liking your second day?"

"I love it."

"Gee's getting you used to the way we do things around here?"

Ryan cleared her throat, "Oh yeah. She's—been great."

"So, where'd you go for lunch?"

"The little café by the mall," Gee smiled.

Regis nodded. "Good, good, good…. Okay. I put a few files on Ryan's desk, Gee. I'd like for you to go over them with her. Show her how we enter the information into the computer. Let me know if there's anything you need from me. And I received a call from the San Diego Police Department. They wanted to thank us for your report on M & C Tactical."

Gee and Ryan did a sideways glance at each other.

"They did?" Gee asked. "That was nice of them."

"Damned good work, Gee."

"Thanks, Reg," she said with a smile.

"Okay. That's all I wanted to say. Good to see you two getting along."

"Yes, sir," they said at the same time, side glanced at each other again, then turned and walked out of the office.

28

IT WAS ALMOST 5:00. Gee told Reese she'd pick her up at 5:15. She poked her head in Ryan's office. "I'm getting ready to leave. Jot down your address for me, so I can put it into my GPS. I'm leaving to get Reese, and we'll meet you at your apartment within the hour. Is that good?"

"Perfect." She grabbed a pen and wrote down her address. "I'll be home by then, and, hey, I really do appreciate you coming to help me," Ryan said.

Gee fanned her hand. "Girl, it's no problem. Moving is always better with friends, pizza, and wine," she laughed.

When Gee stepped outside alone an eerie sensation flooded over her.

She stretched her neck to glance around the parking lot before moving toward her car, picking up speed as she walked. Her quick steps echoed on the pavement and seemed to synchronize with the rapid beating of her heart. "Calm down, Gee." She whispered, but her thoughts kept going back to the car that swerved in and out of traffic, desperately trying to stay behind her. *When did it first start following me? Could he be here?* Her eyes scanned the parking lot again. *Had he been watching me all along?* When she reached the car, she snatched the door open and slid behind the steering wheel. *Why would someone be following me?* A car door slammed nearby, and she whipped around in its direction to see that it was an employee from across the street. She combed the area in every direction, then put the key into the ignition, started the car and pulled out of the parking lot. As she drove, she checked her rearview mirror regularly, looking for familiar vehicles.

Home seemed so far away, but soon she was pulling into her garage. She waited–glued to her seat, watching the garage door fold down and close, before exhaling a relieved breath. The tension in her shoulders relaxed, and she opened the car door and walked inside.

Reese's cheery voice chimed from the kitchen. "Heyyy. How was your day? Don't get upset, I'm making this for tomorrow's dinner, so you don't have to." She came around the kitchen island, wiping her hands with a towel. "I'm— ready—to— " She took one look at Gee's face and rushed to her, her own expression sliding from its ingenuous smile to sheer panic. "Oh, my god, what's wrong? You look like you've seen a ghost."

"I just had the most distressing drive home."

"Why? What happened?"

Gee moved to the couch and eased herself down onto it. "There was a car. This afternoon. It followed me. I don't know why. I'm thinking it's someone Cassandra McClure hired, trying to scare me. She doesn't like that I'm on to her. She's got somebody watching me."

Reese sat beside her. "Are you sure?"

Gee nodded, "Oh yeah, and they wanted to make sure I knew they were there."

"What did you do?"

"I had just left a meeting with Officer Ellis, the officer who took me to the hospital the night I got hurt. Ryan and I were leaving the station when all of this happened. She's the one who had the idea to head back to the station, so we did. Ryan called ahead to Officer Ellis, to let him know what was going on. By the time we pulled in front of the station, Officer Ellis had the whole police force outside waiting for us.

"Did they get him?"

"No. He got away, but the police got his license plate number, so I should get a call sometime tomorrow from Officer Ellis. When I left work tonight, I . . . all of a sudden became jumpy and afraid. I couldn't get to my car fast enough . . . driving home, constantly checking the rearview mirror. I was a nervous wreck and I think that's exactly what they were trying to accomplish."

"They've done a good job of it. I don't think I've ever seen you this frightened."

"It makes me angry."

Reese laughed. "You wouldn't be, Gee Haynes, if it didn't."

"I'm gonna find out who it was."

"Gee, wait for the Officer to tell you how to proceed with this. Don't put yourself in danger."

"Too late. I think I'm already there, but she's going to regret the day she was born by the time I finish with her."

Their eyes met, and a shadow of concern flowed between them.

"Come on. Let's go to Ryan's."

"What did you make for tomorrow?"

"I found the ingredients for my special spaghetti. You've always liked it."

Gee nodded. "You're right. I love your spaghetti."

"I made plenty. We can take some to Ryan, too."

"Great idea. She'll appreciate that."

They filled a Tupperware full of spaghetti, grabbed a bottle of wine from the rack, and left.

29

RYAN'S PLACE WAS a small, two-bedroom, two-bath, luxury apartment. It was located in a secure building and you needed a key card to enter. When Reese and Gee arrived, they had to call Ryan's phone to have her buzz them through the door, an added reason why she decided to move there.

It took them three hours to unpack the boxes and put everything away, and when they finally opened the box holding her coffee pot, Ryan danced around the room with it before setting it in its place on the kitchen counter. She displayed the same excitement when they pulled out her iron, blow dryer, and the remote control.

"You have no idea how spoiled you are until you can't find the remote control," she laughed.

They chatted about everything, listened to music, drank wine, and ate pizza. When the boxes were empty, they broke them down and put them in the garage. With the boxes out of the way, the apartment looked larger, and they sat on the sofa to continue talking.

"What do you do, Reese?"

"I'm in real estate. Buying, selling. I do it all."

"Interesting."

"She's good too. She helped me land my place. Got it at a steal."

"That was because you knew what you wanted. We went through the model and she decided to buy it," Reese laughed.

Ryan leaned forward. "You bought the model?"

"Yep, they made me a deal I couldn't refuse," Gee laughed.

"I hope it didn't include a horse's head."

They laughed harder.

"Ryan, we're going to have to stay in touch, now that Gee's moving to Arizona in a couple of months."

"I know," said Ryan. I can't believe I meet my next best friend, and she leaves me."

"How do you think I feel? Gee and I have been friends since high school. When Regis moved the office from L.A. to San Diego, I was ecstatic. But, now she's moving to Arizona and I don't know what I'm going to do without her."

"I already told Ryan why you were staying at my house. I hope you don't mind." Gee said.

Reese's smile faded. "Not at all. The man is a raving idiot. You want to hear the messages?"

"Sure. Can I?"

Reese reached into her purse and pulled out her phone. She played some of the messages and stopped after the fifth one. "Anyway, you get the gist of it. It continues on and on and on. Nonstop. He threatens to find me and kill me."

"Why don't you just block his number?"

"Because I need all the evidence I can get against him. Sending him to jail is one thing; having him stay there is another. And, as long as he doesn't know where I am, I don't care what he leaves on my machine."

"Are you scared?"

"Shitless."

"I'm so sorry you're going through that. Is there anything else you can do?"

"I already have a restraining order, but he doesn't care about that. Every time I see a silver BMW, I literally freeze."

Ryan and Gee sprang forward and exchanged glances. "What did you say?"

A confused look flashed across Reese's face. "Every time—I –see –a –silver—BMW –I –freeze. Why? What?"

"It was a silver BMW following me today!"

"Oh, my god!" Ryan shouted.

"Wait a minute, Reese. The other day, when you wanted to make spaghetti, we didn't have all the ingredients, and you wanted to go to the store. How were you able to make spaghetti today?"

Reese dropped her eyes, then looked up shamefully.

"No, you didn't."

"The store is *almost* directly across the street from you, Gee. I only needed a few things."

"Reese, what if that wasn't the first time Daxden followed me? What if he was in the area and saw you walking to the store by yourself?"

Reese gave a blank stare. "But your community is gated. He can't get in."

"He's good at tailgating. We found that out."

Ryan stood up and put up her hands. "Listen, what we're going to have to do tomorrow is call Officer Ellis and let him know what we found out tonight. He'll be able to tell us what to do."

"I'll also call Keith and let him know. He'll be here this weekend. I feel good about that."

"Me too," Reese said.

"Reese, you have to understand that this thing is much bigger than a couple cans of tomato paste and a pound of ground turkey meat. Please. Stay inside until it blows over."

"I will. I will…. Promise."

"We'd better get home," Gee announced to Ryan.

"No worries. I understand. We'll talk tomorrow, and Reese, don't be so hard on yourself. This can't be easy for you, either."

Reese got up and moved toward the door. "It's not, but that's no excuse. Gee's right, I should've known better."

"No," Gee said. "It's not like this happens to you all the time. How would you have known? Let's get home and get some rest. We'll deal with it all tomorrow."

They hugged Ryan, wished her well in her new place, and left.

30

THAT NIGHT, WHEN Keith called, Gee told him, "It was Daxden. He's the one who followed me."

"Daxden? How do you know?"

"Reese and I went to Ryan's tonight to help her unpack boxes. We were talking about why Reese was staying with me, and Reese said, every time she sees a silver BMW, she freezes. It was a silver BMW following me today. What do you bet Officer Ellis calls and verifies it after he runs those plates?"

"Daxden."

Gee nodded.

"He's following you, hoping you'd lead him to Reese."

"Which concerns me—"

"Why so?" Keith asked.

"I found out tonight that Reese walked to the store, down the street from me."

"Why's that so bad?"

"I don't know if today is the first time he followed me. What if he did it before and couldn't get through the gate or he got through the gate, but didn't know my house?"

Keith was quiet.

"Keith?"

"I'm calling Pen in the morning. Hopefully, he'll come with me this weekend."

"You think that's necessary?"

"I don't know. We'll see by the weekend."

Gee glanced over at the clock. "You'd better get some sleep."

"You too. You've got a long day tomorrow."

"Keith? I love you so much."

"I know, babe. I love you too. Talk to you tomorrow. Sweet dreams."

They hung up.

Sweet dreams? That was a first. Keith never ended a call with 'sweet dreams' before, she smiled. Nestling into the folds of the covers, she rested her head into the plume-like pillow, gave a slow yawn and closed her eyes. The hum of the night and light tapping of rain on the rooftop, combined with the soft wind brushing against the wind chimes in the backyard created the perfect lullaby, causing her to drift off into the sweetest dream.

When Keith hung up from talking to Gee, he made a call to Pen.

"Hey, what's up?" Pen asked.

"You ready to jump?"

"Only if you are. What's going on?"

"I just found out it was Daxden chasing Gee's car this afternoon. I'm so ready to kick this guy's ass, I can taste it."

"Well hell, I'm in then. When do you want to go?"

"Tomorrow morning, no later than six. I want to try to get there by early noon. You don't think Kelly would mind, do you?"

"No, she'll be okay with it. Especially when I tell her we're going to check on Gee."

"Good. See you in the morning then."

"Okay."

***

In her dream, Gee sat at a small café' with her mother.

"You look so good, Mom."

"I'm doing great, sweetie. There's no reason to concern yourself about me. How are you?"

"I'm good. There's so much I want to tell you."

"Well, I'm here for you."

"I know. I've missed you so much," Gee said, reaching out to hold her hand. "You've got to meet Keith. You're going to love him."

"I know I will." She smiled.

"How long are you staying, Mom?"

"I'll always be in your heart, Gee." She said standing and taking a step back.

"Mom, wait. Don't go. Just one more minute."

"I'll always be in your heart," she said again, and took another step back.

"No. Wait, Mom. Stay longer? Please."

"I'm here for you—I'm here for you—I'm here for you," echoed repeatedly until her mother was gone, and the dream was replaced with the annoying ring of her cell phone. It pulled her away from the suspension of consciousness that had lulled her during the night. Now, stirring fitfully, she reached over and felt around on the nightstand until her hand covered the culprit that intruded her peaceful slumber. It rang again, and Gee blindly picked it up and laid it to her ear. A greeting rolled out of her mouth on a long frustrated breath. "Helloooo?"

"Babe, you're still asleep?" Keith asked.

"Uh-huh," she yawned. "What time is it?"

"It's after eight! Aren't you supposed to be at the office?"

"The office?" she asked, sitting up into a stretch.

"Babe, it's almost 8:30. What are you doing at home?"

Her eyes popped open. "8:30? Oh no! I overslept."

She threw her legs over the side of the bed and hopped up. "Keith, I've got to call Regis and tell him I'm going to be late. I'll call you back when I get to the car."

"Alright. Call me back."

She hung up and immediately punched in Regis's number. He answered on the second ring.

"This is Regis."

"Good morning, Reg. It's Gee."

"Everything okay?"

"Regis, I overslept. I'm going to be late. I don't have appointments this morning, and I'm caught up with paperwork, so there's nothing really pressing. I hope you don't mind. I'm sorry."

"Gee, why don't you go back to bed—take a day off?"

"No, I'll be there. Just going to be a little late. That's all."

"I don't think you're all the way recovered. I wish you'd listen to your body and rest."

"Okay. I'll stay home on Monday. Keith's coming for the weekend. I'll take three days then, but today, I'll just be late."

"Suit yourself."

"Okay. See you in a bit."

She pressed the button and ended the call, then moved from the bed to the bathroom to turn on the shower. Stepping in, she allowed the water to pulsate down her back and up again, increasing the pressure to focus on her neck, then, she closed her eyes to appreciate its full effect—pure heaven.

She was dressed and ready to leave by 10. She slipped out of her bedroom and headed for the door to the garage.

"I thought I heard you in there. Why are you still here?" Reese asked.

"Oh, Reese. I'm *so* late." She fanned her hand. "Overslept. Can you believe it?"

"Yeah, I can. You need to rest. You're going to wear yourself out."

"I'm okay. I'll call you later from work."

"Drive carefully."

"Thanks. I will," Gee said, rushing through the door to the garage. She pulled out of the driveway, tuning in to the oldies radio station that soon blared her favorite hits. Lou Rawls was crooning, "Lady Love," and Marvin Gaye sang, "What's Going On." She pressed the Bluetooth to call Keith. When he answered, he sounded out of breath.

"Hey, babe," he said. "You on your way to work?"

"Yeah, why does it sound like you're in the car?"

"I'm with Pen. So, you overslept this morning. You must have been really tired last night."

She shook her head. "I don't know what happened. My head hit the pillow, and I was *zonked*. It might've been the rain."

"Or maybe you're working too hard—too soon?"

"You've been talking to Regis."

"Uh-huh. He's worried about you."

"He's always worried about me."

"He loves you."

"I know, but I'm okay. I told him I'd take an extra day off when you come for the weekend."

"How about two extra days?"

251

"Keith."

"Okay, okay. I'll take what I can get," he smiled.

"I'm pulling in at work. Talk to you later?"

"Of course. Love you, Gee."

"I love you too, Keith."

She pushed the Bluetooth button, and the radio blasted the last part of, "Ribbon in the Sky," by Stevie Wonder. She turned off the car and rushed into the Ovalton Building.

"Good morning, Ms. Haynes," Gloria chimed.

"Good morning, Gloria. Is Ryan in her office?"

"Yes, ma'am, and I put some messages on your desk."

"Thank you. I'm going to peek in at Ryan first."

"Okay, ma'am."

She walked down the corridor to Ryan's office.

Ryan was sitting with the desk phone to her ear. She glanced up, when Gee opened her door and peeked in. Lifting a finger to her lips and then motioning for her to come in and have a seat. Gee tiptoed to the chair in front of Ryan's desk.

Ryan finished the call then lowered the receiver onto the base. "You okay?" she asked.

"Yep, just overslept. I'm good. How'd it feel to wake up and make coffee in your own kitchen?"

"Ahh-mazing," she exaggerated with a smile. Then she picked up the coffee cup she had taken from Gee's office, and with a slight lift, she said, "I'm going to miss this guy."

"You don't have to miss him. I give him to you as a gift. I have plenty. They're going to be yours soon anyway when you move into my office."

Ryan chuckled. "I don't know, Gee. That's always going to be your office, to me."

"Temporarily – until you make it your own." Then Gee stood and made her way to the door. "I just wanted to peek in and say hi. Gloria put messages on my desk, so I guess I'd better get to them."

"Okay. We'll talk later this morning. Maybe do something for lunch?"

"Sounds good."

Before Gee could close the door, Ryan asked, "Any new cases?"

"Nope. I'm not taking on any new ones. I worked my last one the other day."

"You talking about the M & C Tactical case?"

"Yep. All done."

"Well, I just got a call from—" She searched around on her desk, then lifted a sticky note from it, "an officer— Stevens, in South Carolina. They recovered a gun at a crime scene. It's been traced back to M & C Tactical. Franklin McClure sold it. I think this kind of reinforces your case against them. Right?"

Gee walked back to Ryan and took the sticky note from her hand, then gave her a wink and a smile. "Thanks, Ry. You're a jewel." She turned and left the office.

***

At first, Ryan Parrish wasn't sure she was going to like San Diego. She hadn't told her parents about the move until she was sure her new job was secure and the right fit. Today, she made the call. Her mother answered.

"Hi, Mom. It's me, Ryan."

"Hi, dear. You alright?"

"Oh yeah, I'm good. Just calling to let you and Dad know I got a new job."

"You did? That's wonderful, dear. What are you doing now?"

"Same work—a different place."

"Different place? You mean, you're moving again?"

"Already moved, Mom. I left Florida."

She heard her mom exhale a breath through the phone and call out. "Gordon, Ryan's got another new job. She's moved away from Florida."

Ryan heard her father's voice in the distance, getting louder as he entered the room where her mother was. "What are you saying?" he asked. "She's got a what?"

"A new job. Ryan's got a new job, she moved away from Florida?"

"Where's she going now?"

"Well, I don't know, Gordon. I haven't asked her that."

"What kind of job is it?" her dad asked.

"It's the same job in a different place." her mother answered.

Ryan sat patiently while her parents carried on their own conversation back and forth before remembering she was still on the phone and turned their attention back to the phone call at hand. No different than any other time she called home.

"Ryan, your dad wants to know where you're going."

Ryan smiled, knowing her mother had the same question, and this was her way of asking it without seeming to pry. She chuckled.

"I moved to San Diego."

"She's in San Diego, Gordon."

"Why, that's in California, Millie. Who in the world does she know in San Diego, California?"

"Dad wants to know who you know in San Diego."

Ryan's smile widened. "No one. It's just a fresh start."

"She wants a fresh start, Gordon. She doesn't know anyone there."

"Hell's Bells, she can come home and do *that*."

"Ryan, you sure you don't want to come home, dear?"

"Uh, no, Mom. I'm good. I'm meeting new friends. I really like it here."

"Gordon, how much money's left in the can over there? Do you need money, Ryan?"

"Mom, no—no, I don't need money. Don't send money. I'm good . . ."

"Okay, Ryan. We love you." She turned to her husband. "She's okay with money, Gordon."

"Okay," was his answer, and Ryan could hear his voice trail off as he moved further away from the phone. She could see him in her mind's eye, walking into another room, talking to himself. "I don't understand why these youngsters feel they gotta flit from one place to another. In our day, we bought a house and stayed put in one spot."

Ryan chuckled, "I love you too, Mom. Give Dad a kiss for me," she said and hung up the phone.

31

REESE WATCHED ALEX exit his car and make his way to the front door. Her heart fluttered, and every cell in her body tingled with excitement when he rang the doorbell.

She glanced around to assess her surroundings. She had coffee cups on the counter, cookies on a plate, and brownies on a tray. *Did Alex even like brownies?* She didn't know. What she did know was that she was as nervous as a canary on a cat farm. The doorbell rang again. She rubbed her hands together and opened the door. His magnetic eyes seemed to devour every inch of her, and it took everything she had to tear her eyes away from his; but finally, she said in a hoarse voice, "Come in, Alex." She moved to give him room to enter.

His gaze never left hers.

Not being able to resist, she leaned up and pressed a soft kiss on his cheek, placing them both in the same breathing space, so close she could feel his breath quicken, along with her own.

His arm encircled her and he touched the small of her back. She melded against him while the heat of his hand burned through her shirt. His breath was warm against her ear. "Reese," he whispered,. It gave him pleasure to hear her name roll off his lips.

"I—uhh—made brownies," she said, swallowing hard and taking an involuntary step back.

"I love brownies."

"I wasn't sure," she said, averting her eyes and lifting them to his again. *God, this is silly.* "I—have coffee too."

He smiled and gave a nod. "I drink coffee," he said, still holding her gaze.

She led the way to the kitchen and popped a pod into the coffee machine. "Help yourself to the brownies," she said, as the brew streamed into his cup.

He picked up a brownie and laid it on a napkin, then looked up at her. Are you as nervous as I am?"

She nodded. "Probably more."

He reached for her hand and brought it to his mouth, pressing a soft kiss into her palm. "Good. That must mean you like me too," he smiled.

Reese laughed. "I think we've already established that."

"You talking about the phone call the other night?"

"Uh-huh."

"You never said you liked me."

Reese laughed again. "You don't know?"

"I feel something, but you haven't said."

"Are you saying you want to hear me say, I like you, Alex?" Reese asked with a smile, knowing he was trying to break the ice by teasing her.

Alex leaned forward. "Honestly, Reese. I can't wait to hear you say it."

Reese leaned in too. "Well, here it goes. Pay close attention. I like you, Alex Whitfield –I like you a lot."

"Ahhhh—" he said, leaning back and placing his hand over his heart. "Music to my ears."

She laughed again. "What time do you leave today?"

"My plane leaves at 7:00. I need to return the rental and catch a shuttle to the airport. I thought I'd better leave here at 5:30."

"Oh, good. We have plenty of time."

He met her gaze. "Yes, we do. I like spending time with you, Reese. It feels good."

"I feel the same way."

They laughed and talked through three brownies and a second cup of coffee. Time seemed to speed up and away from them. When Alex glanced at his watch, it was 5:20. He stood and went about helping Reese clean up. She put two brownies in a plastic bag and handed it to him.

"Thanks." He closed his eyes and summoned a breath, holding it in. Then, he let it out slowly. Lifting his head and looking skyward, he said, "This is the hard part."

"What?"

His gaze cut to hers. "Leaving you," he whispered. "I don't want to go. I want to stay –with you."

"We'll see each other again," she nodded. "I need to tie up some loose ends so things don't get complicated and confusing."

He studied her and brushed his thumb across his bottom lip, then shook his head as a faint chuckle came up from his chest. "You must be talking about yourself because I'm not confused about a damn thing, Reese." The way he looked at her made goose bumps rise up all over her skin.

They moved toward the door, and she opened it, stepping out with him. They walked down the driveway to his car and faced each other. Neither of them spoke. Then, once again, she leaned forward and placed a lingering kiss on his cheek. That's when she heard it—one word—almost like a breath. If she hadn't been so near to him—if his lips hadn't been so close to her ear, she would never have heard him, "Please." He whispered, tilting his head inward, and lifting his lips until they covered hers.

Reese surrendered. A low moan escaped her, and she sank against him, lifting her head slightly and opening her mouth to allow Alex's tongue full access—giving him permission to—explore. Then she wrapped her arms around his neck and shuddered when she felt one of his hands on her hip. The other, he placed gently on the side of her face and caressed her cheek.

When he pulled away, he waited, silently pleading for her eyes to open. When they did, Alex got a glimpse of everything he needed to see—longing desire. He wanted her to crave him as much as he did her. At the same time, he needed her to be his—completely his. No one trying to lay claim—completely his. It was as though they both understood. He lifted her hand to his lips and kissed it, then opened the car door and sat behind the wheel. Just as he was pulling out of the driveway, she called to him. He stopped, and she hurried to his car. Alex powered down the window and she leaned in and placed another kiss on his lips. "Please know that I'm going to put an end to this mess, Alex. Come back to me."

He looked deep into her eyes and touched her face. "Try to stop me," he said. "I'll call you when I get situated at the airport."

They kissed again, and he was gone. Reese stood in the driveway, watching his car disappear from sight.

She dropped her shoulders and began to move back up the driveway toward the house.

Behind her, the sudden slam of a car door, and rapid footsteps made her turn around. Ice rushed through her veins. "No!" she screamed and ran for the door.

How could he be here?

Daxden's was quicker. He snatched a handful of her hair and yanked so hard she almost fell backward.

She screamed again, "No, Please."

"Now, I s-see what y-you' been up to. No w-wonder, you ain't been answering my c-calls."

"Daxden stop. You're hurting me. You don't know what you're talking about."

"I d-don't know what I'm t-talking about? I j-just s-sat in my car and watched you, and y-your new boyfriend just about have s-sex in the f-front yard."

"Daxden, please. Stop. Help! Somebody — help!" she yelled.

"He half pulled and dragged her down the driveway and around to the passenger side of his car. When he opened the car door, he shoved her so violently she smashed her face into the car frame with a loud thud.

Reese let out a painful gasp. She reeled back, throwing her hands over her face. Blood oozed around and through her fingers.

Daxden didn't care. He gave her another brutal shove that forced her the rest of the way inside the car. Then he pulled back s fist and smashed it hard into her jaw. The pain seared through her and everything went dark.

***

Daxden had secretly followed Gee home twice and failed. The second time he only missed seeing which community she pulled into. He went back the following afternoon, drove into a gas station across the street from a convenient store, and parked. He'd sit there all day, if he had to. Eventually Gee had to pass this way going home and he'd be ready and waiting for her. He took out his cell phone and skimmed through Reese's social media. Nothing. She'd been like a ghost since he'd seen her at the courthouse. When Daxden looked up, he couldn't believe his eyes; were they playing tricks on him? There she was, walking down the street—carefree—not a worry in the world. He watched her enter the convenient store and waited for her to come out, then he eased out of the car and followed her to a gated community. She punched in the code, and walk through.

"Now I know where you are." He said through a menacing grin.

As an extra bonus, Daxden drove back to the Ovalton building that afternoon and spotted Gee leaving with a co-worker, he followed them to the San Diego Police Department. When they left, he trailed them—recklessly through the streets, wanting her to know she was being followed. He ran up on her car—tailgating her, then he pulled back—toying with her. She didn't know his car, so he could scare the living shit out of her and she'd never know it was him. It served her right for interfering in his life with Reese. Reese belonged to him, and she needed to butt the hell out.

So engrossed in his effort to terrify and teach Gee a lesson, Daxden lost his sense of direction. He realized, too late, that Gee doubled back to the police station, and the police officers were there waiting for him. 'Damn it.' He slid his car into gear, and with his tires screeching, whipped the car around and sped away, leaving black marks smoking on the pavement. He raced home, knowing it wouldn't be long before they'd come looking for him. There was no doubt in his mind that at least one of the officers snapped a picture of his license plate. He threw clothes into a suitcase, called for a rental car and laid low for a while, then set off for the gated community. Daxden smiled when he was able to tailgate a car through it. He drove around the neighborhood – slowly, up and down the streets for hours, until he spotted her. Reese, with a man, walking to a car. They stopped and faced each other. *What the hell? Is he getting ready to put his lips on my girl?* Then it happened. Daxden's brow creased. He couldn't believe what he was seeing.

"She's acting l-like a-a-a t-two b-bit whore." He waited for the man's car to drive away and disappear around the corner, before jumping out of his, and took long quick strides to catch Reese before she got to the door.

***

Reese tried to open her eyes, but the searing pain made it difficult. She adjusted them to the darkness and opened them anyway. *Where am I?* She wanted to scream – but there was something tight wrapped around her mouth. Her hands—bound. Her ankles too. *Where am I?* She struggled to get loose.

"I-It's about t-time y-you woke up."

Reese turned in the direction of Daxden's voice. Her eyes went wild when she saw the eerie darkness that filled Daxden's. He sat back in his chair, cleaning his nails with a knife. Watching her. His legs stretched in front of him and crossed at the ankles.

"S-so, who's the new b-boyfriend, Reese?"

Paralyzed with fear, she shook her head erratically.

"I-I'm sorry, Reese, I-I can't, I-I can't understand w-what you're sayin', probably because of th-the t-tape around y-your mouth," he laughed. His face turned serious. "Y-You're a lyin' bitch. Y-You ch-cheatin' on me? I-I'm s-sick of y-you tryin' ta make a f-f-fool of me. Y-You're gonna learn. You d-don't ch-cheat on me. Y-You, belong t-to me." He stooped down and slid the knife into his ankle sheath, then walked over to her. He got as close to her face as possible, and yelled, "Do-you-understand?" Spitting each word into her face.

She bobbed her head in a desperate attempt to appease him.

"I-I knew we'd c-come to an agreement. You just have to learn." He stood over her. "Lesson number one—" he held her up and gave her an open-handed slap, hard in the face, then followed through with a backhanded one, emphasizing each word. "Women—don't—behave—like—two-bit—whores!" he yelled. Then he stumbled back and wiped his sweaty face with the sleeve of his shirt.

Reese felt her head whip from one side to the other with each stinging blow. She screamed, but the heavy tape caught the sound of it and held it captive, while she pleaded with him through wild eyes and heavy sobs, shaking her head frantically.

32

GEE CALLED REESE'S cell phone for the third time. She didn't answer. *Where could she be?* After the fifth time, she grabbed her purse and headed to Ryan's office. She knocked, then poked her head in.

"Hey, have you talked to Reese today?"

"Earlier. Why?"

"I've been trying to reach her for almost two hours. She's not picking up. I'm worried. I'm going to run home for a minute and check on her."

Ryan jumped up. "I'm going with you."

"I'll let Regis know we're leaving," Gee said.

"I'm driving. You don't look like you're in the condition to."

"It's not like her, Ry. She doesn't do stuff like this. Something's wrong." Gee said, her eyes wide with fear.

She ran into Regis's office and let him know she was leaving; and they hurried out of the building, hopped into

Ryan's car, and drove off. When they reached the gate of Gee's community, Ryan punched in the code. And as they entered, Gee's phone rang. She glanced down at the caller ID. It was Alex.

"Hi, Alex."

"Gee, is Reese with you?"

She let out a long sigh. "No. I was hoping—"

"I told her I'd call when I got to the airport, but she's not picking up."

"I know. I've been calling too. She's not answering. I left work to come check on her. We're pulling into my driveway right now."

"I'll hold on. Please, let me know that she's safe. It's probably nothing."

They jumped out of the car and headed for the garage. Gee punched in the garage code and watched the door power up and they rushed through the garage and into the house.

"Reese!" Gee called out. No answer. She rushed to Reese's bedroom door and tapped on it. "Reese, you in there — ?" Nothing. She opened the door. No sign of Reese anywhere. Her purse still on the bed. *Why would she leave without her purse?*

Ryan yelled from the front door, "Gee. I think you need to come in here!"

Gee hurried to her.

Ryan stood at Gee's front door. "I found it like this—wide open."

"My door was—open? Reese would never do that."

Alex's voice exploded through the phone. "What's happening Gee?"

"My front door is standing open. I don't know what's going on. Reese isn't here, and my front door is open. Her purse is still here. This doesn't make any sense. Something's wrong, Alex."

"There are brownies and cookies on a plate in here," Ryan yelled from the kitchen and two cups in the sink. She must have had company." She lifted one of the cups to her nose. "It's coffee."

"It was me," Alex said.

Gee spoke into the phone. "You?"

"I was there at your house. I went to see Reese before I left. We ate brownies, drank coffee, and talked. When it was time for me to go, she walked me to the car, and I left. She was there. She was good. Listen, I'm on my way back. Give me thirty minutes."

"Oh, my god, Alex, her phone is here. She left it on the kitchen counter. She would never have left her phone and her purse. What the hell? I'm calling Keith. He was coming this weekend. I'm sure he'll come earlier if I need him to."

"Let him know I'm on my way too. I'll see you when I get there."

"Okay."

They hung up, and Gee punched in Keith's number. He answered, "Hey, Babe."

Urgency filled her words. "Reese is missing. I came home from work—her purse is still here— and her phone. My front door was open, and there's no sign of her anywhere."

"Wait—what do you mean—missing?"

Pen faced him. "What's going on?"

Keith whispered over the phone. "Something about— Reese missing."

"Keith, I'm here at the house; she's not here. Her purse is here and her phone, but she's not here!"

"Could she be with Alex somewhere?"

"No, he's at the airport. He called me, looking for her too. He's on his way back here."

"Pen and I have been on the road since early this morning. After you told me about Daxden, I thought we'd come pay him a little visit. We should be there in another hour or two. I'm sure there's a reasonable explanation for this. Just stay calm."

"I can't stay calm! I know this has something to do with Daxden. That's the reasonable explanation."

"Let's hope not. We'll be there shortly."

"Hurry, Keith." She hung up.

Twenty-five minutes later, Gee heard tires screeching into her driveway. Alex jumped out of the car and bounded his way to the door. His frantic look sent a surge through her. She'd always known Alex to be calm and composed.

"Keith's on his way."

Alex pivoted, looking from Gee to Ryan. He ran his hands through his hair and made a nervous attempt to rub the tension from his neck and shoulders. It didn't work. He spotted Reese's phone on the counter. "Did anyone check to see if there were any more calls from him—voicemails—anything?"

Gee picked up the phone and checked it. The blue light flashed to indicate voicemails and unanswered calls. They were from Daxden and all, basically, the same. He was going to find her and teach her lessons she'd never forget. If they were going to be together, she needed to understand how to treat him.

The last message simply said,

"Surprise – Surprise." Followed by a guttural laugh straight from the pits of hell.

"What do you suppose that means?" Gee asked.

Ryan shifted her weight. "It can't be good."

"I think we know where Reese is. Right?" Alex said, stretching his neck. A muscle in his jaw tightened.

When Gee's phone rang, it was Officer Ellis.

"Afternoon', little lady. I got some good news for ya. The license number we traced led us to a man named Daxden Green. We got some information down here that he's not such a nice guy. Kind of loses his temper a lot.

He's been arrested a coupla' times, but nothin' really stuck. I have an address for him.

"Officer Ellis, I need that address. We have reason to believe he abducted a friend of mine. No one knows where she is. She has an order of protection against him, but he's been harassing her—calling, leaving threatening messages. If he has her, we've got to find her before he k—" she turned to Alex, "before she gets hurt." She saw Alex swallow hard. Can you text me the address?

I don't think you should go there without someone witcha."

"I'm not alone. I have back up."

"Okay, it's on the way, but you call me if you decide ta go over there. I think I might be able ta pull together a copula officers and meet you there."

"Okay. Thanks, Officer Ellis."

Alex sat on the couch, his fingers pressed against the corners of his eyes. "So, what are we doing? We can't just sit here—at least—*I* can't. I feel helpless. We have to do something! There's no telling what he's doing to her, if he has her."

Ryan sat forward. "Let's just wait and see what Keith—"

"I can't! Reese could be dead by then. Did he send the damn address?"

"Alex, I—"

He turned to Gee. "If it was Keith, would you wait?"

"No."

"Give me the address, Gee."

Gee turned to Ryan. "I'm with Alex. I say we use our resources and move. I'll call Officer Ellis and let him know we're going to the address. The longer we wait—"

Ryan nodded, "Let's go."

Gee picked up her phone to text Keith:

GEE: Keith, we can't wait any longer. We have to find Reese. Sending you Daxden's address. Meet us there.

KEITH: Okay. Got it.

33

THIRTY MINUTES LATER, they were in front of Daxden's house, waiting for Officer Ellis to show up. When he arrived, he had two other cruisers following him.

Officer Ellis got out of the car and strolled over to theirs. He stooped down to talk to all of them. "I think you should stay put until we see what we're lookin' at here."

They nodded and watched him and the other officers approach the door of Daxden's house. They knocked. "Mr. Green, you in there? Name's Officer Ellis. I need ta talk witcha." No answer. They peered through the windows. There was no movement inside. He turned and gave a shrug, and Gee stepped out of the car.

"Can't we just go in?"

"Not without a warrant."

"Can we check the back?"

"Sure." They walked around to the back of the house. Officer Ellis knocked on the back door and called out,

"Anybody home? Mr. Green, you in there?" He turned to Gee. "Nobody's here," he said. "I wish we could have done more, little lady. I'm sorry."

No problem, officer."

"But if you need anything else, you call. Hear me?"

"We hear you."

Gee went back to the car. She turned to Ryan and Alex. "That was pretty useless. Ryan, drive around the block."

Ryan started the car and drove down the street and turned the corner. When they returned to Daxden's house, Officer Ellis and his crew were gone.

They hopped out of the car and dashed across the street. Alex tried the windows on the side of the house. Locked. They ran to the back and tried those windows. They found one that was unlocked. Alex opened it and heaved Gee carefully up and through it. Ryan was next. Then it was Alex's turn. He found something to stand on and hoisted himself up and through it. Soon, they were all standing in Daxden's kitchen. They started in the basement—searching for -- anything, but there was no sign that Reese or Daxden had been there. They moved up the stairs.

Gee's phone buzzed. It was Keith. She opened the text:

KEITH: Where are you?

GEE: Inside Daxden's house.

KEITH: How'd you get in?

GEE: Back window. We're going upstairs.

They continued up the stairs and moved into what seemed to be the master bedroom.

For the most part, Daxden was an organized sociopath who kept his house neat except for his personal quarters, his bedroom.

Cluttered papers piled high on a mahogany dresser and overflowed onto the floor, the bed was unmade and clothes scattered throughout. Unlike the rest of the house, the bedroom would've given visitors a different view of how Daxden Green *really* lived. Gee walked to the dresser, curious as to what paperwork Daxden thought necessary to pile up in this manner.

They heard footsteps and froze. Then Keith called out, in a loud whisper.

"Gee!"

"In here," she called back.

Pen and Keith entered the room.

Keith moved to Gee's side and picked up a folded paper dated back to 2008. 'Sharon O'Reilly -vs.- Daxden Green:' a case of stalking. Another paper accused him of assault. On each paper –a different name and different charge. She turned to get Ryan's attention. "Check these out."

"Here's another one," Pen said, "A lawsuit. Karen Fisher -vs- Daxden Green – 2012"

"The whole top of his dresser is full of them."

Ryan walked over to Gee. "Are these all—"

276

She nodded. "Cases against him."

Alex came forward with a two by four. "Who keeps something like this in their bedroom?"

"A sociopath," Gee scoffed.

Ryan pulled the two by four from Alex hands. "Let me see that." She turned it over. "Gee, you might be interested in this. Looks like it could be the same wood as the fragment."

Gee turned to examine it. True, she could see that some of the wood pieces had broken off and fallen away. "Yeah, it kind of makes you wonder, Doesn't it? But—" She gave a dismissive shrug and returned to the dresser, searching through the papers.

Gee froze. Amidst the mound of paper, lay a folded bright white envelope. She moved closer at a snail's pace, reached out and pinched the tip of the envelope between her forefinger and thumb, as if it were a disgusting rag, offensive to the touch. Then she lifted it up and away from the rest of the papers.

"Keith," she whispered, "the note. It's the envelope that was taken out of my pocket the night I got hit."

"No way. How can you be sure?"

"I'm certain of it."

She opened the envelope and read the note out load.

"Just as you feared, I think Cassandra knows. We need to cool it. If she does know, I'll need to tell Franklin before she does. Please go. He's going to kill you."

Gee lifted her eyes to Keith's.

"What's it doing here?" He asked.

"Ryan, let me see that piece of wood again."

Ryan brought it over to her and Gee examined it carefully. "The fragment that Officer Ellis gave us the other day, do you think it could fit here?" She turned the piece of wood until she found the exact place. Ryan studied it, lifted her eyes to Gee's and nodded. She slid the note back into the envelope, folded it, and stuffed it deep inside her pocket.

"Are you saying that Daxden is the person who hit you?" Keith asked.

Gee nodded. "Looks like it. How else would he have gotten the note? He doesn't know the people I investigated."

The muscle in Keith's jaw flexed, and he and Pen exchanged knowing glances.

Gee continued her search while Alex and Ryan sifted through the junk on the other side of the room.

"What are we looking for, in particular?" Alex asked.

"Nothing, in particular, just anything out of the norm."

"How about receipts?" Keith asked.

Gee turned. "What kind of receipt?"

"Here's one for a rented storage locker. Daxden rented it a week ago."

"A week ago? Why do you think Daxden needs a storage locker?" Gee asked.

Pen stepped forward. "Same thing I was wondering."

"Does it give an address?"

"Yep."

"Hold on to it," Gee said.

Keith folded the receipt and put it in his pocket.

Ryan moved to Gee's side and handed her a piece of paper, "Here's a familiar one."

Gee lifted the receipt from Ryan's hand and studied it. "This is the same car wash receipt as the one Officer Ellis found."

" I'd say the secret's out, huh?" Ryan shrugged.

Gee nodded slowly. "It was definitely Daxden who hit me. Wow."

"We'd better get out of here. Let's go check out the locker."

They left the same way they got in; through the window. When they were all out, Alex lowered it and they headed for the car.

34

REESE STIRRED HERSELF awake. *Was she having a nightmare. Things like this didn't happen in real life; did they? Wake up, Reese—wake up,* she told herself. She tried to shake herself awake. An agonizing pain singed through her. She groaned, wanting to run from it, but her legs wouldn't move. *What's wrong with my legs?*

"O-Oh, h-here you are."

Reese turned to Daxden, shaking her head, *No, no, no!* She shot pleading eyes his way, begging him to stop but all he heard were broken sobs and gurgles.

"S-See, now, y-you want to b-be my friend, huh? Lesson number two—" Daxden walked over to her. "Can you repeat after me, Reese? W-Women don't play with m-men's emotions." He pulled his foot back and kicked her hard in the ribs. There were no more words—no more pleading, just a hard grunt that emerged from the pit of her stomach and lodged in her throat. She surrendered to the darkness once again.

When Reese tried to wake up again, sheer pain ripped through her body, but she didn't move. She forced herself to lay still. *Noooooo, don't move. Don't let him know you're awake,* she told herself.

She pried her swollen eyes open to survey the area through tiny slits. *Please, God, don't let him know I'm awake. Think—think.* She tilted her head using the tiniest movements. *What do I see? A door, like a garage that rolls up, containing nothing but the chair where Daxden sat. Am I in a garage? What do I smell? Damp earth mixed with rusted metal. Where have I seen this before? Not a warehouse—a storage locker. Yes, that's what it is. Like the one I used for my furniture before my house was ready.'* She closed her eyes and allowed her mind to empty itself of all thoughts except one…*Alex. Her loving Alex.* What she wouldn't give to be in his arms right now. *'Be still, Reese and pray that somebody— comes—Gee—will come. Be still.'* and stay alive.

***

Gee called Officer Ellis. "I think we found Reese."

"You found her? Where?"

"We have a receipt for a storage unit. Daxden has a storage unit."

"Now, how would you know that, Ms. Gee?"

"We—uh—found it."

"And that's all I want ta know about it, little lady. Where's the storage?"

She gave Officer Ellis the address for the storage company.

***

Daxden walked to Reese and stood over her. "Uhhh, Reese," he called out. She didn't answer and didn't move. *How could she still be out?* "Reese," he called to her again. Disappointed, Daxden walked back and sat in his chair. "Damn it!" He wanted her to wake up. He needed to teach her lesson number three, but it's not worth teaching if she can't feel it. Lesson three was his favorite. He got angry. "C-Come on. W-Wake-up, bitch." When she didn't stir, Daxden decided to go to his car for a bottled water.

Reese heard his footsteps leaving the storage unit. *Lie still, Reese. Don't move.* She told herself.

***

When Ryan drove into the parking lot of A-1 Storage, Keith and Pen pulled in behind them. They hopped out of the car.

"Keith, I'm thinking you and Pen are the only two that Daxden won't connect to Reese. Do you think you can go look around? We'll stay here and wait for Officer Ellis."

"No problem," A sly, malicious grin spread across Keith's face.

The large storage units were outside, so they had to walk through gravel to get to them. Keith took the receipt out of his pocket. "We're looking for storage number 1014." He said to Pen.

Pen turned to him and stopped. "You know he's here, don't you?"

Keith stopped too. "I hope he is. There's a good chance."

"I know you, Keith. I know that look. You sure you want to do this?"

"Damned straight."

"What do you want me to do?"

"Just have my back."

"You jump, I jump. So, what's our game plan?"

"No game plan. I'm kicking—his—natural – born - ass."

Pen nodded. "Let's go then."

They continued, counting the numbers on the storage units. Then Keith spotted someone walking away from a car. "Hey, I think that's him."

They got closer. It was Daxden leaving his car with a bottled water in his hand. He turned it up and took a long drink, then wiped his mouth with his hand.

"Well, well, well," Keith said, "if it ain't my buddy from the restaurant."

Daxden squinted his eyes. "Do I know you, son?"

"Pen, this is the buddy I was telling you about. Thought I was trying to 'push up on his girl.' Fancy meeting you out here."

"Oh, shit. I know who you are now," Daxden spat.

"Looks like we might be neighbors," Keith said, waving his arms at all the storage bins. You've got storage here too?"

"Maybe."

"The last time I saw you, you wanted to catch me outside," Keith said, tilting his head to the side. "Well, here I am."

"You must think you're s-somebody to be scared of."

"Pen, what you think. Should he be afraid of me?"

Pen cocked his head to the side, "I'd be," he said, with a grin.

"Tell me something, mister. What happened to that fine woman you were with that night?"

"I think that's none of your business, son."

"Pen, you should have seen her. Fine as they come, and she put him in his place fast."

"Hey, don't n-no woman p-put me in my place."

"That one sure did! Left this bastard sitting by himself, looking like a lost puppy." Keith gave a hearty laugh.

"M-Man, you' getting ready t-to get your ass kicked."

Pen knew exactly what Keith was doing, and he stood by, watching him work his magic.

"Man, I never saw anything like it, Pen. The woman made him look like a punk-ass bitch--."

Keith's last word clipped off with a grunt when Daxden threw his whole body into Keith's torso. Keith stumbled back, whirled around and punched Daxden hard in the chest. Daxden punched back. Keith ducked. Daxden hit nothing but air. Keith came up with both fists. One that sank deep into Daxden's gut, and the other connected with his jaw. Daxden stumbled and Keith lunged at him, tackling him to the ground. Daxden rolled over then came up in one swift movement, pulling his knife out of his ankle sheath. He sprang to his feet and faced Keith with an ominous grin that spread slowly across his face.

"Uh-uh-uh."

Daxden whirled around in the direction of the unexpected reprimand. Pen stood at his side with a gun pointing directly at his head.

"I'm gonna need to ask you to put that down." Pen warned. "I can bet my gun trumps your knife any day of the week unless my gun's not loaded. You want to test me?"

Daxden dropped the knife, and Pen kicked it away from him.

Nearby voices brought their attention to Officer Ellis approaching.

While Daxden and Keith fought, Gee, Ryan, and Alex circled around and came up on Daxden's storage bin from the opposite direction. Alex stepped inside and squinted through the dense lit room.

"Reese?" he called out.

She recognized Alex's voice immediately and struggled to sit up.

"She's there," Ryan shouted, pointing at the movement in the dark.

"Reese, we're here!" Gee called out.

Alex rushed to her and was met with pleading eyes.

"Ryan, I saw a knife out there in the gravel. Can you get it for me?"

Ryan rushed out, got the knife, and ran back in, and handed it to Alex.

He cut her loose and removed the tape from her mouth. His eyes went dark, and his jaw trembled with rage when he saw her bruised and swollen face. Blood caked around her hairline and now with no restraints it oozed from her lip.

Reese cried out in pain when Alex pulled her close—cradling her—shushing her —kissing her.

They could hear Daxden outside. "Hey!" He said. He raced to the door of the locker. "Who's in there? This is *my* bin."

Reese's eyes went wild. "He's coming back. I hear him. He's coming back."

Alex moved quickly and stood in front of her, shielding her from Daxden's view.

Daxden rushed inside and charged at Alex with all his might. Alex brought up a heavy fist that caught Daxden in the face. Daxden staggered back, then he came at him again—fast— throwing a right punch that Alex caught in mid-swing and twisted Daxden's arm behind his back so hard and fast, it forced him to double over. When Alex loosened his grip, he did it with a forceful push that almost knocked Daxden off his feet. Daxden turned and darted forward again, lifting his foot in the air, expecting it to sink deep into Alex's stomach. Alex caught it and ushered him out of the locker, on one leg, with Daxden hopping desperately, in fear of toppling over. When they got outside, Alex shoved Daxden's foot hard then let it go and watched him fall head first onto the ground.

He shot Daxden one last threatening glare and issued his final warning: "Stay away from her, because if there is ever a next time, I *promise*, you won't live through it!" His glare raked over Daxden, and he turned and rushed back to Reese, while Ryan and Gee looked on and exchanged stunned glances.

Officer Ellis and the other officers pulled Daxden to his feet and held him fast.

"W-What the hell is th-this about? I ain't done nothin' wrong. Y-You got the wrong guy. Th-This ain't even my locker," Daxden lied.

"Gee." Officer Ellis called.

"I'm here." She called back, leaving the locker and standing at Keith's side.

"Gee. Is this the man who tailgated you?"

"Yes, sir. It is. He's also the man who hit me the night you took me to the hospital. I found the two by four with the fragment pieces missing. Well, I think it's the same wood but, I also found this in his possession." She pulled out the envelope. "The only person who would've had this is the one who took it out of my pocket that night."

"Wait," Daxden yelled, "that was in my house. You were in my house? S-See, now y-you're a thief *and* a liar. You're a lying', mother f-fuckin' bitch."

Keith's head shot up, and his eyes flashed with an anger Gee had never seen. She watched him move toward Daxden. His icy gaze fixed on the man who insulted his fiancée in a way no man had the right to do. He glared into Daxden's eyes and Daxden glared back.

"What?" Daxden spat.

I underestimated you." Keith said.

Gee moved forward. "Keith. It's all right."

"No, it's not, Gee. I didn't think this piece of shit could do it, but he's managed to throw gasoline on a fire he didn't even know was burnin'." He moved closer to Daxden, shaking his head. "See, I can't let you disrespect my fiancée like that." His fist shot out and slammed into Daxden's face.

Daxden staggered back and threw his hands up. "Owww. Your fiancée? See, y'all play games. Y-You

288

women, y-you're deceiving," he said, turning to Gee. "That's why I tried to kill your sorry ass!" Keith's jaw twitched and he slammed his fist into Daxden's face again.

Daxden staggered back again. He stomped his foot into the ground, then turned to Officer Ellis "Aren't you gonna do something about this, officer?"

"About what, sir? The man is just protecting his wife."

"Somebody needs to put a leash on this dog!" Daxden shouted.

"And somebody needs to teach you when to shut the fuck up," Keith said.

Officer Ellis moved forward and caught Daxden by the arm. "Daxden Green, you're under arrest for violating an order of protection, assault, and probably a bunch of other charges. Somebody slap some cuffs on this piece of shit and escort him ta my vehicle. Stay with him 'til I finish up here."

"I-I didn't v-violate nothing. P-Prove it. Let me s-see you do that. Y-You're v-violating my rights, and I'm gonna s-sue your ass. How about th-that? I'll see *you* in court."

It wasn't long before they could hear the ambulance in the distance, blaring its sirens through the streets.

"Gee's phone chimed. She looked down at the caller ID. It was Regis. She answered. "Hi, Reg."

"Okay, what's up? Where are you?"

"At a place called A-1 Storage. We found her, Reg."

"You did? She was there?"

289

"Some jerk had her, here in a storage bin. They arrested him."

"In a storage bin? Why?"

"Because he's sick. She's beat up pretty bad. We're on our way to the hospital. Keith and Pen are here, too."

"Good, good, good. Ryan? Is she still with you?"

"Yes, sir."

"You two be safe. Don't get too close."

"We won't," she said.

"I mean it, Gee. Don't get too close. Stay your distance and allow the police to do their jobs."

"I will, Regis."

"I want to see you and Ryan in my office, first thing in the morning."

"Yes, sir. I'll let her know."

They hung up.

"Let me know what?" Ryan asked.

"Regis wants to see us in his office, first thing tomorrow."

Ryan nodded and rolled her eyes.

35

THE WAITING ROOM was empty. It was just them, waiting for the doctor to tell them news about Reese's condition.

Gee leaned over to Alex. "Umm. So, you kind of like Reese, huh?"

He nodded. "I guess it's safe to say we like each other. She wanted to clean up the mess with Daxden before we made it official, but I didn't make it easy for her."

Gee laughed. "By the looks of things, she's pretty smitten, herself."

He considered her. "I hope so."

"Can I ask one other question?"

"Sure."

"How'd you learn to fight like that?

"Alex chuckled lightly. "I wasn't fighting. I was—communicating."

Gee laughed, "Well then, how'd you learn to *communicate* so well?"

"When my father passed away, I needed to bring balance back into my life. I became friends with the son of a 10th degree Grand Master. There are only a handful of them here in the United States. I became a student. Tae Kwon Do also taught me to reach inside myself and become the best person I could be. In turn, I could give that as a gift to those who came into my presence and that's what I need in my line of work."

"Impressive."

Officer Ellis strolled in. "So, how things going? Do ya know anything yet?"

"No. Still waiting," Alex complained.

"Well, maybe I can do somethin' ta speed things up."

Alex's face lit up. "You have connections?"

"Just one," he said, walking to the receptionist's desk. "Excuse me, there's a doctor on staff here named Michael Ellis. If he's not too busy, can you tell him his dad's here ta see him?"

"Sure."

Officer Ellis turned and gave a slight wink, and soon they heard Michael's voice coming from the doorway.

"My dad?" he asked, walking into the waiting room. "Dad, what's up? You okay?"

"Oh, yeah. I'm just fine, son. If you're not too busy, there are some folks I want you ta meet."

"We're not too busy. It's been pretty quiet."

"Hi, Michael, Gee said. "I don't know if you remember me? Your dad brought me in the night someone hit me in the head. You took care of me."

"Yes, I remember. How've you been?"

"A lot better. I'm here for my friend tonight. Her name's Reese Cunningham. She's back there. These are my friends. This is my fiancé, Keith Jenison, my friend, Ryan Parrish, and Dr. Alex Whitfield. Alex really wants to go back to see about Reese. Do you think you can make that happen?"

Did you say, Dr. Alex *Whitfield*?"

Alex nodded. "Yes, I'm Dr. Whitfield."

"You spoke at a seminar the other day."

"Yes."

"I was there. I actually became interested in psychiatry after hearing you speak at a conference some years back. Now, I never miss one. I have a copy of your first book, *Reflections from Within*, on display in my office."

"So," Alex said, matter-of-factly, "do you think I can get back there to see my—um –friend?"

"Oh sure," Michael said with a nod. "Come on. I'll take you back."

"He walked to the receptionist window. Can you open the door? I'm bringing Dr. Whitfield back to see a patient."

Alex pivoted and gave a sheepish look to the rest of the group, then turned and walked through the doors.

He made his way to the head of Reese's bed, leaned close to her ear and whispered, "Hey, beautiful."

Her swollen eyes tried to open, but remained mere slits.

"It's okay. Relax. Keep them closed." He bent down and kissed her lightly. "I just want you to know I'm here. I'm not leaving you."

Her voice was weak from pain. "They gave me medicine. I can't stay awake."

"Then, sleep."

"I want to see you, though."

He studied her fondly. "I know the feeling. I don't think I could've sat out there one more minute."

Reese attempted a smile and winced. "It hurts when I smile."

"Oh, sorry."

"Is everybody still here?"

"Yes, they're here."

"What about Daxden? Did they get him?"

"They did. He won't be bothering you anymore."

"I hope not. I just—want my life back. The way—it was before."

"Really?"

"Except—for one slight change," she said, lifting her arms to wrap them around his neck. Her movement stopped abruptly when a surge of pain ripped through her rib cage, she winced again.

"Let me help you with that," Alex said, and he leaned down and laid his lips gently on hers.

36

MORNING SEEMED TO come quicker when Keith was there. They got home late from the hospital and fell asleep fast. Now, all she wanted to do was stay wrapped inside his warm arms, but she couldn't. She swung her legs around, sat up on the edge of the bed, and pulled herself out of it. She heard Keith stir so, she tiptoed quickly into the bathroom.

Her thoughts went to Reese, wondering how she was feeling this morning after a few doses of pain medicine. Although the bruises on her face would heal quickly, the ribs were going to take time. X-rays showed that Daxden's kick fractured two of them. By the time they were allowed to see her, she was sedated and didn't even know they were there. So, while she slept, they slipped out. Everyone but Alex. There was no budging him. *Alex—nice, quiet Alex— who has fire in his fist and a temper to boot. Who knew?*

She laughed to herself and stepped into the shower, closing her eyes and allowing combinations of a rhythmic stream to etch down her back and cascade around to her neck, relieving the tension in her muscles. She stayed in the shower as long as she could, appreciating the nozzle's varying patterns and modes. Finally, she stepped out, wrapped herself in a towel, and walked into the bedroom to get her clothes. She decided on the electric blue pants suit with gold, double-breasted buttons—a good color for the mood she was in today.

"Come back to bed," Keith pouted through a stretch.

Gee smiled. "I can't. I have a meeting with Regis this morning."

"Oh, he'll understand."

"Really?"

He laughed, "Okay, maybe not."

"I'll try to get off early, though," she said, balancing herself on the edge of the dresser to put her heels on.

He sat up on one elbow and watched her hurry around the room. "You look ravishing."

"Keith. Don't start," she laughed.

"And you smell good too."

"Keith." She warned and rushed to her jewelry box. She picked out a pair of gold hoops, and leaned closer to the mirror to put them on.

"I'm just admiring what's mine," he said, pulling the covers back.

"I'm watching you, Keith. Don't do it."

He sat up on the edge of the bed. Gee giggled and put her hand up. "Stop."

He stood and walked toward her. "I just want a kiss before you go."

"Keith. Oh my god," she laughed. Then she tried to get serious, but her laughter broke free.

They kissed, and warmth spread through her body like hot lava. Breathless and thirsty for him, she pulled away and slid him a lusty glare. "You are *so* wrong for this, Keith Jenison. You're actually going to make me go to work like this?"

He lifted an eyebrow, "A little preview of what's waiting for you when you get home."

She glared at the amused look on his face.

He moved toward her again, and she hopped backward and held her hands out to stop him. "Huh-Uh! Stay back, you mean man," she said, and ran out of the bedroom. She listened to his ear-splitting laughter from behind the closed door.

She was in the car and on her way to work when the phone rang.

"I'm sorry."

"No, you're not, Keith."

"I am. I just couldn't resist it."

"That's what you say every time. You're ridiculous," she teased.

"That's why you love me."

Her phone beeped. "Keith, let me call you back. Reese is calling. Is Pen up yet?"

"I don't think so, Tell Reese I said hello and we'll probably see her later today.

"Okay. I will."

She switched over. "Reese?"

"Hi, Gee." She spoke barely above a whisper. "You on your way to work?"

"Yep. I have a meeting with Regis first thing this morning. How are you feeling?"

"Like I've been – hit in the face and — kicked in the ribs," she said, trying to laugh. "Ow. Oww."

"Sorry."

"Why are you sorry? You didn't do it," she said, trying to laugh again. "Ouch."

"So, I had a little conversation with Alex last night at the hospital."

"And?"

"He really likes you. But you already know that. Don't you?"

"I like him too, but I had to get Daxden out of the way first."

Gee laughed. "And I guess you've done that."

"Alex and I have been—talking on the phone since the day I went to the seminar. He wanted to see me before he left for Arizona, so he came over yesterday. We had refreshments. I walked him to his car, he— kissed me. It was amazing."

"Was it, Reese?"

"Uh-huh. Sometimes, when he looks at me, it's like he's seeing my soul. Sounds corny, huh?"

"No, it sounds wonderful – Reese, I'm at work and I've got that meeting, so," she sucked air through her teeth, "I'm sorry, I've gotta run. We'll try to get over to see you, if not today, definitely tomorrow. And Keith says to tell you hello."

"Okay. And Gee, thanks—for—being there. I don't know how you found me, but I'm glad you did."

"I'm glad we did too. Love ya, Reese. Talk later?"

"Of course. Love you too."

They hung up, and Gee hopped out of the car and hurried into the building.

"Good morning, Gloria. Any messages?"

"Morning. Just two, Ms. Haynes."

"Is Ryan here?"

"Yes, ma'am."

She opened the door to her office and walked to the window, taking in the striking end of the early morning sunrise. Its oranges and yellows blending against the blue canvas. Like so many mornings before, it created a breathtaking, golden haze across the horizon. "I'm going to miss you," she whispered.

Adele Hewett Veal

"You don't have to, I'll take a picture every day and text it to you. If you want me to."

Gee whirled around to see Ryan standing in the doorway. "Will you?"

"You know I will," she smiled fondly.

"Did you already have coffee?"

"Yep, you'd better grab some now, before we go in to see Regis."

Gee rushed to the coffee pot, inserted a pod, and watched the brew stream down into her cup. When it was ready, she lifted it to her lips, blew the steam away and took a few quick sips. Setting the cup on her desk, she picked up a folder and the two walked together to Regis's office.

Regis looked up as they walked in. "Well, I see you're both in one piece. You found your friend and brought down the perpetrator, and nobody got hurt. That's a good day. Have a seat, ladies."

They sat in the chairs in front of his desk.

You two seem to be getting along well. Are there any questions for me, Ryan?"

"No, sir. Gee has been very helpful with getting me situated."

"Good, good, good. So, with that out of the way," Regis sat back, steepled his fingers and considered them both. "I had an interesting conversation with an Officer Ellis, who said you had evidence to prove Daxden Green was the one who hit you a couple weeks ago. Did you press charges?"

"No, sir," Gee said.

Regis shrugged, "Why not?"

"Well, I figured there was no need."

Regis gave a curious look, "What was the evidence?"

Gee took a breath and opened the file. "I have it right here. It's the envelope I told you about when I was at the hospital. The one I thought I lost." She handed it to him.

Regis opened it and read it aloud. "*Just as you feared, I think Cassandra knows. We need to cool it. If she does know, I'll need to tell Franklin before she does. Please go. He's going to kill you.*"

Gee rushed on, "Why would Daxden have that particular note in *his* possession?" she asked, sitting forward. "He had no connection to the people I happened to be investigating. Officer Ellis also found a wood fragment that looked like the same wood as the two by four we found in Daxden's possession. And, there was a car wash receipt that matched the one Officer Ellis found at the scene. I know he's the one who hit me. I'd bet my life on it."

Regis turned to Ryan. "And do you agree?"

"Uh—yes, sir. I do. Gee's a superb investigator. If she'd bet her life on something, I'd bet mine too."

The two women exchanged glances. Ryan gave a quick nod, and they turned back to Regis.

Regis studied them both, then took a breath and sat back. "Two peas in a pod," he muttered. "So—once again, I'm going to ask you. Are you pressing charges?"

Gee shifted her weight. "Well, I don't see any reason to, since he's already been apprehended."

"Wait a minute. You were so adamant about finding out who hit you the other night at dinner, and now that you know, you're ready to just move on?" he said, waving his hand through the air. "Let bygones be bygones?" He studied her then sat up quickly. "Gee, how'd you get your evidence?"

Gee's eyes widened. "What do you mean?"

Ryan cleared her throat while Regis continued.

"Officer Ellis said when they got to Daxden's house, no one was home, and they didn't have a warrant to enter his property; but you say the evidence was in his possession. Was the envelope in his pocket when they apprehended him? The two by four: was it under his hat?"

Ryan sat forward. "I don't think he was wearing a—"

"That's not my point!" Regis said, slamming his hand down hard on the desk,

Both women stiffened their backs.

"How—did—you—get—the evidence?"

"We got it from his house," Gee said.

Regis glared at them. "How'd you get in?"

Gee surrendered her answer. "We went through a window."

"A window."

She nodded. "Yes, sir."

Ryan took a breath to speak. "After Officer Ellis left, we doubled back and went through a window." She said, nodding as she spoke.

"This is the reason you can't press charges. You gathered the information *illegally*."

"But sir, we were looking for Reese. I mean, what if he had her tied up in there. We didn't go into the house to find the note or the two by four. That was just a divine bonus. We went there to find Reese."

Ryan finished for her, "Had we not gone in, we would never have found the storage locker receipt, and we might not have gotten to Reese in time. We knew it was wrong, but we were desperate. Desperate times call for desperate measures. Right?"

He studied them, steepling his fingers together again and laying them against his lips. "And, what if he had come home? Had you thought about that? He could have shot you both for trespassing, and he would have been within his rights."

"That was a chance we were willing to take—sir," Gee said. "Nothing happened."

"I keep telling you, Gee. You get too close. You take dangerous chances. Use your resources, but do things right, so people don't get hurt. If he'd come in and shot Ryan, is that a pang of guilt you could've lived with? Or . . ." He turned to Ryan, "What if he had shot Gee, would you have been able to live with the guilt? All because you didn't follow the rules . . ."

Gee sat forward. "What if it had been me?"

The question stung Regis, and a disturbing look etched across his face.

"If it had been me, *you* would've gone in, Regis. I know you would've. The same as you did when I was in the desert. You combed that desert for days, looking for me, even when everyone else had given up. And, when I was in the fire, looking for the little girl, they held you back from coming in after me. You were willing to take chances to rescue me, regardless of the danger. And you're saying you don't understand why I would take the chance to save my friend, who is the only family I have?

A sudden shadow of pain marred his face.

"Look," Regis finally said, "I get it. I just want the two of you to be safe. Think before you act, and for God's sake, stay out of trouble."

"Deal," Gee agreed.

Ryan pulled herself forward and glanced from Gee to Regis. "Are we done here, then?"

"We're done," Regis said.

Ryan stood and walked with Gee to the door. Then she leaned over and whispered, "That was good. You're a real pro."

Gee snickered with a wink, "When all else fails, reverse the guilt trip. I find it works every time. You might want to remember that."

Gee turned to see Regis lean his head back and pinch the bridge of his nose. She knew his outburst was because he cared, and she loved him for it. Her heart swelled as they walked back to their offices.

37

BY 4:00, Gee felt her body growing tired. She decided to finish the last report and let Regis and Ryan know she was heading home. She'd welcome some rest and knew that Regis would be all over it, since he'd been reaming her to slow down.

She picked up her phone and called Ryan's office.

"Hey, Gee."

"Hi Ry, did you have lunch already?"

"I brought some fruit from home. Want some?"

"No, I think I'm going home early."

"You okay?"

"Just a little tired. I'll finish up here and call it a day."

"Okay, I'll call you later. You goin' to check on Reese?"

"Oh, yeah. Keith and I may shoot by there tonight. You?"

"Sure, but I won't be there until later. My desk is piled to the max."

"Anything I can help with?"

"No, Gee. Go home. Get rested. I've got this. Plus, you've got Keith there. Go enjoy your man." She laughed.

"K. Talk to you later."

Gee pressed the button to end the call. She picked up a stack of papers and put them together. Then she opened her drawer, in search of her stapler. No staples. Exasperated by the inconvenience, she went to the door.

"Gloria, do we have staples in the supply closet?"

"No, sorry. I have them on order, though. The delivery won't be here until tomorrow."

"No worries. I'll get some from Ryan." She moved down the hall and tapped at Ryan's door, then peeked in. "Hey, Ry, have any extra staples?" she asked, raising the stapler over her head.

"I don't even have a stapler yet. I've been using yours," she laughed.

Regis passed Gee on his way out the door.

"Are you gone for the day, Regis?"

"No, I'll be back. What's up?"

"I was thinking about leaving early, if that's alright with you. I'm a little tired today."

"Good. You need to rest. Go home."

"I just finished my last report. I need staples. You got some?"

He continued walking toward the stairs, talking to Gee over his shoulder. "My top drawer. Left side. Take what you need."

He stopped abruptly before getting to his car. "No." He said and turned to hurry back into the building. He took quick steps up the stairs and through the hall, his pace increasing to a slight jog. "No—no—no—no!" he repeated. He reached his office door, hoping for the best. Bracing himself for the worse, he opened it.

Gee stood with the black velvet box opened in her hand. Color drained from her face and her eyes glued to the familiar content inside. "I—thought it was a—gift for Helen. I only wanted to peek at what you bought her."

"Gee—I can explain." He stepped in and closed the door.

She reached up and touched her butterfly wing, never lifting her eyes from the matching one in the box. Confused, Gee asked, "But how?" She shook her head. "I don't understand. Where…?"

"Gee, you've got to understand, I didn't know about you."

"What are you talking about?"

"She never told me." He shook his head desperately. "I didn't know about you."

"Didn't know what, about me?" she asked, afraid of the answer.

"Your mother. She never told me."

"Wait. You knew—my –"

"Please, let me explain."

Gee's voice elevated. "Explain what?"

"We were in love, Gee."

"Wait. I don't understand what you're saying."

"Your mother and I – we loved each other, but she was still married. Her last name was Jackson. I never knew her maiden name, although she mentioned she would be going back to it after the divorce, Haynes was not a name I knew. I didn't make the connection until – you."

We were together one time. One — very special time. I would've stayed with her for the rest of my life, and she knew it. My career took me out of the country for a few months. I didn't want to go, but she swore she'd wait for me. I thought, by the time I got back, her divorce would be final, and we could begin our lives together.

I had the charm made special before I left. Your mother loved butterflies. So, I designed a butterfly charm for her with wings that came apart. We went out with friends and, when I finally got her alone, I gave it to her. I kept half for myself, and put her half on a gold chain, and fastened it around her neck. I told her the necklace meant we belonged to each other for as long as we had them. When the time was right, the two parts would come together as one. She agreed.

I left the country, and when I returned, she was gone. Didn't leave a forwarding address or anything. It broke my heart, but life moved on. I opened my own firm, and one day, years later, a young girl sashays through my office doors, with a big smile and big bright eyes, looking for a job. You wormed your way into my heart and into my life. I didn't understand why, until one day, we were going over a case. Something caught my eye—the gold chain around your neck … that dangled the half of a butterfly charm.

Do you remember that day? I asked you where you got your necklace, and you said your mother gave it to you before she died. I asked your mother's name. When you said, Rosalyn, my heart crumbled into a million pieces.

I started my search. Could *my* Rosalyn Jackson, be *your* mother, Rosalyn Haynes? Could your butterfly necklace be the other part of mine? Or was it rational to believe that somewhere in the world someone had designed the same charm? I searched the internet until I found the obituary, Rosalyn Grace Haynes. Her face—my Rosalyn's face, wearing the necklace I fastened around her neck, years ago. I read the obituary over and over again. 'Left to mourn, daughter, Georgie Haynes.' No husband listed. She never remarried. I was confused. Where did the daughter come from? Did she meet someone else? Is that why she disappeared? Did she get pregnant by another man? I checked your birth certificate. *Father's name: N/A.* But, it was your birth date that kept coming to my mind, and I wondered if it was possible; a shot in the dark, I needed to know—needed to be sure. So, I took your coffee cup and had the DNA checked. It came back a 99.9% match. She never told me. I—didn't have a clue."

Gee lifted her hand, wiping her tears with the back of it. "Why didn't you tell me?"

"Tell you? How? What could I have said? I couldn't even make sense of it myself."

"But, all this time—"

"What was I supposed to say to you, Gee—'Oh, by the way, as fate would have it, I'm your father?'"

"I don't know what you could've said, but you should've said something!" she yelled.

"What? Tell me what I could have said. Please. Because I'm at a loss here. Tell me what I should've said." Regis reached up and brushed tears from his eyes before they had the chance to course down his face.

Gee focused her eyes in the distance, recalling something she had thoughtlessly tucked away in her brain. "Mom had a gold pocket watch in her jewelry box with the initials 'RGO'. I always thought it stood for Rosalyn Grace, and whatever her married name was, but you say her married name was Jackson. Do you have any idea whose watch—?"

"It's mine. I gave it to her. The initials stand for Regis George Ovalton. She named you after me. Georgie."

Gee lifted her hands. "I've got to get out of here," she cried, putting the box on his desk and moving toward the door.

"Gee, please. Don't leave. Not like this."

"I-I have to. I can't think." She opened the door and rushed through it.

"Gee."

She brushed by him and rushed to her office, grabbed her purse, and ran out of the building.

Regis's heart shattered, then he cursed under his breath and sat down in the chair behind his desk. He covered his face and allowed every despondent thought and emotion to take their liberty and ravage through him. His body shook with unrestrained sobs.

He had no idea how long he'd been sitting there, but now the building was dark and quiet with nothing but grief holding onto him like an unwanted tenant. A dim light shone from the corridor. Taking an exasperated breath, he stood and gathered his things to go home. He shook his head at the unexpected turn of events, then a slight movement caught his eye. It was a small, petite shadow that moved slowly into the room and traveled to stand in front of him. Her eyes searched his for acceptance. She took a deep breath and lifted her shoulders. "So—what do I call you now? Dad?"

A small sob escaped him, and he reached out with trembling hands, pulling Gee against his chest and cradling her in a warm, fatherly embrace, "I would love that—call me whatever you like," he whispered.

38

THEY PROMISED TO come together and talk. "I have so many questions," Gee said.

"I do too, and I've been waiting a long time to ask them."

"Does Helen know?"

Regis gave a reluctant nod. "She does."

"Can we get together tomorrow? I'd like to have Keith with me, so since he's here ---"

"Of course."

"I told him I was coming home early, but I guess that's shot to hell," she laughed nervously.

Regis smiled, "Yeah, you're a little late."

She stood to leave, then turned back to him. "Regis?" she said, "can I get another hug?"

"You never have to ask that. I have a lifetime of hugs saved up just for you," he said, opening his arms to her.

***

Gee slid into her car and drove home with overwhelming thoughts weighing heavily on her mind. *I have a father. My father's name is Regis Ovalton.*

Sometimes, when she least expected it, the universe would surprise her with a fragmented memory of her mother's lingering hugs—worries melted, problems vanished, and she'd be strengthened by just the simple thought of the act. Today, Regis took her worries and her problems, and with his hugs, made them evaporate into thin air. How could two people be so much alike?

She thought about the similarities she shared with him. Signs—clues—that she thought were peculiar . . . but fanned her hand at them, chalking them up as coincidence. They had the same drive, the same aspirations, and the same optimism. They'd finish each other's sentences and laugh about it. She'd shrug it off, calling it a 'God wink,' when it was actually a family trait.

To drown out the thoughts, she turned the music up in the car and filled the night air with the soulful sound of Donny Hathaway. "I Love You More than You'll Ever Know." She hit the Bluetooth button to call Reese.

Reese's voice was still weak and strained. "Hey, you on your way?"

"No, sorry, Reese. Something came up at work. It's late, so I'm headed home. How are you?"

"Ribs—still hurt. Alex has been here, though."

"Oh, really?"

"Yes—really." she smiled.

"Can't wait to talk to you about him."

"Yeah, I could use some sisterly advice."

"Then I promise to be there tomorrow to give it."

"You—okay?"

"What do you mean?"

"Something – in your voice. Something's wrong."

"No. I'm good." Of course, Reese would pick up on her strange mood. "Promise. I'll be there tomorrow. Okay? Gotta go," she said, hurrying Reese off the phone.

"Okay. See you tomorrow."

Gee hung up, pulled into her garage, and sat watching the door roll down before getting out. Keith came to the door and waited for her.

"Hey, thought you were coming home early."

She rushed to him and buried her face in his chest and sobbed – not tears of sadness, but tears of acceptance and knowing. For the first time since her mother's death, she realized she'd been trying to dig herself out of a large hole with a shovel. Today, Regis handed her a ladder. This was the raptured connection of family, in every sense of the word.

Keith's voice rolled over her ear, like a gentle caress, "Hey, hey, babe. What is it? Come on. Let's talk about it?" he said, holding onto her.

"Is Pen still here?"

"No, he left this afternoon. Something about Kelly not feeling well. I let him take the car. I'll just catch a flight out."

She cleared her throat and lifted her eyes to meet his. "I love you, Keith," she said.

He guided her into the house. Concern carved its way across his forehead, and he brushed the bangs from her face. "I know you do, babe. What's wrong?"

"I-I need to tell you something."

He gave a curious look. "I'm—listening."

"You'll need to sit down for this one."

He creased his brow again then took a seat on the sofa. "You're scaring me."

"I'll be right back," she said, rolling her eyes toward the ceiling.

She went into the bedroom and pulled down her old photo album, and she opened her mother's jewelry box to retrieve the pocket watch. When she returned, she sat beside him and opened the album. "This is my mom. Did I ever show this to you?"

"Briefly."

"You see her necklace?"

"Uh-huh. The same one you wear. Your mom gave it to you before she passed."

"Right. It's only half of a butterfly," she said, reaching up to touch it. "I used to search for the other half, thinking Mom put it away somewhere—for me."

Keith sat forward, "Okay…uh-huh."

"Well, I found it today."

"Oh, okay. That's good? Right?"

"I found it today in Regis's desk drawer."

"Uhhhh, Now, you kinda lost me."

"Regis has the other part of my butterfly."

"You mean he has one—like yours?"

She shook her head. "He has the other half."

"What are you saying?"

"I opened his drawer to get staples. I thought the box sitting there was a gift for Helen, and I wanted to see what Regis bought her. So, I opened it and couldn't believe what I was seeing. It was the other half of my butterfly."

"How did Regis get it?"

"They were in love, Keith."

"Who?"

"Regis and my mother! He designed the butterfly charm and put half on a gold chain for her. He kept the other half. My mom was still married and in the middle of a divorce. Regis was being sent out of the country on business. He gave her the necklace with the plan that the two parts would eventually come together again, when the divorce was final. There's so much more to this story, but here's the most important part." She laid the pocket watch on the table and brushed her fingers across the initials. "These initials, 'RGO'? They stand for Regis George Ovalton. I was named after my father."

Keith's eyes slid from the watch to the picture and finally to Gee, "Huh?"

"Regis Ovalton is my father!"

"You can't be sure, Gee."

"I am. Regis told me. He took a DNA test, and it came back 99.9%. You can't argue with DNA, Keith."

"Holy shit!" he shrieked. "What the hell?"

"I know. Regis tried to explain it, but I didn't want to hear it or accept it. I ran out and sat in my car with his words reeling in my head, but they were wrapped in such sincerity and love. Love for my mother and love for the child he never knew he had. I couldn't leave."

"God," Keith said, pulling her into his arms. "You must have been devastated."

"I was at first. I sat in my car for hours, and when I saw Ryan and Gloria leave, I knew I had to go back in. I could just see him sitting there in the dark, hurting, and I didn't want him to hurt anymore. He grieved the loss of my mother long after she passed away, and now, he probably thought he'd lost me too. I couldn't let him grieve anymore. He didn't deserve that. Oh, I miss my mother! Why she felt she had to keep such a secret, we'll probably never know. But what I do know is, Regis has *always* been like a father to me. What's worse than finding out that the man you considered a father figure is *actually* your biological father? I love him, and he's my—dad."

"So, now what?"

"He and Helen are coming over tomorrow to talk. I can't say I don't have questions. But for right now, all I want to do is relax—with you. I'm so tired."

"You got it, babe. What about Reese? You want to call her and tell her we're not coming?"

She took a breath and nodded. "I already did."

"Good. How about a glass of wine?"

"Sounds great."

He went to the wine rack and pulled out a bottle of Cabernet Sauvignon, returning with two glasses.

"What's the smile for?" he asked.

"It just amazes me. I had often wondered if my mom felt deprived in not finding true love, but now I know she did. She knew there was someone out there who loved her more than life itself. If you could've heard the way he talked about his love for her, you'd understand."

He poured the wine into her glass. "What makes you think I don't understand?"

"I mean . . . you know."

"I understand it because that's how *I* feel. I love you, Gee, more than life itself." He lifted her hand and placed a warm kiss on the back of it.

Her smile widened.

39

THE NEXT MORNING, Gee woke up wrapped in Keith's arms. She tilted her head to look up at him and his eyes met hers.

"How long have you been awake?" she asked.

"Long enough," he smiled and pulled her closer, "You going to work today?"

"I don't think so. I'll call Regis, I mean my dad—I mean --" She fanned it away, picked up her phone and dialed his number.

His gruff voice answered. "Regis Ovalton."

Gee's heart leaped at the sound of his voice, and she smiled. "Good morning."

"Morning. Is everything alright?"

"Yeah, just fine. I thought I'd take some time off today. I'm exhausted, and I want to go check on Reese. Do you mind?"

"Nope. Not at all. You need some time off, so good for you."

"Thanks." She held the phone closer to her face, "You okay?"

"Better than okay."

A warmth spread through her. "I'm glad. Looking forward to seeing you and Helen today."

"Sure thing. Do you want us to bring anything?"

"Helen's tenderloin."

His voice elevated. "Her tenderloin?"

She laughed. "Just kidding. No. You don't need to bring anything. We're good."

"We'll pick up a bottle of wine."

"That'll work. Can you do me a favor and transfer me to Ryan's office?"

"Sure thing. Hold on. And Gee? Take the time to really rest. You need it."

"I will."

Regis transferred the call to Ryan. There was a long pause before she picked up.

"Hey, Gee. You're not coming in today, huh?"

"No. I need to rest. I'm exhausted. Also, I want to go see Reese later."

"Good for you. Let Reese know I'll drop by after work. I went last night. Alex was there. What do you think about that? I like him for her. "

"Alex is great. I just hope they're not moving too fast, but who am I to say anything. I knew right away, Keith was the man for me. I just had to convince *him*." She laughed and snuggled closer to Keith. His arms tightened around her.

"Guess who I ran into at the hospital?'

"Can't guess. Tell me."

"Michael Ellis. Officer Ellis's son."

"Ohhhhhh," she smiled. "What's up with that?"

"Nothing—yet. We'll talk later."

"Sounds intriguing. Okayyy. We'll talk." She laughed and hung up the phone.

"Now, I'm all yours," she said, turning to Keith. She wrapped her arms around his neck and pulled him down until his lips covered hers. Her body melted against his, and he nestled close to her ear, whispering words of love and adoration, making her feel like liquid in his arms. Then he made love to every inch of her.

***

It was noon when they walked into Reese's hospital room.

"It looks like a florist took up residence in here!"

Vases of white lilies filled every empty space, and an arrangement of red roses sat near Reese's bed. "

"I know–it's Alex," Reese smiled. He asked me what my favorite flower was—but I had no idea he was planning this. A new arrangement comes every couple of hours."

Keith moved to Reese's bedside. "How you doin'?"

Her speech was broken, followed by quick breaths as she spoke. "I'm good, Keith. Really."

"Have you spoken to the police?"

"Yeah, they were here yesterday – took my statement. Daxden's arraignment is tomorrow morning. Apparently, I'm not the only one. This is what he does –he's a stalker."

Gee stepped forward, remembering the many orders of protection they found sprawled on Daxden's dresser. "He'd better get a good attorney."

"He has one. He's been advised to plead guilty."

"Uh-huh. So, now what?" Keith asked.

"Now, I go back—to living my life— no more looking over my shoulders."

"That's good, Reese. And what about Alex?"

She smiled. "I like him –a lot. But right now, we're just feeling our way around each other. You know?"

He nodded. "Okay," and gave an awkward pause and shifted his weight, then slid his eyes over to Gee. "I guess I'll let you two have some girl time. I'm sure you've got plenty to talk about. I'm going downstairs to get some coffee." He moved to Gee and placed a light kiss on her forehead, then walked out the door.

They waited until they were sure he was out of earshot, then Gee widened her eyes and laughed.

"He's just concerned."

"I know," Reese said fondly.

Gee sat in the chair next to Reese's bed. "What are the doctor's saying?"

"Not much of anything yet. Mom called. She's on her way. She should be here soon."

"That's good. It's been a long time. I can't wait to see her."

"He fractured two of my ribs."

Gee winced then reached up and touched Reese's face. "What about these bruises and the gash across your nose?"

"It looks—worse than it is. I thought my nose was broken, but it's not. The bruises will eventually go away. But enough about me. What about you?"

"What?"

"Ryan was here yesterday. You've been busy."

"Yeah, I have."

"She said you helped bust up a group selling illegal guns."

Gee nodded.

"Then you go over and above the call of duty and find me?" The pain in Reese's ribs made talking difficult.

"That wasn't just me; it was Alex and Ryan, too. We worked together. Then Keith and Pen came. Between the two of them and Alex, Daxden didn't have a chance. "

"Alex calls it 'communication," but I thought he was going to kill the man."

"Me too," Gee said, covering a shame-faced smile. "Actually, Daxden caught it from both sides because Keith had a little *conversation* with him too."

"Good." Reese shifted her weight around in the bed and winced from the pain. "Serves him right."

"So, anyway, I decided to take some time off...come up to see you and spend time with Keith."

What's—Regis saying?"

"He says I went back to work too soon, and I work too hard."

"Are you—listening?"

"Well, yeah."

Reese met Gee's gaze and held it, studying her.

"What?" Gee asked.

"Ryan said she heard raised voices coming from Regis's office. Did you and Regis have an argument?"

"I guess you can say that."

"Something's wrong, Gee. What is it?"

"Yeah, there's something, but it'll keep."

Reese breathed deep and winced. "Tell me."

"Reese, I..."

"Tell me, Gee," she half whispered through the pain.

Gee looked at her and shook her head, then she took an exasperated breath, dropped her shoulders, and told Reese all about Regis.

40

DOWNSTAIRS IN THE small café, Keith filled a coffee cup and sat at a table close to the door. He took out his cell phone and called Pen.

"Hey, man. You home yet?"

"Oh, yeah, I've been home for a while."

"How's Kel?"

"She's good. I guess I should tell you. I'm sure you'll hear it from Mom or Pop. Kelly's pregnant again."

"So, that's why she hasn't been feeling well?"

"We suspected it for a while, but she wanted to wait for me to get home, to take the test."

"That's great news! Are you excited?"

"I am, but the morning sickness is horrible."

"Can't the doctor give her something for it?"

"It's not her, it's me. They call it sympathetic pregnancy. I'm experiencing the same symptoms as Kel, and it's just not right."

"Keith laughed so loud that Pen had to hold the phone away from his ear.

"Glad you think that's funny. How's Gee?"

"She's dealing with a lot right now. I'll fill you in later." He looked up at the door and saw a familiar face passing by. "Hold on, Pen." Keith rushed to the door. "Hey, Doc," he called out. "Pen, I'll call you back," he said and hung up the phone.

Alex looked around and spotted Keith at the door of the café. He pivoted and moved toward him. "Hi, Keith. What are you doing down here?"

"Giving Reese and Gee a chance to talk. I'm having coffee. Join me?"

"Sure."

Alex got coffee and sat down at the table with Keith.

"So, You're going up to see Reese, huh?" Keith asked.

Alex nodded, "Yep."

"I saw all the flowers. Good move."

Alex smiled, shifting his gaze to a couple entering the café and then back to Keith. The moment seemed awkward, somehow.

Keith cleared his throat. "Reese and Gee. They've been best friends for a long time. I kind of took her under my wing, when Gee and I got together."

Alex nodded then gave a deliberate shake of his head.

"You won't ever have to protect her from me, Keith."

"I didn't think so," he laughed.

328

"I've already let her know I'm not going anywhere. Especially now."

"I hope it works out between you two. I really do, man."

"I need it to," Alex smiled with a nod. "I've never thought of myself in a relationship. I mean, there've been women: a dinner here, a movie there, but nothing serious. I was focused on my studies and speaking engagements, trying to convince doctors of my diagnoses and theories. But, I go over to see you and Gee and I get sideswiped by this beautiful woman who I can't get out of my mind. It was as if a switch turned on, and a neon sign pointed in her direction, blinking the words *missing piece.* The more I see her, the more I want to see her."

Keith nodded and gave a slow smile. "So, now what?"

"I'm not sure, we'll figure it out. I, at least, want to try."

"I think that's kind of obvious with all the flowers," Keith laughed.

They finished their coffee. "Come on, I'll walk up with you. They stood and walked out of the café together.

Alex regarded Keith and shoved his hands in his pockets.

"You don't think it was too much, do you?"

"What? The flowers? Are you kidding, man? Women love that kind of stuff."

***

Reese had fallen asleep again and Gee was standing at the window, gazing out. When she turned and saw Keith and Alex, she placed a quick finger to her lips.

"Shh. She just fell back to sleep," she whispered. "The doctor came in. He said they've ordered a CT scan and an MRI because when there's more than one fractured rib they get concerned that it could cause other problems for internal organs, blood vessels, and nerves. It could also cause a complication called pneu-mo-thorax."

"What the hell is that?" Keith asked.

Alex stepped forward. "It's when a sharp edge of a broken rib punctures the lung."

Gee turned to Keith and laid her head on his chest. "She didn't deserve this," she said.

"Sh-sh," Keith whispered against her hair, "she'll be okay."

Alex leaned over and placed a soft kiss on Reese's forehead.

"Thank you," Reese said through a low whisper.

Surprised, Alex looked closer. "Are you awake?"

"Uh-huh," she breathed.

"Did you hear what the doctor said?"

"Yes, I—heard everything."

***

Alex shoved his hands into his pockets and leaned against the wall, watching as the interns came in and wheeled Reese's bed through the door. Keith walked to him and placed a hand on his shoulder. "You okay?" he asked.

"Oh yeah, I'm good." But the crease in his forehead told them differently. Uncomfortable silence continued to rest in the room until Gee spoke up.

"These are beautiful, Alex," she said, admiring the red roses by Reese's bedside.

He turned to her and nodded, trying to smile but failing miserably. Instead, he lifted his hand, raked it through his hair, and then, taking a cleansing breath, he walked over to the vase and gently brushed a finger across one of the petals. "My father used to send my mom roses every Friday. Eleven of them. He said, she was his original rose, so he'd send eleven to make an even dozen."

"That's so romantic."

Keith lifted his brow and winked at Alex, then he mouthed the words, "I told you."

They laughed.

"Keith and I were talking about the wedding plans on the way up here. Is there anything I can help with?"

"No, I think we're good. We're having the wedding in mom and pop Jenison's backyard. Kind of a family tradition. Her landscaper transformed one side of the backyard into a gorgeous flower garden. It's beautiful this time of year. We've covered everything. The only thing we need to do is show up and get married."

"Regis, Pen, and I went together and took care of our tuxedos. We've set up a time for our final fitting. If I didn't know better, I'd think Regis was more excited than me."

Gee tried to cover her smile.

"Isn't that your boss?" Alex asked.

"Yes, it is." She said, sliding a knowing glance to Keith.

***

Alex stayed at Reese's bedside until she woke up again.

"Hi," she said.

"Hey, you," he answered, pulling his chair closer.

"Is everyone gone?"

"No, Gee and Keith just stepped out for a second. They'll be back."

"Does that mean—I have you to myself?" Reese asked.

Alex smiled and lifted an eyebrow, "For the time being. What did you have in mind?"

"Come here."

Alex stood and leaned over the bed. "What do you need?" he teased.

She reached up and caught him by his shirt and he allowed her to pull him down until their lips met.

"Feels like you're getting stronger," he smiled, and leaned in for another one.

"Can't leave you kids alone for a second."

Alex turned to see Gee and Keith standing at the door. Then he turned back to Reese.

"Looks like we have company."

They laughed.

"So, tell me something how long do you think it takes for ribs to heal?" Gee asked.

Alex shifted. "Usually up to six weeks."

Gee gasped. "What does that mean for the wedding?"

"Nothing." Reese whispered. "I'm not missing that."

"Here's another news flash for you. Kelly's pregnant," Keith announced.

"Oh no, it's good news, but is she going to be able to fit into her dress?"

"She's only a couple of months. She should be okay."

"Keith?" Reese said through a wince. "What do you think about Regis?"

"It was a shock at first, but it explains why he's been so protective."

"What is this about, Regis?" Alex asked with a shrug.

Reese turned to him. "Gee found out—that Regis is her biological father."

His face scrunched. "You just found this out?"

Gee nodded. "Yeah, afraid so. He's known it for a while, but I just found out. If I wasn't such a snoop," she laughed, "I wonder if he would've told me at all. I've always felt connected to him somehow anyway. The problem I'm having is…I don't have any idea what to call him. I find myself not calling him anything."

"What do you want to call him?" Keith asked.

She brushed her bangs to the side, tucked them behind her ear, and pulled her shoulders up into a light shrug, "Something we'd both be comfortable with."

"You don't think you'd—feel comfortable calling him, Dad?" Reese asked.

"I guess it just sounds weird coming out of my mouth."

Alex shoved his hands in his pockets. "Why?"

"Because all this time, I was under the impression that my father left when he found out my mom was pregnant with me."

Reese struggled to stay awake, "Well, now—you know that's not true."

"If Regis had known he had a daughter, do you think he would've left?" Keith asked.

Gee smiled fondly. "There's no way my mom would've been able to keep him away."

Reese smiled. "Your—mom was an amazing woman, Gee. It's hard to believe she didn't prepare you for this."

"Yeah, I know."

"He's your father. Why do you have a problem calling him *Dad or Pop*?" Keith asked.

"We'll see after today."

"Today?" Reese asked.

"Yeah, he and Helen are coming over this evening. I'll see how things go then."

"How do you think he'd react to you calling him Dad?" Alex asked.

"He'd love it," Gee smiled.

"Let me know what happens," Reese said.

She smiled again. "I will."

41

AT 4:00 THAT afternoon Regis and Helen rang the doorbell at Gee's house.

Gee turned to Keith. "Why am I so nervous?" she shook her hands in front of her, trying to calm herself.

"I'll get the door. You go sit down."

"Okay."

Keith greeted them. "Hey," he said, opening the door, "good to see you. Come on in."

Helen chimed in lovingly. "Where's my girl?"

Just the sound of her voice immediately put Gee at ease. "I'm in here, Helen," she said, standing up and rushing to her. I'm so glad you were able to come too."

"Sweetie, I wouldn't have missed this for the world."

"Oh, Helen. You are amazing."

"Well, come on, sit down. Where do we start?"

Regis took a breath. "I have no idea."

Keith sat next to Gee and draped his arm around her shoulders. "Well, let's start with when you had the first inkling about Gee."

"At first, I thought it was a coincidence that she was wearing the necklace."

"I remember the day you asked me where I got it," Gee said. "For some reason, that day stuck in my head because you seemed preoccupied after I told you my mother had given it to me before she passed away. The look on your face was pure confusion. Like you were trying to pull information out of thin air."

"I was. I couldn't wrap my brain around the fact that, if your mother was my Rosalyn, it meant she was no longer here on this earth."

Helen reached over and covered his hand with hers, and Regis met her gaze and nodded. "I'm good, sweetie," he whispered but, still a muscle flinched in his jaw.

Helen sat forward. "When Regis came home and told me what he suspected, I thought he was crazy. The whole thing sounded too far-fetched, but he was convinced of it. Then the DNA results came in."

Regis turned to Gee. "I don't understand what Rosalyn could have been thinking. Why she just didn't tell me about you. Why wouldn't she have wanted me to have a relationship with my daughter –my *only* daughter—my *only* child*? What could have been going through her head?"

"No telling. And I'm convinced we probably will never know. Mom had been going through bouts of cancer since I was six years old. All I knew was that mom was sick, and then she got better. She was back to being Mom. Five years later, she got sick again. That last time took its toll. I watched her grow tired and weak and in six more years she was gone."

Helen sat forward again, "You poor dear."

"No, Helen, I had a wonderful relationship with my mom. You remind me of her. Did I ever tell you that?"

Helen shook her head slowly. "No, you never did."

Regis lifted his eyes to Helen too. "Such a gentle soul." He said, squeezing her hand and then he turned back to Gee. "Would you mind if I take a look at that pocket watch?"

"No, not at all." She got up and went into the bedroom, returning with the pocket watch and the photo album, and put them both on the table.

Regis picked up the watch. "I never thought I'd see this again," he chuckled, more to himself than anything.

Gee opened the photo album and turned to the picture of her mother. Regis swallowed hard and blinked back the tears that brimmed his eyes. "Yep, there's my Rosalyn. The same picture you chose for the obituary on the internet. May I—?" Gee nodded as he lifted the plastic and pulled the picture from its place. He smiled a knowing smile. "This was the night I gave her the necklace. She was so happy. She swore she'd never take it off."

"And she never did, until she gave it to me."

"You can't see me," Regis stated, "but I was standing over there looking at her." He pointed to an area off to the side.

"So, mom was looking at you? All this time, I wondered what she was thinking, but it wasn't what she was *thinking* at all. It was— who she was *looking* at."

"Can I see that?" Keith asked.

"Sure," Regis said, handing him the picture.

Keith studied it and then looked at Gee. "You look so much like her," he said proudly.

"Yeah, that's what people say, but I don't see it. I used to think, *I must look like my dad*." She smiled at Regis, who tried to smile back, but instead, his eyes dropped to the floor and then back up to meet hers.

In that moment, he felt cheated — deceived. *Why had Rosalyn deprived me of something so precious? Why didn't she trust me enough to tell me about the child we created together? Why did she allow Gee to go through the misery of thinking she was alone in the world, when she wasn't?* He was angry, and he didn't know what to do with the anger or where to direct it. The muscles in his jaw clenched. But, out of nowhere, an unexpected hand lay gently on top of his, and he turned to meet Helen's kind eyes. She gave him a slow smile, and every bit of his anger vanished. He

339

took a cleansing breath and realized, although he had his own feelings of emptiness and loss, it didn't matter. Nothing he could do would bring back the time or love he'd lost. It was permanent, and now, thank God, there was Helen.

Keith's eyes lingered on the photograph. Then, out of instinct, he turned the picture over and was surprised to see numbers written on the back. He studied them. The numbers, faded by time, laid heavily on his mind through dinner and even after Helen and Regis left. Of course, Gee noticed, and after they were gone, she turned to him.

"Okay, what's up? Something's bothering you."

"Yeah."

"What is it?"

"Gee, I believe your mom may have left you something."

"Left me something?"

"I need you to focus on something," he said.

"Sure. What is it?"

"I was looking at your mom's picture; then I turned it over and found this." He held it out to her. "What is this?"

Gee took the picture and looked at the back. "Numbers?"

"Right, but what kind of numbers?"

She was exasperated. "Come on. Just tell me."

"Gee, don't they look like numbers for a safety deposit box? Did your mom have one?"

"I don't know. I've never thought about it."

"Let's take another look at her jewelry box?"

She rushed into her bedroom, pulled the jewelry box down from the shelf and took it to Keith.

He opened a drawer.

"That's the drawer mom kept the pocket watch in."

"Do you mind if I take a closer look?"

"Of course not. What are we looking for?"

He pulled a loose piece of velvet away from the drawer, and there it was.

What is it?" He picked it up and laid it carefully into Gee's hand. "A key."

"What do you suppose it's to?"

"Let's find out. Do you remember where your mom's bank was?"

"Sure. I've been there many times with her."

"Where is it?"

"L.A."

"Call them. See if they have safety deposit boxes with these numbers."

Gee Googled the number and put the phone to her ear. After going through a series of automated prompts, she finally got a representative.

"Hi, my name's Georgie Haynes. My mother and I used to bank with you before she passed away. I've since moved away but found a key that looks like it opens a safety deposit box. I have the number and I was wondering if my mother still had one there. Can you check it for me?"

"Of course. I can tell you if we have a safety deposit box with the number, but as far as the contents, I can't share that information over the phone. You'd have to come in for that."

"That's no problem. Thank you."

Gee gave her the numbers, and it was confirmed that it was there. "Do you have the key in your possession?"

"Yes, I do."

"Then, all you have to do is come in with your identification. Your mother would be considered the tenant. If you are a co-tenant, in possession of the key, you can come in and remove the contents from the box."

"Is there a way you can check to see if I'm a co-tenant?"

"What is the name again?"

"Georgie. Georgie Haynes."

"Georgie Haynes *is* one of the co-tenants."

"Then, I can come in with my key?"

"Yes, ma'am."

"Can you tell me who else is on that list?"

"I'm not sure if I can give that information over the phone, but I can tell you there were only two keys. One for Rosalyn Haynes and the other for Georgie Haynes. I'd suggest you come in and judge for yourself what information you want to share with the others."

"Others?" She slid curious eyes to Keith.

"Yes, ma'am."

"Thank you for your time. I'll get there as soon as I can."

She hung up and slowly turned her attention to Keith. "What do you think?"

He lifted his shoulders. "Let's go."

"When? Now?"

He turned to the clock. "No, not now. They'll be closing soon. Let's go tomorrow. We can get an early start and get there before noon."

"Sounds good to me."

"I didn't ask them who had been paying the lease on it."

"We can ask tomorrow. Do you think they'll tell you?"

"I don't know, but it's worth asking."

***

That night, Gee slept fitfully. The thought of being only hours away from her mother's most valuable and secretive possessions gave her such anxiety that Keith had to reach over and rub her shoulders. Even when she finally slept, her dream was controlled by someone chasing her through a dark tunnel and then down a, never-ending, spiral staircase and she didn't understand why.

Dawn came whispering away the night and Gee jerked herself awake. She turned over to face Keith. "Keith," she called out quietly. He stirred. "Keith," she called again.

He opened one eye slightly.

"Hmmm?" he said through a sigh.

"Come on. Let's get ready to go. We have a two-hour drive ahead of us."

They showered and dressed and were soon on their way to L.A., stopping only once for coffee and gas. Their conversation was light and mostly about what they might find in the box.

"Wouldn't it be funny if we go all this way and find nothing?" Gee asked.

"Why would your mom have a safety deposit box with nothing in it?"

She nodded, knowing her comment made no sense.

At noon, they pulled up in front of the bank, and Gee reached over, grasping Keith's hand. She swallowed hard.

He lifted her hand to his lips and kissed the back of it. "Calm down,"

Finally finding a space, he parked, and they hopped out and hurried inside.

Gee spoke to the teller and showed her driver's license. It wasn't long before a tall woman, wearing a navy blue suit, came from the back offices and stood at Gee's side. She smiled. "Would you please follow me?"

She led them to a room that held many safety deposit boxes. Gee took a deep breath and followed her through the door. She glanced around, reading the numbers on the boxes until she found the one that matched the numbers on the paper in her hand. She walked to it, slipped the key into the keyhole, turned it, and slowly opened the box. Inside laid three envelopes. One addressed to her, another for Regis Ovalton, and the third for Reese. Gee's hand trembled as she lifted the envelope addressed to her. Quick breaths came as she whirled around to explore Keith's face. He nodded, as if giving her the permission. She slid the note out of the envelope and began to read.

My dearest Georgie,

I'm sitting here watching you sleep. Listening to your shallow breathing makes me smile, but I know that soon this privilege will be taken from me. You will grieve, but I also know how strong you are ... so strong that you will get through this and allow fond memories to replace your grieving heart.

My time is limited. I feel it in everything I do and in every breath I take. Even my words have become difficult. So, I'm using the time while you're sleeping to write these letters.

It gave me great pleasure this evening to give you my gold necklace. I want to explain how important this piece of jewelry is to me. Someone I will go to my grave loving with all my heart gave it to me. You don't know him yet, but he is a significant person in your life too. He is your father. His name is Regis George Ovalton.

I struggled with the thought of telling you about him earlier and decided against it. I waited for you to get older, not knowing I wouldn't last that long. I wanted to make sure you understood that what I had with your father was pure love, not a dirty love affair or something immoral. It was a love that only comes around once in a lifetime, but still too late for me. Most importantly, it was a love that created you, such a precious life.

His job sent him away for a couple of months, and during that time, I finalized my divorce and found out I was pregnant, all in the same week. I was thrilled because I knew your father loved me! I loved him too, but I wasn't sure if he wanted a child at all, especially since he had just been promoted to the position he had worked so hard to get. Who was I to ask him to put his life on hold and raise a child he might not even want? I couldn't do that to him, and I couldn't do that to you. So, I let you believe you were the child of the man I was married to, who left when he found out I was pregnant. Was it the right thing to do? I guess I'll never know.

When I decided to tell Regis about you, you were six. I had a doctor's appointment. My plan was to go to the doctor and then to Regis's office to let him know about this beautiful life we had created together. That day I found out about my cancer. That changed things drastically. It was no longer the right time to discuss my pregnancy. So, I waited until I finished my last round of chemo and looked him up again. He was gone. To Italy.

When he got back, he opened his agency in L.A. I read it in the paper, and I was so proud of him. Grand opening— Regis Ovalton –Private Investigator. I went to his office and stood at the door. I saw him with a woman who he leaned down to kiss, then his eyes met mine through the glass door. The shock on his face was enough to send me reeling. I didn't have the right to interrupt his happiness. I left as quickly as I could. Time passed, and the cancer returned. I lost track of Regis, and, in a way, I was relieved that I wasn't putting him through the agony of caring for me. The only picture I had in my mind was the one of him—happy.

I'm leaving you his name because I want you to find him. Tell him who you are, and I hope he has enough love to carry you through the remainder of your life. You deserve it. You've brought so much joy to me even when you were being stubborn and annoying (a trait I'm sure you get from your father). I look into your sleeping face and see his, and it makes me smile, because I know that I had him, through you, for my lifetime.

I do want to tell you that you are going to grow up and love hard, and someone is going to come along who will know exactly how to love every part of you. He will give you the love that I felt for such a short time. When it comes, hold onto it with both hands. Don't throw a shadow over your happiness by making excuses for it. Just be happy. Kiss your children for me every night.

My prayer is that you carry the things I've taught you in your heart. I pray my words become echoes whenever you need to hear them.

Take the other two letters. One to Reese, the other to Regis. Find Regis - and tell him that I'll love him always and through eternity.

My love Always, Mom

Gee folded the letter neatly and placed it in her purse, then lifted the other letters from the box. She turned and handed the key to the bank manager.

"I won't need this anymore," she said with a slow smile.

Keith stepped forward. "You okay?"

She turned to him and nodded. "Better than I've been in a long time. She really was remarkable, ya know? I wish you could've known her."

He studied her. "If you're anything like your parents, I think I *do* know her."

She held up the other letters. "She wants me to give these to my father and Reese."

"Okay. We can do that."

"Yeah," she said, with another nod and moved toward the door. Then, as an afterthought, she turned to the bank manager and thanked her for her time.

***

The ride home was a quiet one. Gee reached into her purse, pulled out her letter, and read it to Keith. When she finished, she turned to him. "A lifetime of questions were answered on these pieces of paper."

"I'm surprised you didn't cry. I thought, for sure, you would."

Gee smiled, "I feel like I'm walking through a dream. It's all so surreal, like Mom came down from heaven to let me know everything's alright."

"I can see that."

"I'm curious to know what she wrote to these two," she said, holding up the other letters.

Keith gave her a side-glance. "Me too."

She grasped his hand and gave it a squeeze, and Keith squeezed hers right back. Studying her periodically during the drive home, he noticed there was something different about her—she was more content, somehow.

"I've been thinking about something," Keith said.

She turned to him. "Okay?"

"Remember the discussion we had about you giving up everything and moving to Arizona?"

"Uh-huh."

"I have a suggestion."

"You do?"

"Yeah, why not start your *own* agency?"

Her eyebrows lifted in sudden surprise, "What?"

"You'd be great at it."

"I wouldn't know the first thing to do."

"Ask Regis. He'll help you."

"I know he would, but—"

"But—what?"

"But where would I get the money? I don't have that kind of money…and I'd have to hire employees. Where would I—?"

"I can be an employee."

Her eyes widened. "You?"

"I think we work well together. Don't you?"

"W-Would you want to do that?"

"I think it's the perfect solution. You can continue to do the work you love, and we can do it together."

She was quiet. Thoughts swirled around in her head, flooding her brain. "How—?"

"It was just a suggestion, Gee. Just give it some thought."

"No. I love the idea. I'm—just wondering—how?"

"We'll figure it out."

***

By the time they reached home, Gee had the answer. She would talk to Regis about opening an extension of his office in Arizona and allow her to run it. It wouldn't be *hers*, but it would definitely be a solution and a way to stay connected. Not like she needed one, but that's what she'd say when she spoke to him about it.

"When do you think I should talk to him about it?"

"Hmmm. I'd feel it out. Go with your gut."

"Yeah, you're right—my gut," she said, nodding her head repeatedly.

"Do you want to take the letters to them now?"

"Don't you think we should?"

"Yeah, I do."

"I'll call Regis." She took her phone out of her purse and punched in his number.

He answered. "This is Regis."

"Hi—it's me, Gee."

"I know." His voice softened.

"Umm— yesterday, when we were together, Keith and I came across a number on the back of the picture of Mom. Turns out, the numbers belonged to a safety deposit box, and in the jewelry box, where Mom kept your watch, we found a key."

"Yeah, yeah, Gee. What are you trying to say?"

"We went to the bank where mom did her banking and found the box. I'm trying to tell you that she left something—a letter—for you."

She could hear him taking in a mouthful of air, in and out, in and out.

"Are you alright?" she asked, knowing he was, but needing to hear him say it.

"Did you read it?" His words came out in a whisper.

"Of course not. It's for you. She left me one too, and there's one for Reese. I can bring it over to you."

"Are you at home?" Regis asked.

"Almost. You want to come over?"

"Yes, I think that's best."

"Okay," Gee nodded. "Sure. What time?"

"I can be there in about thirty minutes, if—if it's okay with you."

"Sure. I'll be there by then."

"I'll need a few minutes. Then I'll be on my way."

Gee knew that meant he would talk to Helen before he left, to reassure her of his love, but also his curiosity. She would understand, as usual. She'd want to go with him, but she'd never suggest it, knowing, if he didn't ask, it was something he felt he needed to do alone. She'd understand that too. Gee smiled and pushed the button to end the call.

***

She was in the bedroom when she heard Regis at the door. Keith opened it, and the two men embraced in a man-hug, as Regis slapped Keith lightly on the shoulder.

"So, she left a letter, huh?"

"Looks like it."

Gee crossed over to Regis. "Hey," she said with a hug, "come on in."

He followed her into the family room and sat down. Nervous tension laid heavily upon Regis's shoulders.

Gee walked to the table and pulled the letter out of her purse then returned to Regis and handed it to him.

Regis stared at the envelope before reaching out to touch it. Then, finally taking it from Gee's hand, he gave a heavy sigh and tapped the corner of the letter on his knee.

"I'd—like to read it in private, if you don't mind. Is there somewhere I can go?"

"Of course." She pointed to the guest bedroom.

He stood, walked into it and closed the door. Sitting on the edge of the bed, he opened the letter and began to read.

My dearest Regis,

Since you're reading this letter now, I have to assume you've met our daughter. Let me tell you a little about her. She's both determined and loving. She's optimistic and such a jokester. She'll make you laugh until your sides ache and, yet, she's so compassionate it could bring tears to your eyes.

Regis stopped reading and stared through the air as if he were collecting data from the files in his brain. He chuckled. "Now you tell me."

Lifting the letter, he continued to read:

There are several reasons I didn't tell you about her, but none of them seem rational now.

First, You had just started your dream job. You didn't deserve to be approached by someone you had a one-night stand with, accusing you of being the father of her baby. I made myself scarce on purpose. I know that wasn't fair either. Please forgive me.

When Gee was six, I decided it was time to tell you about her. It was that very day I found out about the cancer and I was devastated.

Months of Chemotherapy and Radiation filled my days. I couldn't bring myself to ask you to be a part of such an ordeal but when it was over —when the doctor's gave me the news that I was in remission, I knew I was going to find you and run into your arms. I realized how precious life was and I didn't want to live another day without you.

On the last day of treatment, I rang the Bell of Hope so loud and listened to it chime through the hallways of the hospital, giving other cancer patients hope for their own cure; but it also rang in my heart, with a sincere hope that you would understand what I had done and still accept us into your life. I was in remission, but you were in Italy. So, I had to wait.

I read in the paper when you opened your office in LA, a 'Grand Opening.' I was so proud of you! And I was there. I stood at the glass door that led into your building and saw you, sitting on the edge of your desk. The smile on your face melted my heart. There was a woman with you. I watched you lean forward and kiss her so gently on the lips. As far as I knew, she could have been your wife? I froze. I had no right. And, when I thought you saw me, I ran.

Regis whispered, "I did see you. I knew it was you. I thought my mind must've been playing tricks on me." He brushed a tear from his cheek, took another exasperated breath, and read on…

So often, I'd wonder, how two people could know such a love in one night. We loved each other. I will go to my grave remembering the night we shared, so full of passion.

I felt cheated when the cancer returned and the doctors gave me the news that there was nothing more they could do. After Gee went to bed, I sat in the dark for hours with so many questions going through my mind. I wondered how to tell her I wasn't going be around to see her grow up, fall in love, or get married. I will never hold my grandchildren, but, Regis, you can and you will. How bittersweet this is to write.

She has no idea you're her father. I let her think she was the child of the man I divorced. We never discussed it any further. I know I didn't do the right thing by holding on to this secret. I wanted to make it right, so when she developed the desire to get into the field of investigation, I pointed her in your direction. I told her about your great company and encouraged her to research you.

I know she will eventually come to you. You will see the necklace --our necklace -- and know.

So love her, Regis. That's all she's going to be looking for.

"I do, Rosalyn," Regis said aloud. "I loved her long before I understood why. Why didn't you just—tell me?" He cried. "Why couldn't you give me the chance to love you both?" He closed his eyes, "I remember that passion too, and how we didn't want to leave each other. I would've stayed with you forever. I could've been there for you. It was my decision to make, not yours."

Regis crumpled the letter and pressed it against his face, allowing fresh tears to course over it, soaking into the paper -- blurring the words. "My decision—mine...not yours." He repeated.

Gee listened for as long as she could and then she turned to Keith, "I need to go to him."

He knew the unshed tears in her eyes were more for Regis than herself and he nodded.

"Go."

She rushed through the bedroom door and ran to Regis. Holding onto him, the two cried uncontrollably. "It's okay, Dad. It's okay. Really, it is." Gee assured him over and over again. "Don't cry. Please, don't," she pleaded.

Regis pulled back and looked at her. He exhaled a long breath and tried to smile. Heavy tears stained his cheeks, and he shook his head. "That mother of yours—whew."

"I know, huh?" she said, wiping his face.

"She sent you to me."

"Yes,I know that now."

"She went to my office when I opened the agency in L.A."

"She did?"

"She was coming to tell me about you. I saw her."

Gee nodded curiously.

"She was standing at the glass entrance door. I was with a woman who came to celebrate my grand opening. I kissed her, and when I looked up at the door, I saw your mom. I thought, 'I must be dreaming.' She ran, and I ran after her, but she was gone. From that day on, every time I looked at that door, I'd remember her standing there. I always wondered if she'd come back. I hoped—she would. But, time moved on. Two or three years later, I hired my first employee—you. What were you then, about eighteen—nineteen years old?"

"Mom passed away when I was just coming out of high school. I was turning eighteen. I started working for you a year later. So, yeah, I was about nineteen."

"So precocious and sure of yourself."

Gee looked down, then she lifted her eyes back to his, with a smile.

"I remember the day I met Helen. I thought, not including my Rosalyn, she was the most beautiful woman I had seen in a very long time. You were in my office, and you said, "Regis, just call her.""

Gee laughed. "I remember that day."

"I said, 'you don't just call a woman like that out of the blue.'"

"And I said, 'you do if you like her,'" Gee quipped.

"A week went by. Then you came storming into my office, picked up my phone, dialed a number, and shoved the phone into my hand. When I asked you who it was, you said, 'Helen,' and walked out."

"I knew you'd never call her on your own."

"Helen and I were married a year later. I love her, Gee. She's everything to me."

"I know," she smiled.

"But, every day, I'd go into the office and be reminded of your mom, standing at that glass door, looking at me."

"That's why you suddenly moved the office to San Diego."

"I had to get away from that glass door. I was constantly watching it. Helen didn't deserve that."

"Did you already know about me?"

"No. Not exactly. I was beginning to put things together after seeing the necklace. I believe we were waiting for the results of the DNA test, but in my heart, I knew."

Gee took a breath. "I told Keith that it was as though Mom came down from heaven to let me know everything was alright."

"Exactly. Regis said, shaking his head. "Well, I'd better go. Helen's waiting for me, and I don't want her to have to wait too much longer."

"Are you going to show her the letter?"

"Of course … if she wants to see it."

"Good. Did she tell you I asked her to sit in for Mom at the wedding?"

He nodded. "She told me."

"You know, if I had the choice to choose another mom, it would be Helen."

Regis just nodded his head, stood, and moved toward the door. "I believe she feels the same way about you." He walked out of the room and over to Keith. "Thanks, Keith."

"For what?"

"For sharing." He said, nodding toward Gee.

Keith laughed, then walked over and draped his arm around Gee's shoulders, "She's *your* daughter. I should be thanking *you*."

He left, and Keith pulled Gee into his arms and held her for a long time.

***

Gee and Keith's footsteps seemed to echo through the corridor as they approached Reese's room. They stood in the doorway and watched Alex walk to her with a glass of water. He handed it to her. "Careful, I may have made it too full. Don't spill it."

"It's just fine, Alex. Thank you."

Gee turned and looked endearingly at Keith. "They look good together," she whispered.

Alex turned to the door. "Hey, you two."

"Hi," Gee said, moving into the room. "Look at you, Reese! They've got you sitting in a chair now? How does it feel?"

"It—hurts."

"But it's progress. Right?" Gee said with a smile.

"I guess I should be thankful, huh?"

"She's doing well. I'm proud of her." Alex smiled and bent down to place a kiss on her forehead. "She walked down the hall and back, too."

Gee folded her arms, "Really? Reese that's great."

"That was Mom's doing. She's here."

"Oh, she is? Where?"

"Yeah, she got here this morning."

"Did you get a chance to meet her, Alex?"

"Oh, yeah," he smiled and gave a wink. "She likes me."

"Of course she does." Gee laughed. "I can't wait to see her."

"She's still here somewhere. Probably at the nurse's station, giving them a hard time."

They laughed.

"Have you seen Ryan?" Gee asked.

"Every day. She—stops ...," Reese winced through a sudden pain, before finishing her thought, "down to see Michael first."

"Oh, sounds like that can turn into something special," Gee said.

Reese's mom came to the door. "My goodness. I thought I heard familiar voices," she said, sashaying over to Gee and Keith for a quick hug. She stepped back and studied Gee.

"You look more and more like your mother every time I see you."

Gee smiled.

***

Maggie Cunningham became a fast friend to Rosalyn Haynes during her final days. She sat by her bedside and listened to her ramble on and on. In her terminal state, Rosalyn repeated herself constantly, but Maggie didn't mind. She'd answer her questions as if it was the first time she had asked.

"Promise me you'll take care of her, Maggie. Don't let her grieve long. She'll want to shut down, don't let her do that either.

On her wedding day, give her the gift along with my love."

Maggie, nodded passionately. "I promise, Rosalyn. I'll take care of it," she said, wiping fresh tears from her cheeks.

"Don't let her grieve long, Maggie. Promise me you won't let her grieve long."

"I won't, Rosalyn. I promise."

Maggie held onto her friend's hand and sometime during the night, Rosalyn Haynes passed away.

***

"Mom Cunningham." Gee chimed and hugged her back. "It's good to see you!"

"How long have you been here?"

"Just got here this morning."

"You look good. How long are you staying?" Gee asked.

"For as long as I'm needed, but it looks like Alex has everything under control."

Alex smiled. "I do my best, but nothing can ever take the place of a mother's love."

"That's the truth." Gee chimed in. "I'm glad you're both here. I've—got something to give you."

They turned their attention to Gee as she reached into her purse and lifted out the last letter, addressed to Reese. She stepped forward and handed it to her.

"It's from Mom."

"Your mom? What--- for me?" Reese asked.

"Yep. I found three of them. One for me, one for Regis, and this one's for you."

"You found them—where?" Reese asked.

"Mom had a safety deposit box. Keith and I found the key and went to the bank this morning."

Reese examined the letter. "Gee—I—"

"You don't have to read it now. You can wait."

"No, it's not that. I—why would she—?"

"I don't know why. You'll have to read it to find out."

Reese opened the envelope and pulled the letter out. She unfolded the paper and read the first part. Tears welled up in her eyes and spilled over onto her cheeks as she dropped her hand into her lap. She lifted her eyes and slid them over to meet Gee's.

"The letter's not for me," Reese stated.

Gee shook her head, "Sure it is. It's got your name on it."

"But it's not for me. It's for—Keith."

Gee's eyes widened. "Keith?"

"Me?" Keith asked, just as shocked.

"Your mom writes that she knows she can depend on me to give the letter to the man you would marry."

Keith's eyes became like tiny slits, and he creased his forehead as he moved forward to take the letter from Reese's hands.

For some reason, although unexpected, it didn't surprise Gee that her mother had left the letters behind. She was that type of mom to cover all her bases and leave no stone unturned, even in death. However, to find the letters at *this* precise time in her life—the perfect time, made her wonder if—perhaps—her mom—could be— her eyes lifted and she scanned each corner of the room, remembering the echoed voice in her dream— 'I'm here for you—I'm here for you—I'm here for you.'

She watched Keith move to an area alone to read.

My dear son-in-law,

My heart swells every time I think about my daughter walking down the aisle to meet the man who has captured her heart. I know that kind of love. I've only had it once in my life, but I know it. I also know, whoever you are, you must be—some kind of special.

I have held my little girl's hand to lead her to the park, to school, church, stores, and other places. Now it's your turn. Lead her, son-in-law. Take her hand, to have and to hold and –lead her.

She loves hard and spends too much time questioning her own worth. You probably already know that (and I'm laughing as I write it). You might have to tell her a thousand times that you love her. Not because she's insecure and feels the need to be convinced of it, but just because she likes to hear it.

Tonight, as I lay next to her, I pray for you. I pray that you not only listen to her dreams, but that she hears yours as well. I pray that you both remember the words you speak during your vows. Those words are going to be the ones that help you through the hard times.

By now, you've probably been told about my love for butterflies. I pray that you feel them in your belly, more than a dozen times during your marriage, because it means you're anticipating something great—and exciting.

If I know my daughter, you are a man full of loyalty and love. Integrity and character. You're brave and intelligent, and I pray that you are a great father of faith and leadership.

Although my marriage didn't work out, I still tried to raise my Gee to understand the seriousness of the blessed union between two people. I taught her that marriage is a genuine commitment of love and, while she's honoring you, I pray that she maintains her own strength and character.

I believe you come from a loving family, or Gee would never have been drawn to you. Your mom and I probably share some similar traits, and she prays too, because that's what good moms do.

I wish you both the best life together, and I welcome you to the family.

Love always from above,

Your mother-in-law (Rosalyn Grace Haynes)

Gee watched breathlessly, waiting for him to finish reading. When he looked up, he considered each person in the room and he shook his head in disbelief.

"What is it? What did she say?" Gee asked.

Keith gave an amused look and held the letter up. "She gave us her blessing."

42

GEE WATCHED THE second-hand on the clock sweep down from the twelve, past the three, to the six, and back up to the twelve. "One minute," she whispered. "Just thirty more of these, and I'll be Mrs. Keith Jenison."

She walked to the full-length mirror and turned to the side. She'd lost count of how many dresses she tried on— how many bridal shop appointments she made, only to leave disappointed. She wasn't trying to be difficult; this was the most important day of her life. The dress had to be perfect.

It was Helen who found the dress and called her.

"It's got your name written all over it," she said.

"Helen, are you sure?"

"It's perfect. You're going to love it. You have to come right away."

"I'll get Reese and meet you in an hour."

"I'll have them put it on hold."

When Gee and Reese walked into the bridal shop, Helen's face lit up with an excitement Gee was familiar with. The bridal attendant escorted her into the dressing room where they had already hung the dress. She put it on.

"Helen," Gee squealed, sucking in a breath "I love it. This is it!"

"Come out, so we can see it!"

She stepped out of the dressing room, smoothing her hand over the beautifully beaded Venetian lace and tulle fabric. She faced the mirror. The dress fit her tiny frame perfectly and flared to the floor in an elegant chapel train. She lifted her hand to the off-the-shoulder neckline and swept it across the sweetheart detail that lay on top of an illusion bodice. The long illusion lace sleeves matched the sheer back.

When she turned back to Helen and Reese, priceless silent nods let her know they approved.

Time seemed to stand still as she waited for her wedding day. Now, here she was, staring in the mirror, feeling the same excitement. She glanced up at the clock.

"Twenty-five minutes," she whispered.

She heard a knock at the door. "Hey, you decent?" Reese called out.

"I am. Come in."

Kelly, Ryan, and Reese stepped in. They wore the same gold, off-the-shoulder bridesmaids' dresses. Kelly's was a little different, because she was the matron of honor.

They hugged, doting on how elegant Gee looked in her dress.

Ryan did a spin and struck a snapshot pose. "I told you I'd find it."

"You look great, Ry, and Kelly your skin is glowing, you are absolutely radiant."

"That's what pregnancy will do for you," she said, rubbing her baby paunch. Hopefully, *you'll* find out the same, very soon."

"And I'd love it."

"I know you would." Kelly smiled and gave Gee another hug.

"And Reese—"

Reese hadn't said anything. She stood, looking at Gee in her dress. "You look beautiful, Gee. Your mother would be so proud."

"I know. Thank you for saying that. What's going on downstairs. Is everything ready?"

"Of course. Mom Jenison made sure of it."

"Think about this." Gee said, "A few months ago, I had my doubts about moving here to Arizona. I thought about how different things were going to be and wondered how I was going to fit in. But, today, I don't have a doubt in my mind. I have never been so sure of anything in my life. I'm not alone. I have a father who I love, a stepmom who I adore, *and* Keith's family." Then, gesturing to Reese, she said, "I also have you and your mom, and I have Ryan, my newest sister friend. I'm so lucky."

Ryan smiled. "Yes, you are lucky, and so are we."

"I'm glad you were able to be a part of my wedding."

"I wouldn't have missed it for the world, Gee," Ryan smiled.

"So, Michael's here with you, huh?"

"Yes, he's here," she said shyly.

Gee looked from Reese to Ryan. "Which one of you are going to be next to walk down the aisle."

They both turned and pointed to each other then laughed.

Another knock brought their attention to the door.

Helen called out, "It's Helen and Regis."

Reese opened the door and let them in.

Helen's hand went to her mouth. "You look stunning," she said.

Regis moved to her and gave her a kiss on the forehead. "You nervous?"

"Yeah, a little. I keep looking at the clock. Time is going by so slow."

Regis laughed. 'It'll be here before you know it. But, listen, I've got a few things I need to say to you before I escort you down the aisle."

"Is this a private conversation? Should we leave?" Reese asked.

"No, it's nothing I wouldn't want you girls to hear. First, I want you to know that, although I wasn't there to be the father you needed when you were growing up, I'm here now. You come to me if you need anything."

"Okay," Gee nodded. "I've always felt that anyway, but I understand why you feel the need to say it."

"The other thing is," he reached into his pocket, "it's time for this to be in its rightful place."

Helen went behind her, reached up, and unhooked her necklace and handed it to Regis.

Regis took Gee's half of the butterfly, and, connected it to his half, then slid it back onto the chain. Helen placed it back around Gee's neck.

Gee tried to stop the tears, but they continued to flow freely down her cheeks. "This is perfect," she cried. "Thank you so much."

"Now it's where it's supposed to be," he said.

"I hope you don't mind," Helen said. "I brought this for you. You don't have to wear it if you don't want to. I—just thought—" She lifted a box to her.

"Helen, what is this?" Gee asked, reaching out and taking it.

"Open it."

She lifted the top. "It's beautiful."

"It's my gift to you, dear. It belonged to my mother."

"Oh, Helen. Are you sure?"

"I have never been surer of anything."

Gee rushed over and pulled her in for a long embrace. She removed the aquamarine hair comb from its box and handed it to her. "Can you put it in my hair?"

"Sure."

Helen slid the comb into Gee's hair. Then she turned and hugged her again.

"I think it's about that time," Regis said, looking at the clock.

They turned and walked out of the room.

The first one to go down the aisle was Kelly, Gee's matron of honor. Following her were Reese and Ryan.

Kelly's little girl, Lizzie, came down the aisle sprinkling rose petals from side to side. Then the wedding march began. Everyone stood.

Gee looped her arm through Regis's and started down the aisle. She leaned toward him and whispered, "I need to talk to you about something."

He glanced down at her. "Now? What?"

"It's business."

"Business—now?"

"I was thinking about opening up my own agency here in Arizona. Keith said he'd help me. Would you consider starting an agency here and letting me run it?"

Regis stopped in mid-stride and turned to her. He had no idea how long they stood staring at each other. Gee's eyes were unwavering and fixed on his, waiting for his answer.

The guests looked from one to another and soon began probing the situation, buzzing with whispered questions and shrugs.

Regis examined Gee's face. "You would want to do that?"

"Of course I would. I love my job, and I'm not ready to give it up."

He brushed her hair to the side and tucked it behind her ear. Gee smiled, it was the first time he'd ever done that.

"Well," she asked, "what do you think?"

"We can definitely look at it. Check things out and see if it's going to be cost-efficient. We'll talk after the ceremony. Okay?"

"Okay."

"They turned and continued down the aisle, with Gee's eyes glued on the handsome man waiting for her at the altar. She smiled the biggest smile when they had almost reached him and Keith walked up to meet them.

Regis handed her over, "Gee," he said, "I guess this is a good time to say, 'I love you.'"

She smiled, leaned forward, and placed a kiss on his cheek. "I love you too, Dad."

Regis felt as though he floated on air to the empty seat beside Helen. He leaned over and whispered, "I love it when she calls me 'Dad'," he brushed a tear from his cheek.

Helen patted his hand and smiled, "I know, dear."

***

With the wedding over, Keith and Gee sat at the bride and groom table, watching everyone they loved laughing and celebrating this day with them. She watched the tender way Alex held Reese during their slow dances, every now and then leaning down to steal a kiss or two. Gee smiled.

"You happy?" Keith asked.

"I am," Gee answered. "I think you're going to have to scrape this smile off my face."

Keith laughed. At least yours can be scraped off. I think *mine* is permanent."

He leaned over and gave her a long kiss that ended in the crowd erupting with hand clapping and hoots, embarrassing them both.

"So, what was the pause in the middle of your walk down the aisle?" Keith asked.

"I had just asked Dad about starting an agency here."

Keith's eyes widened. "And he said—?"

"He's going to think about it. See if it's going to be cost-efficient."

Keith nodded, "That's fair enough. Right?"

Gee nodded back. "Right."

Keith leaned over and gave Gee another kiss. "I'll be right back," he said, and walked across the yard to talk to Kelly and Pen.

"You two look great over here," Keith said, slapping Pen on the shoulder and reaching over to give his sister a hug.

Kelly smiled. "It was a beautiful ceremony, Keith."

"Yeah, it was, wasn't it? Did you find out your due date yet?"

"Probably February or March." Kelly's smile got bigger as she rubbed her baby bump.

Keith turned to Pen, "You ready for this, Daddy? Two kids?" Keith laughed.

"As ready as I *can* be. There's nothing like it, man. You ought to try it."

Keith's smile stretched across his face, and he gave a wink. "I plan to. We need to get settled first, but you know me —you jump, I jump."

They laughed, and Keith pivoted, glancing around to find his bride.

The reception was coming to an end, and Gee was saying her good-byes to those leaving.

"I was trying to wait for everyone to leave, but it doesn't look like that's going to happen anytime soon." Mom Cunningham said walking up behind her.

Gee eased around and hugged her.

"I'm sorry, did you need me?"

"Yes, I have a gift for you."

Gee smiled. "You can just put it on the gift table."

"No, I don't think it should go on the table."

"Why not?" she asked, lifting her champagne glass to her mouth and taking a sip.

"It's a special –gift from—your mom."

374

Gee's eyes widened, and she covered her mouth to keep from spraying champagne into the air. "My—mom?"

"She made me promise to give it to you on your wedding day."

"W-What is it?"

She reached inside her bag and pulled out a large envelope. "She took this insurance policy out for you when you were born, and before she passed away, she made me the trustee; I've continued to pay the premium, but it's yours –from her."

Gee opened the envelope and looked over the policy. "W-Wait—what? Is this saying what I think it's saying?"

Mom Cunningham smiled. "That's right, Gee. Your mother left you a policy for a half a million dollars, sweetie."

Keith turned toward Gee. His smile faded when he saw the stunned expression on her face. Something was wrong. Her face had drained of all color, and it appeared as though she'd forgotten how to breathe. He excused himself and rushed to her side. "What is it?" he asked. "What's wrong?"

Gee couldn't speak. She handed the policy to him, and he read it. He then lifted his eyes to Mom Cunningham, his expression mirroring Gee's. "W-W-What is this?"

"It's a policy that Gee's mom took out for her when she was born. She made me the trustee and asked me to give it to her on her wedding day.

Keith's expression went from disbelief to shock and then to pure elation. He turned to Gee and let out a hearty laugh. "Do you realize what this means? I guess we can tell Regis, opening an agency here in Arizona has just become cost-efficient."

At that moment, as fate would have it, a single monarch butterfly lifted from the nearby flower garden. It swirled gracefully around Gee and, ever so lightly rested upon her shoulder. Gee smiled, watching its wings wave up and down, granting her full view of its beauty before lifting off her shoulder and dancing its way into the sky. Gee studied it until it flew completely out of sight.

"Okay, Momma," she said, with a slight shake of her head. "Now—you're just showin' off." She lifted her eyes to the heavens and smiled.

EPILOGUE

REGIS FOUND A building in Arizona that would serve the purpose of the new agency there.

Gee and Keith were at the Ovalton building three weeks after their wedding, to finalize the agreement between them.

Regis leaned forward and slid the agreement across the desk for them to read. "Are you sure you want to do this, Gee? You have the money to open your own agency, and if that's what you want to do, I'd completely understand."

"No, Dad, I want to stay connected here. You've taught me everything I know about this business, and we're family. If it hadn't been for your encouragement, I wouldn't have my degree in Criminal Justice, and I definitely would've dropped out of that political science class. Why would I want to leave?"

Regis slid his eyes to Keith's, and he shrugged.

"We've discussed it, Regis. You're stuck with us. She's not going to budge."

A tap at the door drew their attention. Ryan came in and tiptoed to Gee to give her a hug. Gee hugged her back.

"It's good to see you, Ry," Gee said with a smile.

"You too," Ryan said, moving to Keith. She hugged him too.

Regis lifted his eyes to Ryan, "Did you get it?"

"Sure did," Ryan answered, holding up the file she brought in with her.

Gee looked from Ryan to Regis. "What's up?"

Ryan handed the file to Regis, who handed it to Gee.

"Your first case," said Regis. "It happens to be in Arizona."

Gee opened it with Keith leaning over to read along with her, while Regis went on explaining.

"She's a young girl—bought a gun and took it to school."

Ryan sat forward. "Bet you can't guess where she bought it."

Gee turned to her. "No. Where?"

Ryan reached over and showed Gee the sticky note on the next page. "Online. M & C Tactical sold it to her. No background check and she lied about her age. There was an altercation at the school, and people got shot."

Gee sucked in a breath. "Not children!"

"Her mom called here, wanting to hire us to investigate the situation that wouldn't have happened, if M & C had been more responsible. She says she thinks Lace bought the gun because she was scared." Ryan said.

"Scared of what? Please tell me she didn't shoot any children!" Gee asked again, waiting impatiently for an answer.

Ryan shook her head, "We don't know who all got shot, Gee. We just know that the girl needs help. Her mother says she has a small anxiety disorder."

"Small? "How small?" Gee asked. "Is she on medication?"

"Sometimes," Regis said, clearing his throat.

Keith shook his head. "Having an anxiety disorder and being scared is not a good combination."

"Especially if you're not taking your medication," Gee added.

"Another reason she said she needed a gun was to protect her sister. She claims her sister means the world to her."

Ryan leaned over. "The girl's name is there at the top of the first page. Lasandra Carter. They call her Lace."

"Lace," Gee repeated, flipping back to the first page. "So she was protecting her sister, huh?"

Ryan nodded. "Yep, that's what she said. Lace alleges her sister found the gun, and did the actual shooting. She's adamant about it. "

"I can see that being the case. Could there be truth to it?"

Regis shifted in his chair. "Yeah, but there's only one problem,"

Gee turned back to him, "What's that?"

"After talking to the police on the scene, the teachers, and her mother, we discovered one crucial fact—Lace doesn't have a sister."

The room went completely still.

Made in the USA
Columbia, SC
08 July 2021